Death AT WHITEWATER CHURCH

Death AT WHITEWATER CHURCH

AN INISHOWEN MYSTERY

ANDREA CARTER

OCEANVIEW PUBLISHING
SARASOTA, FLORIDA

ISBN 978-1-60809-353-3

Oceanview Publishing
Sarasota, Florida
www.oceanviewpub.com
10 9 8 7 6 5 4 3 2
PRINTED IN THE UNITED STATES OF AMERICA

For Olive, my grandmother

Chapter 1

THE WIND WAS bitter. There was snow in the air. I looked up at the sky. It was gray, that ashen gray that imbues the landscape with an eerie, otherworldly quality. Three o'clock in the afternoon and the light was fading already.

"Why the hell would anyone want to live in a church?" Paul Doherty wrestled with the padlock on the old iron gate.

I shrugged. "Not sure I would."

"Clients really pushing for this report then?" he asked.

"Liam is, anyway. First sale he's had in a while. He nearly had a fit when he discovered you didn't have the map."

Paul grinned. "He'll get it tomorrow – if we ever get in, that is."

He gave the key a last tug and the padlock released. He shoved the key into the pocket of his anorak and dug out a woolly hat, pulling it down over his ears as he lifted the gate just high enough for it to pass a foot or so over the rough grass, allowing us space to squeeze through. I waited while he arranged his camera bag and other equipment across his shoulders, and then we set off in single file up the overgrown driveway. It didn't take me long to regret not wearing gloves. My hands were scratched repeatedly by the briars that crept out towards us from the moment we left the gate. I regretted, too, the skirt I was wearing; I had come straight from court. Suddenly, I heard a loud expletive ahead of me, uttered with considerable feeling.

"Paul," I mock-scolded him.

"Ah, Jesus. Who's going to hear me up here?"

He had a point, unless you counted the cattle in the next field, a cluster huddled together against the cold. As we climbed higher, I could see the cliffs and the Atlantic Ocean crashing against them. Never the most hospitable of waters, today the ocean looked as hostile as I'd ever seen it: dark, inky-blue with white horses riding the waves. It was always rough here, where the River Foyle met the sea at the north-east corner of Donegal.

We kept going up the hill, managing eventually to find a less uncomfortable route through. And then it appeared, looming high ahead of us, silhouetted against the pale sky. We stopped in our tracks, simultaneously.

Paul exhaled loudly. "Whitewater Church."

I stared up at it, blowing on my hands. "Impressive. Do you still call it a church once it's been deconsecrated?"

"No idea."

He rested his bag on the ground and fished out his camera. He screwed on a lens and flipped the switch to turn on the flash.

"It's been unused for a long time, but I'm still surprised by how much it has deteriorated," he commented.

"How old is it?"

"Hundred and fifty years, give or take a few. Built of fine local granite."

"I'm sure it was beautiful once," I said.

"See the quoins at each corner and the bell tower? Typically Victorian features."

The church was in bad shape. The gable end we were facing was completely covered in dark ivy, and there were places where the walls were starting to crumble. The stained glass, which must once have resided in the two arched windows, was long gone, but the stone cross on the eaves was still there, defiant.

The building had a heartbroken look about it, as if grieving for the parishioners who had abandoned it, the people who would have come to worship every week. I dismissed the thought as fanciful nonsense. Whitewater Church was to be revived – I supposed that must be a good thing. It was to become someone's home.

Paul stopped taking photographs. "Do you have those maps?"

"Map singular, I'm afraid." I opened my bag, produced a flimsy sheet of paper, and handed it to him. "I'm going to have to get my office scanner fixed."

"Don't worry about it. You're the one who had to hand-deliver it. And to be honest, I'm happy to have some company."

He unfolded the map. It was little more than an old drawing with some rough measurements.

"Is this all there is?" he asked.

"Yes, sorry. I doubt this place has ever been properly mapped. That's what was attached to the old Registry of Deeds conveyance."

He folded it back up and put it in his pocket.

"Okay. I'll just need to measure the boundaries on the ground and ensure that they match the boundaries on the map as best I can." He looked around him at the overgrown site. "It's not going to be easy. Right, the light's fading. I'll do the inside first."

He picked up his bag, hoisted it over his shoulder, and started to walk towards the main entrance, cursing again as his foot caught in a stray briar. The ground was covered in rubble, bits of metal and weeds – lots of weeds.

"The original door must have been impressive all right," Paul said, looking up.

"Wood?" I asked.

He nodded. "Carved, probably."

It was hard to imagine it now. It had been replaced by an ugly corrugated-iron gate about ten feet high by eight feet across, which was starting to rust around the edges. The salty sea air couldn't be good for it. Another padlock. Paul rooted in his pocket and retrieved the keys.

The door swung open easily when the lock released and we went inside. There was more rubble underfoot and a smell of damp decay, but still there was growth: weeds were sprouting from the walls and in patches here and there on the floor. It was less dark than I had expected; light was coming in through the windows, as was foliage. The ivy that was climbing the external walls had found its way inside, and the remains of a bird's nest rested on what was left of the windowsill.

"It's not very big for a church," I said.

Paul shrugged. "The population here would never have been terribly high – a few families at most. Almost like an island population."

While Paul took some measurements and photographs, I wandered slowly around the interior, looking at the walls. Here and there were the remains of memorial plaques to in-dividual families. Fishermen who died prematurely, farmers who lived long lives: a community. A community that no longer existed. We eventually gathered our things and left. Outside, the light was fading rapidly.

"It's going to be dark soon," I said. "Have you much left to do?"

"I'm nearly done. I have a torch – if we're really stuck, I can use that. Not that I fancy the idea of being here after nightfall."

I stood and watched while Paul walked around the perimeter of the building measuring the external walls. A loud fluttering made me jump. I looked up to see a rook fly over my head and land on the cross on the eaves. There were four of them, in a neat row, spectral and silent. As I watched them, I lost my footing and stumbled backwards. The heel of my boot hit something metal. I looked down. I was standing on some kind of iron grid about two feet square and very overgrown. I called out to Paul, and he came over to investigate, pushing the weeds aside to get a better look.

"Damn it," he said. "Does the church have a basement?"

"No idea. Anything on the map?"

"I doubt it." He took it out, unfolded it, and checked again. "No, no mention of a basement."

I followed him as he walked farther along the perimeter of the church.

Suddenly, he stopped dead. "Oh, Jesus." He pointed to a small iron gate at the base of the rear wall. "It's a crypt. The church has a bloody crypt."

I looked at him.

He sighed. "Now that I've seen it, I'm going to have to go in."

There was a bolt across the gate but no padlock this time. It slid across easily, and the gate swung open. He turned towards me with a resigned expression on his face as he took the torch from his bag and switched it on, illuminating a number of narrow stone steps leading down into the gloom.

"This shouldn't take long," he said briskly. "I'll take a quick squint inside, a couple of photographs, I'll do the site measurement and we can head home."

"Okay."

He looked at his watch and then at me. "Sure, why don't you head off, for God's sake? There's no need for you to be here now."

"You must be joking. It's just getting interesting."

The truth was that the prospect of making my way back down the overgrown driveway in the half-light did not appeal in the slightest. He saw through me immediately.

"Actually there's a second torch in my bag," he said. "You could grab that, just in case."

Gratefully, I found it and switched it on. I hovered beside the gate as he slid his legs through the entrance and sat on the top step.

"Can I come with you?"

"Absolutely not. You stay put," he said. "The steps might not be safe. At least I'm insured to do this." He disappeared through the gate.

"You okay?" I called.

"Yep. I can stand, sort of."

Although the ground was damp and cold, I knelt and watched as he went slowly down the stairs, each step reverberating against the walls on either side. They led into a small chamber no more than seven or eight feet high, with what looked like stone drawers on either side. He was right, it was a crypt. I shivered.

"How long are you going to be?" I called.

I heard him chuckle. The echo made it sound like some Bond villain's evil laugh. "Don't worry. I'm not going to stay down here a second longer than I have to."

Halfway down he shoved the torch under his oxter to lift the camera. He took one photograph, then seemed to hesitate.

"What's wrong?" I asked.

"There's something at the bottom of the steps."

He lifted the torch again and directed the beam. He was right, there was something lying on the floor of the chamber. In the gloom it looked like a pile of rags. Paul slowly went the rest of the way down and then stood for a second at the foot of the steps.

"What is it?"

"It's a blanket," he said.

"A blanket?"

"Yes. An old brown woolen blanket, rolled up like a carpet."

I leaned in further, lying on the flat of my stomach, propped up on my elbows. I was almost entirely in the chamber now, with nothing but my feet outside. I inhaled the dank, earthy scent.

Paul poked the blanket gently with his foot. "I can't feel anything inside it."

"Have a closer look."

He looked up at me, an exasperated expression on his face.

"I'll come down." I struggled to twist myself around so I could get my feet onto the step.

"*No*," he said. He shot me a warning look. "I told you to stay put. You shouldn't be here at all."

He went down on his haunches. Even from this distance I could see that his hands were shaking. But he managed to pull the top of the blanket aside, just a little. Immediately, he leaped back, almost losing his balance, dropping the torch. The thud made me jump.

"Paul? What is it? What's the matter?"

He put his hand against the wall of the chamber for support. His torch rolled a matter of inches and came to a stop close by, its beam hitting the wall next to him. Slowly, he bent down and picked it up.

"Paul?" I said again.

He still didn't reply. I stood up and went down the steps as fast as I could, trying not to slip on the uneven ones. Then I squatted beside the rolled-up blanket and carefully moved the top of it to one side, just as Paul had done, directing the beam of the torch to illuminate what he had seen seconds before.

It took everything I had to suppress the scream that rose in my throat.

Chapter 2

"HELLO?" SERGEANT TOM Molloy said again, his voice sterner this time. "Who is this?"

I had made the mistake of dialing the garda station before catching my breath. Leaning against the wall of the church for support, I breathed in deeply, relishing the clean, icy air.

Finally, I managed to speak. "Tom, it's Ben."

His voice softened. "Jesus, Ben, you sound a bit odd. What's going on?"

"I'm up at Whitewater Church with Paul Doherty."

"That deserted place on the cliff? What on earth are you doing up there?"

Paul watched me from a couple of feet away, looking agitated, shifting his weight from one foot to the other. I raised my eyebrows as he withdrew a pack of cigarettes from his bag and lit one, the wind causing the flame of the lighter to flicker.

"Paul was doing a survey . . ." I started, then caught myself. "Look, never mind about that. We've just found a skeleton in the crypt beneath the church."

"You've *what*?"

"I'm serious. A human skeleton. And crypt or not, I'm pretty sure it's not supposed to be here."

"Okay. Stay put. Wait for me in Doherty's jeep. Whatever you do, stay together. I'll be there in ten minutes."

I thought that was optimistic. Whitewater is a good fifteen miles from Glendara, along some of the worst roads on the Inishowen peninsula. I shoved the phone back into my coat pocket, grateful to be able to leave my hand in there with it for a while.

I turned to Paul. "I didn't know you smoked."

"I don't," he replied, sucking on the cigarette with a kind of grim desperation, his face ghostly in the light of the torch he had placed upright on the ground. "Gave up five years ago, but I always carry a pack with me to prove to myself I don't need one."

I smiled. "I can't really begrudge you one in the circumstances."

I came to sorely regret those words. In the confined space of the jeep, Paul chain-smoked one cigarette after the other, giving me a pounding headache. The second the headlights of the Glendara squad car appeared in the rearview mirror, I climbed out, relieved by the blast of Arctic air. Molloy was beside me before I even closed the door.

"You all right?" he asked.

I was surprised by how comforted I was to hear his Cork lilt, to see the concern on his face. Things had been strained between us of late. I remembered the look in his eyes, his hasty retreat. I shook it off. Right now I had more pressing concerns.

"Fine. Just a bit of a shock. I think Paul's pretty shook."

Paul acknowledged Molloy's presence with a barely perceptible tilt of the head but made no move to get out of the jeep. His hands still gripped the steering wheel.

"Right, let's get up there and have a look. You can tell me your story on the way."

Molloy waved at the squad car and Garda Andy McFadden emerged from the driver's seat, phone in hand. He took a luminous yellow garda jacket from the back seat and strode over to Paul's door.

Choosing brute force over planning, McFadden led the way, beating briars away with a large branch he had broken off one of the ash trees along the road. Every bush and bramble looked twice the size it had in daylight.

"First of all, tell me exactly what you two were doing up here," Molloy said.

I took a deep breath. "Liam McLaughlin the estate agent asked Paul to do a survey of the old church and the site. The owners are selling."

"Are solicitors usually present at surveys?" Molloy asked, in a tone that implied he already knew the answer.

"I have the deeds. I had to bring a map up for Paul," I replied defensively. "Our scanner's on the blink."

Molloy gave me a wry look. He's more familiar with my nosiness than most.

"So you act for the owners of this place?" he said.

"I do."

Watery moonlight guided us back to the bell tower, and Paul went ahead along the perimeter of the church to the low iron gate. It was bolted, as we had left it. Molloy pulled back the bolt and the gate swung open. He nodded at McFadden.

"Right, you stay here with Ben, Andy. Paul, you come with me."

I protested.

"The fewer people down here the better," Molloy stated.

They were gone only a matter of minutes. Paul reemerged first, lighting a cigarette again before he was even fully upright. Molloy stepped out after him, looking somber.

"Well, you're right," he said. "They're definitely human remains. It looks like they've been here for some time. And they certainly don't appear to be part of the official, buried remains . . ."

I interrupted him. "Actually, I don't think there are any official remains here anymore. They would have been removed and reburied somewhere else when the church was deconsecrated; that's what usually happens."

"When would that have been?"

"The church was deconsecrated back in the 1990s sometime. I'm pretty sure there was something about it on the deeds."

"What are your clients' names?" Molloy asked, producing a notebook and pen from his pocket.

"Kelly. They're a couple – Raymond and Alison Kelly. I think Liam said they're away in the States at the moment. Not sure when they're back."

Molloy took a note. "I'll need their contact details."

I produced my phone from my pocket. The battery was dead. "I don't have them on me but I can get them from the office."

"I'll need them as soon as possible."

Molloy transferred his attention to McFadden, who had begun fixing crime scene tape to the wall. "Andy, did you get hold of the State Pathologist's office? We're going to need someone up from Dublin as soon as possible."

"Aye, I did." McFadden straightened himself, rubbing his lower back. "There's a pathologist in Letterkenny at the moment, up to give a lecture at the college. I lost coverage down at the gate but I reckoned I'd ring again when we knew what we were dealing with."

"It's okay – I'll do it. From what I've seen of the bones, we'll need a forensic anthropologist." Molloy took McFadden's mobile and walked away with it.

The beam from McFadden's torch flashed on the bolted gate of the crypt as he struggled with the tape. I found myself staring at it, the memory of what I had seen half an hour before returning with a vengeance. My stomach lurched.

"How long have the Kellys owned the church?" McFadden asked, jolting me back to the present.

"I'm not sure. I didn't act for them when they bought it."

He shook his head. "I didn't know it belonged to anyone. I assumed the church still owned it."

"The couple bought it with plans to turn it into some kind of heritage centre, as far as I know, but they ran into some problems."

"Money probably," McFadden said. "The sorry end of our Celtic Tiger."

"Probably, or planning permission," I said. "I think it's lain derelict ever since."

McFadden whistled. "Jesus, I wonder if they knew what they had in their cellar?"

Molloy shot McFadden a look of disapproval. In the dim light, I hadn't noticed him return.

"Stroke of luck," he announced. "It turns out we have a forensic anthropologist and pathologist rolled into one, just down the road. She's on her way."

He turned to me. "Not that I approve of McFadden's crude analysis, but do you think there is any chance your clients did know about this?"

"It seems a bit unlikely they'd have someone out to inspect the church if they did, doesn't it?" I said.

"Sarge," McFadden said suddenly. "Take a look at this." He shone his torch on the ground in front of the entrance to the crypt. There was something glinting in the grass.

Using a handkerchief from his pocket, Molloy picked it up. It was a padlock, similar to those on the gate and the door of the church. It had been roughly sawed open. He rubbed his chin. "Looks like you might be right. Maybe they didn't know."

He handed the padlock to McFadden, still in the handkerchief. "We'll need one of you here when the pathologist arrives; I'm sure she'll have some questions."

"Of course," I said immediately.

"There's no need for you to stay," Molloy told me. "Paul was first on the scene."

Paul hadn't uttered a word since he'd come back out of the crypt. He nodded unhappily, an expression of resignation on his face.

"I don't mind staying, honestly," I said.

"I'm sure you have work to do," Molloy said firmly. "And remember – I need to get your clients' contact details as soon as possible."

"Okay, I'll ring you back with them. Then I need to give them a call and let them know what's happened."

Molloy frowned. "I'd rather you didn't. That's my job." He handed me his torch. "And Ben?"

I looked up.

"I don't need to tell you, keep the details of what you've seen to yourself."

* * *

I made it back to Glendara and the old terraced house that accommodates O'Keeffe & Co. Solicitors half an hour later. O'Keeffe & Co. is my firm, since I took it over from my retiring predecessor six years ago. It's the most northerly solicitor's office in Ireland. *Last legal advice before Iceland*; I've always thought I should put that on my notepaper.

As I crossed the road and watched people scuttle from shop to shop, weighed down with children and bags, people with busy lives and families to feed, I felt a familiar emptiness. Being an outsider in a town where most people have spent their whole lives is not the easiest way to live. Sometimes, in my darker moments, I felt as if my role here was limited to that of an observer and facilitator for other people. That my own life was a sort of half-life, as if I didn't really count because no one knew my "people." But I have my reasons for being here. I have made my choice.

I'm Ben O'Keeffe. Benedicta, actually, thanks to my parents' fondness for an obscure fifth-century Italian saint, but the full version rarely gets an outing. "Ben" does me just fine, although it does create some interesting misunderstandings.

Leah was engrossed in accounts when I walked into the office. Leah McKinley is my receptionist, legal executive, and everything else rolled into one. One quiet afternoon she managed to identify a job description for herself for each letter of the alphabet – aide-de-camp, bookkeeper, coffee-maker . . . You get the picture. It's a two-woman operation.

Molloy had told me to keep my mouth shut, but I'd trust Leah with my life – plus she's bound by the confidentiality clause in her contract. So I filled her in on what had happened, watched her jaw drop, then headed upstairs to my desk. I found an address and telephone numbers for the

Kellys and dialed Molloy's mobile. It went straight through to voice mail so I left a message. Then I went over to the filing cabinet and took out a fat conveyancing file.

I extracted a large bundle of deeds, untied the pink ribbon keeping them together, and spread them out on the desk in front of me, reading through each of the titles until I found the one I was looking for: the most recent conveyance of Whitewater Church, from the Catholic Church Trustees to Raymond and Alison Kelly. I unfolded it and checked the date. The Kellys had bought the church on December 14, 2005. Back in the days when everyone had been full of big plans and easy money.

I shuffled through the earlier title documents until I came across a Deed of Deconsecration from 1995. I was starting to read through it when I heard voices downstairs. Leah was talking to someone with a loud voice and a very distinctive accent. It was one I had been expecting, although not yet. I couldn't hear what they were saying, but from the decibel level, it sounded as if Leah was struggling to calm some frayed nerves. The expression of relief on her face when I appeared at the bottom of the stairs confirmed my suspicion. Standing at the reception desk, looming over her, was Raymond Kelly.

"I can't wait!" he was shouting. "I have to see her straight away."

"Mr. Kelly?" I said.

He whirled around to face me.

"What the fuck?" he said, spreading his hands in a gesture of helplessness. "I turn my phone back on when I land in Belfast, and there's a message from some guard called Molloy. What the hell's going on?"

"Come upstairs," I said.

He followed me up the stairs. "I'm on my way to the station now. That guard said something about a body. A body, for fuck's sake?"

In my office he refused the seat I offered him and started to pace up and down like a caged lion. One, two, three steps to the left, one, two, three to the right.

"Human remains were found in the crypt under the church," I explained. "I was there at the time, as a matter of fact."

Kelly stopped in his tracks and turned to face me, an accusatory expression on his face.

"What in God's name were *you* doing there?"

"Liam asked me to go and give Paul a map."

"Sounds like the whole fucking town was up there tramping about."

I counted to ten. "Paul needed it for the survey," I said as calmly as I could. "As for the bones, they don't know how old they are nor how long they've been there. They won't know anything much until a pathologist examines them." I looked at my watch. "She's probably there now, as it happens."

"Jesus Christ." Kelly ran his fingers through his thinning hair. "Why do they want to talk to me? Do they think I have something to do with it?"

"They didn't say that."

"How am I supposed to know how the hell the damn thing got there?"

"Look, why don't you sit down?"

He shook his head. "I mean, why do they think I'd allow the place to be surveyed if I was hiding a fucking body there?"

"I did say that, actually. I expect they need to speak to you because you're the owner."

He stopped pacing. For a second he looked like a little boy. "Will you come down to the station with me?"

"If you want me to."

His shoulders relaxed slightly. He sat down, put his elbows on the desk, and held his head in his hands.

"Why did I ever buy that damn place? It's been nothing but a headache since I first set eyes on it. Paid far too much for it, couldn't get planning permission, and then the whole bloody economy collapses. A more superstitious person than me would think that the place was cursed. That I was being punished for buying a secularized church and trying to make something of it."

I smiled. "I don't think Whitewater Church can be blamed for the collapse of the whole national economy."

"I suppose not. Still . . . It hasn't brought me much luck. You can't deny that."

"No," I conceded. "But then you couldn't really have predicted this latest development."

Kelly looked gloomily at the stack of papers on my desk. "Those the deeds?"

"Yes, why?"

"Anything in them about a hex?"

McFadden was on his knees searching for something behind the counter when we walked in.

I leaned over to speak to him. "Is the sergeant back, Andy?"

He looked up. "Nope. He's still up at the church."

Kelly groaned beside me.

"This is Raymond Kelly," I said. "The owner. Tom wanted to speak to him."

McFadden stood up. "Aye, okay. I can start taking some details from you if you like, Mr. Kelly."

He managed to get as far as Kelly's address by the time the door of the station opened and Molloy strode in, accompanied by an attractive blond woman, dressed in a dark trouser suit and flat shoes. They were deep in conversation. Molloy glanced briefly in our direction as they walked past and the woman looked up. Our eyes met and I found myself staring into a face I had hoped with all my heart never to see again. Without warning I was transported back eight years, to that awful courtroom where I had last seen her. I gripped the counter and looked away. Seconds later, I heard the door of the interview room at the back of the station slam shut.

Time stood still until they reemerged. My gaze followed them as they walked together towards the door, Molloy leaning forward to catch what she was saying. Pins and needles started to work their way up my neck. I forced myself to look away again, and tried my best to concentrate on Kelly's replies to McFadden's questions until I heard the front door of the station close and felt Molloy beside me.

"Was that . . . ?" I asked. My voice sounded odd.

"That was the pathologist." He looked at Kelly. "And this is?"

"Raymond Kelly, the owner of Whitewater Church."

"Thanks for coming down, Mr. Kelly. I'm sure this is very distressing for you, but we'd be grateful for any assistance you can give us. I'll be back to you in a few minutes to ask you some more questions."

Kelly nodded miserably. Molloy looked at me and cast his eyes in the direction of the interview room. I followed him, unsure if my legs would even work. He leaned against the door with his arms crossed.

"Nothing much yet," he said. "Deceased was male. And according to the pathologist, from the level of decomposition, he's been dead for at least five years. The body was completely skeletonized. But you knew that."

I looked down, the grisly image still clear in my mind.

"That's it so far. She's only done a preliminary examination. No cause of death yet. We don't even know whether the bones were put there by somebody or if the man died down there."

I struggled to refocus. "God, I hope he didn't. What a place to die."

"If he did, it wasn't an accident – we can be sure of that. The gate was bolted from the outside when you arrived, wasn't it?"

"Yes."

"That confirms what Doherty said. With or without the padlock, that gate can't be opened from the inside. The bars are too narrow. He'd have been trapped."

"Christ."

"Yes, Christ. The pathologist has arranged for the bones to be taken down to the hospital in Letterkenny. She's going to do a full examination and postmortem there tonight, so we should have more in the morning."

Molloy opened the door. "Your client – I know him, I think. He owns a few pubs over the west of Donegal, doesn't he, and one in Buncrana. Big into fund-raising for the hospice?"

"That's him."

"Do you want to stay while I talk to him?"

Chapter 3

I STAYED. THE interview didn't last long. Kelly wasn't exactly forthcoming. His responses to Molloy's questions consisted mainly of him insisting that he hadn't been in the blessed place since he bought it and he was damn sure there weren't any skeletons there then. And, in case they were wondering, he was sure his wife hadn't seen any either. And yes, there had always been padlocks on all of the gates, including the crypt.

Molloy didn't seem to want to press him any further at this stage, and so after half an hour, Kelly and I left the garda station together. I walked him to his Mercedes and left him wearing the expression of a man who has won the lottery and lost the ticket.

Alone for the first time in the driver's seat of my old Mini, I put the key in the ignition but couldn't turn it. Instead, I found myself staring at the windscreen, frantically trying to rein in my emotions. A cold hand reached down my throat and clutched at my insides. I knew there weren't too many female pathologists in Ireland, so when Molloy had said *"she's on her way"* up at the church, how on earth could it not have occurred to me that it might be her? Was it the "forensic anthropologist" bit that had thrown me? She had obviously acquired an extra qualification, and there was no law against that. But I had never imagined for a second that I would see her again – and certainly not here.

My phone beeped, making me jump. It was a text reminding me about a Drama Club meeting at seven o'clock. Pathetically grateful for the distraction, I looked at my watch: nearly half six. No point in going home, and as I hadn't had anything to eat since lunch, there was time for a quick sandwich and a coffee.

As I hurried on foot across the square, I wondered if news of the discovery at Whitewater Church had reached the Oak. Now *that* would be a true test of the town's radar. But the pub was deserted. The only live body in the place was behind the bar building a house of cards with beer mats. Although "live" might be pushing it, as a description of Eddie Kearney. I knew, too, the second I saw the cellophane-wrapped sandwiches left over from lunch, that my stomach was not yet ready for food. The choice seemed to be egg mayonnaise or egg mayonnaise.

"Hi, Eddie. Is the boss about?"

He looked up at me all acne-faced and bleary-eyed. "He's gone home for a wee while and then he's going to some meeting in the hall, I think," he said vaguely.

"Grand. I'll see him there. Can I get a black coffee, please?"

I had just taken a seat by the fire when the door opened and a tall man in a pink shirt and blue tie stuck his head in and surveyed the room. It was Liam McLaughlin, the estate agent. He made a beeline in my direction.

"I've just been over to your office. It's shut. I've been trying to ring you there," he said indignantly.

"It's twenty to seven, Liam."

"That didn't stop Ray Kelly ringing me, so it didn't."

"Oh God, yes. I'm sorry. I wasn't sure if I was supposed to tell anyone yet."

He sat beside me and lowered his tone. "Kelly says Paul found a body up at the church, is that right?"

"Well, yes, bones. Human remains anyway, in the crypt underneath the church. They've been there for some time, apparently. The guards don't know anything about them yet, how long they've been there even. The state pathologist is examining them in Letterkenny."

Liam whistled. "Jesus. Kelly's not happy. My ears are still burning."

"I know. I've just left him."

"Do they know who it is? Or how they got there? I mean, did someone get trapped down there or what?"

"No idea yet."

"Jesus," he said again.

I hesitated. "You would have been up there a few times, wouldn't you, showing the place to people?"

"Well, no. You see, the first people I showed it to was that English couple we were getting the survey done for. Fell in love with the place when they were driving by it. Called me out of the blue." He grinned. "No accounting for taste. Why do you ask?"

"Did you show them the crypt?"

He shook his head. "No. Didn't know it existed, to be honest. I just assumed that wee gate led down into some kind of an air vent."

I raised my eyebrows at him as I took a gulp of my coffee.

He caught my look and his face fell. "Oh, Jesus, you're not saying them bones were there the whole time I was showing those people around?"

"Looks like it."

"Fuck."

"Whoever it is, the pathologist reckons the person's been dead at least five years."

"That English couple will hardly go ahead with it now, will they?" Liam sighed. "Not really what you want for your new home, is it – a body in the cellar?"

"Suppose not. Although I doubt if they know about it yet."

"It's not something I can exactly keep from them."

"No."

He stared into the fire, his expression glum. "I'm never going to be able to sell the damn place now, am I?"

"It's not going to be easy," I agreed as I took another gulp of my coffee.

Liam groaned and made his way up to the bar to order a pint.

Ten minutes later I finished my coffee, pulled on my coat and scarf, and reluctantly left the Oak and its fire to head down to the Beacon Hall, leaving Liam chatting to Eddie at the bar. The icy wind hit me as soon as I opened the pub door; the temperature must have been well below zero. No snow yet, but it was coming. You could feel it in the air.

As I walked down the hill, the footpath ahead of me glistened under the street lamps as if someone had sprinkled tiny crystals everywhere. I always liked the town at this time of the evening. It was quiet and still. The shops were closed; it was time for TV and homework and indoors. I felt calmer.

I reached the bottom of the hill, crossed the road, and walked in through the high pillars to the old hall, stone chippings crunching beneath my feet. The car park was shrouded in grainy shadow, and I picked my way carefully between the cars. Condensation was forming on their windscreens; in an hour they would be opaque, laced with spiders' webs of ice. I looked up at the huge Georgian windows, which were dimly lit. The main door was slightly ajar, a chink of light casting a white line across the footsteps.

I pushed it open and ran up the warped wooden stairs. It was impossible to tell if it was colder inside or out. In the main hall I was greeted by a friendly wave from a large, yellow-clad arm near the stage. The only heat in the room was coming from an old gas Superser heater fizzing bad-temperedly and ineffectively in the corner, impotent against the hall's high ceilings and old wooden floors.

Two men and two women in heavy coats and scarves were huddled around an old card table, ragged strips of green baize hanging from the edges like a fringe. They stopped talking as I approached, and the older of the two men got up and dragged an extra chair to the table.

"Thanks, Hal. Always the gentleman." My breath came out as a white mist.

"Chairman's duty." He tipped his cap at me with a grin. Hal McKinney, master of the pun. It was Hal who had persuaded me to join the drama group. As well as being the local undertaker and mechanic, he was also a Commissioner for Oaths. I sent clients to him to have documents sworn. It was a running joke that Hal could bury you, sign the probate papers, and then sell your car.

Looks were exchanged as I took my seat. I was beginning to feel as if I had interrupted something.

"How is everyone?" I asked cheerfully, examining the faces around me.

"Baltic." Phyllis Kettle, the owner of the yellow-clad arm and the town's secondhand book shop, stated the obvious. She was wearing an incredible ensemble of yellow coat, mittens, and blue shawl, which, weirdly on someone of her considerable size, worked. The dark skin helped, and the kind eyes. She had a notebook and pen in front of her, though how she planned to write with mittens on I had no idea. She certainly seemed disinclined to take them off.

"Right, let's get this over with as quickly as possible," she said. "And that means no big speeches." She directed her comment at the mournful-looking, long-faced man with the beard sitting opposite her. Tony Craig, local publican, owner of the Oak and enthusiastic raconteur, had the ability to make a riddle last the length of *The Iliad*.

Well aware of his reputation, he grinned back at her, his smile transforming his face.

"Are we all here?" I asked, looking around. Claire Devitt, the club's set designer, poster artist, and general publicity person, was missing. Not that surprising. Claire was unreliable and had become even more so of late.

"Claire's not coming," said Eithne O'Connell, as if reading my mind.

"Oh?"

The local chemist's quavering tone always irked me for some reason. There was something almost parasitic about the tragic air she adopted when passing on someone else's personal drama. As if she herself were personally affected by it.

"They think they might have found Conor," she said, her eyelids fluttering closed as she spoke.

"Who is Conor?" I asked.

"Conor Devitt. Claire's brother," Phyllis said. "He disappeared six or seven years ago."

I looked up. "Disappeared?"

"Vanished. Without a trace. It happened just before his wedding," Hal said.

"You wouldn't have met him." Phyllis patted my forearm. "It would have been the summer before you came up."

Hal coughed. "As a matter of fact, we thought you might know something about it."

"Me, why?" I asked.

They looked at each other. Phyllis was the first to transfer her gaze to me. She held it there as if waiting for something to register. And it did, of course. I can put two and two together. While they all looked at me expectantly, I played for time, Molloy's words echoing in my ears.

"When you say they think they've found him . . . ?"

"Up at Whitewater." Hal's eyes narrowed suspiciously. "You were up at Whitewater yourself with the sergeant earlier on today, weren't you?"

I had been seen. "Ah, that's why you think I might know something," I said. "Well, I don't, I'm afraid. You know more than I do."

A short silence ensued during which all four regarded me doubtfully.

Phyllis sighed. "Well, the family thinks it might be Conor they found up there. Eithne was just telling us before you came in. As soon as word got out about the body, Claire was on to the guards to see if it might be him. They're all up at the mother's now, waiting to hear."

"God, that's pretty grim," I said. "Are they doing DNA tests?"

Eithne nodded solemnly, her face a picture of tragic concern. "Claire said the guards were looking for the name of his dentist to get his dental records," she told us, her eyelids closing again. "It's just so awful."

There was a collective shiver around the table.

"Should we postpone the meeting, do you think, out of respect?" Tony said after a few seconds. "Till we find out if it is Conor? Seems a bit callous to carry on as normal and start choosing plays while Claire's going through something like this."

"Agreed," said Hal immediately. "Same time next week, instead?"

"Or what about Monday night?" Tony suggested. "We could have our meeting in the pub. I might even stretch to a few sandwiches, if one of you manages to buy a pint."

There was a nod of agreement around the table and everyone stood up. The sense of relief seemed to lift the temperature of the room.

"Careful. They look pretty lethal," I said as Phyllis made her way precariously down the glistening steps outside. Eithne put her hand out to help, but Phyllis waved her away impatiently.

"I'm not an invalid, you know. I'm fat."

Eithne's hand flew to her mouth, a wounded expression on her face.

Phyllis' tone softened. "Entirely self-inflicted, Eithne, and much fun doing so. Save your charity for someone who deserves it."

Somehow she managed to reach the foot of the steps without incident. She leaned against the wall for a minute to catch her breath.

"Speaking of deserving charity, why is it that some families seem to get it so much worse than others?" she said. "They've had such a rough time of it, those Devitts."

"Dreadful to have someone you love disappear like that," Eithne said in a whisper. "No closure. It's been so terrible for poor Claire."

I decided to keep my views to myself on this occasion. I knew they weren't objective. You see, I have never been too sure about the need for closure. I know it is a common thesis, but I've always been of the view that if there's no body, at least there's hope. But I guess that can't go on indefinitely either. Six years is a long time.

"And for his mother and brother," Phyllis said. "Awful for his fiancée, too, of course. God love her. Day of her wedding and he just didn't turn up. No explanation. Can you imagine?"

I shook my head. I couldn't.

I jumped suddenly when a dance music track blared into the night and Eithne scrambled to find her phone. She retrieved it from her bag and hurried away to answer it, heading towards her car – an old Fiat Punto parked by the gate.

"Odd ringtone for someone like Eithne," I commented as I walked with Phyllis in the other woman's wake.

Phyllis grinned. "I know. You'd expect it to be a hymn or something." She lowered her tone. "I think that was Claire, by the way."

"How could you tell?"

"The expression on Eithne's face."

I smiled. "Seriously? You're good."

"Okay, a guess then. Did you know Claire used to work for Eithne when she was a student?"

"No, I didn't."

"They're very . . . close."

There was something about the way she said it that I couldn't quite decipher. She crossed her arms and rested her large rump against the back door of Eithne's old Punto as Eithne paced up and down in front of the gate and I stamped my feet to avoid losing the feeling in them completely. Phyllis didn't seem to notice the cold anymore. She appeared distracted, studying Eithne with great interest as she finished her call, and slapping the car door with her gloved palm as the chemist walked back towards us.

"Still driving this old rust-bucket, Eithne?"

"As long as it gets me from A to B, it does me just fine." Eithne's lips were pursed.

"Fair enough. That's me told." Phyllis grinned at me.

Eithne opened the car door, got in, and turned on the engine to defrost the windscreen, clearly anxious to get off.

But Phyllis wasn't going to let her leave that easily. She held the door open, leaning in. "There were those who said he'd done a runner, weren't there?"

"What was that?" Eithne said distractedly.

"Conor. People thought he'd just upped and gone to England. But Claire never believed that, did she? Claire never believed he just left?"

Eithne looked up blankly. It seemed to take her a couple of seconds to register the question.

Eventually she replied, "She said he'd never have left their mother like that. It wasn't in him."

"Looks like she might have been right," Phyllis muttered ominously, as Eithne revved the engine and drove out through the gate in front of us.

Chapter 4

THE NEXT MORNING I had that nauseous, dry-mouthed feeling that comes from too little sleep. Between the blond pathologist in Glendara garda station and flashbacks of what I had seen in the crypt, the night was haunted by images I could have done without.

I was sure I had seen a spark of recognition in the pathologist's glance. It wouldn't take her long to work out where she had seen me before, if she hadn't already. I was disturbed by the idea that when she did, she would feel the need to share that information – and I wasn't sure what I could do about it. In the meantime, that woman had brought with her a raft of memories I had worked hard to suppress, and I needed to hammer them back down to a safe level if I was to function in any way normally.

By midday there had been no new developments to do with the discovery at the church. According to Leah, Kelly had called twice looking for news. I let her take messages each time. I wasn't ready to speak to either Kelly or Molloy. Eventually, I gave up trying to concentrate on work and crossed the square to Paul Doherty's office.

I was glad to see he looked a lot less green than the last time I had seen him, but infinitely more hassled. He was on the phone, so I sat in his reception area and flicked through a magazine. When he finished his call, he left the receiver off the hook and raised his eyes to heaven.

"Kelly ringing you, too, by any chance?" he asked.

"Twice. Was that him?"

"Not that time, thankfully."

"How are you doing?"

"Okay." He perched on his desk and stretched his arms. "Jesus, I wasn't expecting that yesterday though."

"Me neither, I can tell you."

"Any news from the postmortem?"

"Not yet."

He shook his head. "Did you not think that was the strangest thing you've ever seen?"

"I guess it's not something you'd come across too often in your line of work."

"It'll stay with me a long time, I can tell you." He shuddered. "God, the way it was left. Creepy as hell."

"You mean rolled up in the blanket?"

"Aye, with the pillow under the skull."

I inhaled sharply. "I didn't notice that."

He smiled weakly. "Really? That's not like you." His brow furrowed. "Actually, I didn't see it the first time either, come to think of it. But that second time when I went down with the sergeant I got a clearer look. He pulled the blanket back further than either of us did. You could see there was a pillow squashed up underneath the skull."

"Are you serious?"

"Absolutely serious. It looked like some kind of macabre sleeping bag."

"Jesus." I paused. "Do you think the bones were put there by someone then, in the crypt?"

"I suppose they could have been." He braced his shoulders, as if gathering courage to revisit the image. "The blanket was an old Irish wool blanket, the kind most of us had on our beds before duvets. Half the houses in the country would have one like it."

I nodded. A flashback to my childhood bedroom.

"I'd say that bolt had been used recently enough, too. It opened a bit too smoothly for my liking. And then of course there was Andy finding that cut padlock."

"So you think someone broke in and left the remains there?" I asked.

He shrugged. "God only knows. I'm no expert, but the blanket looked fresh enough to me. And the bones sure as hell didn't."

"Maybe I'll give Molloy a call and see if there's any news."

Paul gestured towards the phone. "Kelly's not happy."

"I know."

"I think he holds me responsible for finding the body." He smiled ruefully.

"Sounds like him all right. You're just too thorough, Paul." I looked around the office. "You on your own?"

"Yep. Both of them off sick at the same time. Typical. Claiming the winter vomiting bug."

"And the cigarettes?" I asked.

"Haven't had one since yesterday." He grinned. "I ran out."

I called Molloy on his mobile. I didn't block the number like I usually do when calling a client, so he must have known it was me. But still he answered in his usual formal way.

"Molloy."

Sometimes it bothered me more than others. Today it bothered me – paranoia, maybe. I didn't like the idea of him having cosy chats with the pathologist.

"Tom, it's Ben. Any developments on the postmortem? You said you'd give me a shout when you were finished up at the church."

"Where are you?"

"In the square. Outside Paul Doherty's place. Why?"

"Come down to the station. I'll be here for another half an hour or so."

Molloy was eating a tired-looking ham sandwich at his desk. He didn't look much better himself: there were dark circles under his gray eyes. He offered me a tea, which I accepted, despite my better instincts. I was handed a mug with a big red heart and the words *I love Montenegro* scrawled across it. As expected, the tea was strong enough to chew.

"I've been talking to Paul Doherty about the way the bones were found," I said.

"Right."

"Pretty strange, wasn't it?"

"Certainly."

Molloy has always been hard to gauge. For five years our professional lives have intersected. I like his kindness, his commitment to his work, his quiet intelligence, the fact that his sense of humor surfaces when least expected. He has made me laugh when I least wanted to, when I most needed to.

I like to think that he regards me as an ally, a friend even. But there are times when it isn't so clear-cut. He is a guard and I am a solicitor, after all. I guess there are limits – it just feels sometimes as if it is always Molloy who remembers them. And then six weeks ago, something changed between us. New Year's Eve. There was a moment. A moment that seems to have cleaved a distance between us I don't entirely understand. So I hesitated before asking my next question.

"Were they put there by someone?"

He didn't respond. I tried again.

"I mean, presumably the man didn't die like that. Wrapped in a blanket with a pillow beneath his head."

He relented. "It seems that the bones may have been moved into the crypt from somewhere else."

"From where?"

"There were traces of soil on them. Minute, but not matching what is in the crypt."

"So they were buried somewhere else first?"

"We don't know that yet."

"Where?"

"As I say, we don't know. We're looking."

I thought about that for a minute. "So we're not talking about grave robbers then. The bones weren't buried in a coffin if there was soil on them, were they?"

Molloy's eyes flashed at me. "Is this general curiosity, or are you asking these questions for the benefit of your clients?"

I colored, aware that Molloy was under no obligation to give me any information at all. As he continued to chew on his sandwich, I tried to read his face. It was only then that I realized he must have had his own reasons for asking me to come down.

His expression softened. "Would it be okay if I asked you a question for a change?"

"Sorry. Of course. Go ahead."

"Thank you. Did you see Doherty touch the bones at all before you called us?"

"Paul?" I said in surprise. "No. He just did what I did. He moved the top of the blanket aside so he could see what was underneath. That's all."

"And where were you when this was happening?"

"At the entrance to the crypt. It was pretty dark, but I had a torch. Then I went down after him."

Molloy nodded and took a bite of his sandwich. I decided to risk another question, this time in what I hoped was safer territory.

"Is it true you think it might be Conor Devitt?"

Molloy raised his eyebrows.

"Claire, his sister, is in the drama group."

Molloy sniffed. "Not many secrets in this town," he said.

I smiled. "No."

"The family seems convinced it is him," he said. "And the bones do belong to a male who could have been Devitt's age at the time he disappeared. Conor was thirty-three. But they could also belong to someone ten years older or ten years younger."

I whistled. "Pretty broad range."

"It's the level of decomposition that's the problem. It means we can't be absolutely precise about the date of death either. Or cause of death for that matter, at this stage, although that may be established by the postmortem. But the date of death is also in range of when Devitt disappeared."

"Are you doing DNA testing?"

"Yes. It's the only way we can be sure. The Devitts have all been called to the hospital in Letterkenny to give swabs. The mother, your friend Claire, and the other son. We're using dental records, too. We should have some idea by Monday morning."

"God love them."

Molloy threw the remains of his sandwich in the wastepaper basket and leaned back in his chair. "We tried our best to find out what happened to him at the time. Without much success, unfortunately."

"Was there anything missing?" I asked. "Money, passport?"

"He'd taken out some money over the previous couple of days, but he was about to get married so that was hardly surprising. And his passport wasn't missing. But then you don't need a passport to go to England on the boat."

"Must have been rough on the family."

"I'm sure it was."

I sipped cautiously at my tea. "So someone dug up a set of bones from somewhere, wrapped them in a blanket and put them in the crypt, with a pillow beneath the skull?"

I was back in dangerous waters. Molloy threw me a warning look. "There are things I can't tell you at this stage, Ben, you know that."

"Okay," I said reluctantly. "Can I ask one more question?"

Molloy sighed.

"Is the skeleton intact?"

"A couple of the smaller bones are broken, and some are not in the right position – but yes, it's almost intact."

"I presume no fingerprints on anything?"

Molloy gave me a *what do you think* look.

"Well, you did say that the pathologist is still working on them," I said brightly.

"Yes."

"So something else may come to light."

"Possibly."

I got up to leave, then remembered what I had come to ask him. I cleared my throat. Molloy looked up.

"Any idea when you'll be finished up at the church? Kelly is going to want to know."

He looked away. "It'll take as long as it takes."

It was as if I'd tipped my cold tea over him.

Chapter 5

I LEFT WORK early, before darkness fell. I needed to clear my head. I live in Malin town, which is a bit of a misnomer since it's actually a small village, about five miles north of the real town of Glendara. I parked on the green in front of my cottage, ran in, did a quick change, and collected together what I needed.

I drove out along the winding coast road, making for Malin Head, past the steep, grassy hills, each one dotted with small white patches of gravity-defying sheep. After three miles or so, I slowed down and took a left towards the sea, following the sign for *Trá na gCuig Méar – Five Fingers Strand*. Five Fingers Strand, or Lagg as the locals call it, is one of my favorite places on earth. I could feel my spirits lift as I drove down the narrow twisting lane, over the bridge and tiny stream, and past the little white chapel and myriad rabbit holes.

After a while I felt the ground under the car soften, and soon I was driving on sand. I caught my first glimpse of the sea through the dunes planted like sentries at the entrance to the beach, turned off the engine, and sat for a minute. The gray hulk of Glashedy Island dominated the horizon. The sea was a deep, greeny blue, the sand beneath it golden. In the heat of the car it was possible to imagine I was looking at a tropical Caribbean scene. But I knew that was deceptive. This was Donegal. And the Atlantic Ocean. In February.

The beach was deserted. Today that suited me perfectly. I grabbed my towel and clothes from the passenger seat and got out, not bothering to lock the car. I wouldn't be long. This was not going to be a leisurely swim, more of a quick medicinal dip. I negotiated my way over the remains of the concrete path wrecked by erosion, and down onto the beach. As soon as I was out of the protection of the dunes, I was hit by a blast of biting sea breeze and I shivered, despite my warm jacket and scarf.

It was always at this point that I doubted my sanity. But I knew the benefits of swimming in the sea the whole year round, and one of them was to *preserve* whatever sanity I had left. My grandparents had done it, and my parents did it, and it seemed to work for them, kept their hearts healthy. Although they had always done it a few degrees' latitude farther south – and those few degrees can make a hell of a difference. Still, it made me feel closer to them on some level. Less guilty.

I stood for a moment and looked, as I always did, across the bay to the five regal rocks that protruded from the sea to give the beach its name, and watched as flocks of seagulls swooped and dived off the cliffs above them. The towering Knockamany Bens.

It soon hit me that standing still wasn't such a good idea. The icy wind was numbing my face. I made my way down towards the shore over the smooth rocks and twisted kelp. The tide was on its way in, the water already halfway up the beach. Generally, Lagg is not a safe place to swim. The currents in the bay are dangerous and unpredictable. But all I needed was a quick dip: a tea-bag swim, or a three-stroker. One to get you out, one to turn, and one to bring you back in.

I stopped at a large rock covered in green moss and put my towel on the driest patch I could find. The wind was whipping my hair about my face. I found a clip in the pocket of my jacket to pin it back, took a deep breath, and started to undress, pulling on my swimming togs and the pair of ancient blue flip-flops I've had since I was a teenager. I picked up my towel and put it around my shoulders for a minute, but hesitation is unwise when tackling a winter sea swim in Donegal. Gritting my teeth, I threw the towel off and ran down the beach towards the sea, discarding my flip-flops a couple of yards from the nearest encroachment of the tide and crying out at the freezing cold of the stones beneath my feet. Suddenly self-conscious, I scanned the beach to see if anyone was around, but it was still deserted. I hopped along towards the sea, and yelped again when the icy waves washed up against my ankles. Then I heard my father's voice: *Straight in, girl, that's the only way to do it.*

I waded in until the water was up to my waist, hyperventilating all the way, then plunged in headfirst. As I submerged, the cold hit me like a ton of bricks; I thought my heart was going to stop. I managed two strokes of crawl out, turned in one, and two strokes back in, relieved when my feet found the bottom again. Desperate to get back onto dry land and into some kind of warmth, I splashed my way back in towards the beach like a drowning animal and staggered up the stones, shuffling into my flip-flops. Not easy, considering I could no longer feel my feet.

But even though my teeth were chattering and parts of me were completely numb, I knew it had worked. I stumbled back up to where my clothes were and started to dry myself off, struggling out of my swimming togs and into my jeans and shirt. My head felt free, my mind clear. Always for these few minutes, and to a lesser extent for an hour or so after, I felt alert and happy. Short-lived but highly effective. I hummed to myself as I dressed.

A voice interrupted my humming. I raised my head but couldn't see anyone and decided it was probably the wind, although I did notice that darkness was falling. I went back to getting dressed. Again, I heard a voice – this time, I was sure someone called my name. I looked up to see a hunched figure walking towards me, waving. I dragged on my boots and coat and scarf, wrapped my togs in the damp towel, and set off to meet them. To my shame, when I finally recognized the face, I experienced that second of panic you get when you struggle to find the right thing to say.

Claire Devitt was wearing a long tweed coat that was far too big for her and a huge green woolen scarf. Her high-pitched voice reached me long before she did. She sounded appalled.

"What in God's name were you doing? Did I see you get in for a swim?"

"It's something I do every so often," I told her. "I'm not usually seen."

She was smiling but the strain was etched heavily on her face. Her skin had a waxy sheen and her long dank hair looked like it hadn't seen shampoo in a week. Her mouth was smeared with bright purple lipstick.

"Are you a lunatic or what? It must be completely freezing."

"It is," I said.

"Some old Dublin habit, I suppose. You wouldn't find too many around here doing that. Unless for charity on Christmas Day or something."

She was speaking very quickly, as if she was trying to fill the air with noise to avoid giving me the opportunity to mention the obvious.

"It helps to clear my head sometimes," I said.

Her smile faded. "Aye, I know what you mean. I could do with something like that. I thought a walk might help. I had to get out of the house."

"We've been thinking about you."

She looked down at her feet, clad in sturdy black workman's boots. "Aye. Phyllis called me this morning."

Not for the first time it hit me that Phyllis' nosy though caring approach was so often the kinder route than respectful distance.

"I know Eithne's been worried about you, too."

"Has she?" Her expression was hard to read.

"How is your mother?" I asked.

"She's getting old, needs taking care of. I've been doing it since Conor disappeared. Not that I mind doing it, of course, but it's not easy." She stared off into the distance. "In a way we've been mourning him for six years. At least if we knew . . ."

"I know what you mean. So . . ." I hesitated. "When will you know?"

She clutched at a strand of her hair and started to pull at it. The skin around her fingernails was torn and red.

"Monday. But I know it's him. He used to go up to Whitewater Church sometimes. He must have gone up the morning of the wedding for a walk and fallen or something."

I looked down. It seemed Molloy hadn't given any details yet about the way the bones were found. I presumed he wanted to wait until they were formally identified.

She studied my face. "I know what people were saying when he disappeared, that he'd just taken off. But we knew he wouldn't have left us to cope without him. He wasn't that kind of person. Conor always took care of us."

"I believe he was about to get married, too," I said.

She frowned. "That wouldn't have changed anything. He had responsibilities to his family."

"Of course. You have another brother, haven't you?"

"Aye. Of a sort," she said bitterly. "Danny. God knows where *he* is."

"He doesn't live with you?"

"Not anymore. He's never around when we need him. After Conor went missing, he took off, too. The rest of us were going through hell, not knowing if Conor was alive or dead, and where was Danny? We'll never know. Came back weeks later looking like a tramp. And now he's done it again."

She started to chew on her bottom lip, getting lipstick on her teeth in the process.

"I come down here to dream." Her voice drifted, and she looked off into the distance. "I have to allow myself to just *be* sometimes, you know?"

I nodded.

"Then I saw you and I thought . . . I suppose I just wanted to have a semi-normal conversation with someone for a few minutes."

"I'm sorry. I'm not sure I've entirely managed that for you," I said gently.

"Not to worry." She turned to face me again. "I'd better go and get some groceries. Who knows what next week will hold. We may have a lot of visitors." Her expression was suddenly brighter, as if she were relishing the thought of a party.

I frowned. "Yes, I suppose you might."

"In a way we've been mourning him for six years, you know," she said defensively.

But she had said that already.

Chapter 6

By Saturday morning, the long-threatened snow had arrived. I woke early to the sound of Guinness complaining loudly on the sill outside my bedroom window. Guinness is an enormous black tomcat with a patch of white on the top of his head, who deigns to live with me and eat my food. When he feels like it. This morning he had managed to make his way up the lilac bush in the front garden and onto the windowsill.

I pulled back the curtains and opened the window, shielding my eyes against the startling brightness. He leaped down onto the carpet and shook out one paw after the other in an indignant fashion, as if the whole winter wonderland outside was a conspiracy against him. Then he tried to clamber up onto my bed, which I strenuously resisted. There are limits.

I leaned my cheek against the glass and gazed out the window. Malin is never exactly a heaving metropolis, but this early on a Saturday morning there wasn't a soul around to spoil the view. Here and there seagulls hopped about, almost completely camouflaged by the layer of white icing that covered the houses, church, and park benches dotted about the green. Everything was perfect and still. Even the gulls' cries were muffled by the snow. I live in a picture-postcard village at the best of times, but when it snows, no Christmas card can beat it.

Guinness weaving impatiently in and out through my bare legs made me shiver and prompted me to shut the window and head downstairs, the cat trailing after me. As I warmed some milk, I replayed my conversation with Molloy from the day before and came to the conclusion that it was vintage Molloy, nothing more. The usual struggle between us. There was no need for me to suddenly be bothered by it now. That pathologist was here to do a job. She'd be gone in a day or two and that would be the end of it; I'd never have to see her again and I could close off those memories. In the white stillness of day I could rationalize, but it had not been so the night before. The swim had helped me sleep but hadn't managed to block the dreams.

I opened the blinds over the kitchen sink. The weather wasn't going to make the guards' job at Whitewater Church any easier. If they were trying to establish whether the bones had been buried somewhere nearby before being moved to the crypt, they would make no progress today.

I had spoken to Kelly before I left the office. Liam was right about the buyers. The English couple who had been so sure that Whitewater was the home of their dreams had executed a rapid U-turn when the news of the discovery in the crypt had reached them. Which it had, apparently, without Liam ever having to tell them. News travels fast in Inishowen. They had returned to England on Friday morning, having withdrawn their offer.

Needless to say, this hadn't helped Kelly's mood. I had promised to let him know when the guards were finished with the church so he could get it back on the market as soon as possible. But I wasn't about to ring Molloy again yet.

I poured milk into Guinness' dish, turned on the radio, and was just starting to make some coffee when the phone rang. When I answered it, I could hear kids squabbling loudly in the background. A female voice shouted at them to keep quiet.

"Sorry about that."

It was Maeve, the local vet.

"You not working today?" I said.

"Nope. I was on call last night but managed to escape with about six hours' sleep. Which isn't bad for this time of year."

"Well done."

"And the good news is that my dear husband has promised to take the boys to their birthday party this afternoon. So I was wondering if you fancied a run into Derry? Lunch out, a bit of shopping, that kind of thing."

"Maybe. What are the roads like?"

"Not too bad. The main ones are all salted. Should be grand into Derry. The sales are probably still on. It's about six months since I've spent any money."

"Okay, then. Sounds good."

"One o'clock in the Tavern?"

"Great. I'll meet you in there. I've a couple of things to do first."

The main roads may have been salted but the secondary roads weren't so healthy, I discovered, while maneuvring my poor old Mini back up the hill to Whitewater Church. The sky had turned a deep blue, the day was utterly still, and the snow was crunchy underfoot and precariously slippery. I had a couple of close encounters with the ditch. When I finally arrived at the church, a figure dressed in something resembling a boiler suit was closing the main gate. As I rolled down the window it took me a second to recognize Andy McFadden. McFadden must be thirty at least, but out of the garda uniform he looked like a kid.

"I like the gear," I called out.

He grinned, making him look even younger.

"Protective clothing. We all have to wear it now. Can't be trampling all over the crime scene."

"You on your own?" I asked.

"I am now."

"Last one to leave turns out the lights?" I said.

"Something like that. The crime scene lads have just finished. It was pretty crowded earlier on." He looked around him. "Just as well they got most of what they needed done last night. The ground's completely frozen."

"So I see. They're done then, are they? Can I tell the Kellys that you're finished with the place?"

"I think so. For the moment."

"I'll contact them this afternoon. Did you find out anything about where the bones came from?"

McFadden looked uncomfortable.

"It's all right," I reassured him. "Molloy told me it was likely they were moved into the crypt from somewhere else."

He relented. "Aye, well, they found some disturbed ground in the old graveyard. A good bit away from the graves, over by the trees."

"A shallow grave, you mean?"

"They're not sure. But they've taken some soil samples away to be tested anyway. From there and from other places around here. See if they match the soil found on the bones."

I knew from the deeds that the tiny graveyard had been separated from the church property before Kelly had bought it. The church trustees had retained it and continued to maintain it. I presumed it was to that graveyard that most of the human remains from the crypt had been moved when the church was deconsecrated.

"Any idea when they'll have the results?"

"Monday evening, I think. Same as the DNA results, they hope."

I pulled my jacket and scarf from the back seat and locked the door.

"Did you know Conor Devitt, by the way?" I asked.

"Aye, I knew him surely." McFadden looked at the ground and kicked the gate to dislodge some snow from his boot. "I've known the family all my life. Conor was a good few years older than me, but we played football together. Good player he was. Always thought it was strange, him disappearing like that. Didn't fit. I've never met a more responsible kind of a fella, if you know what I mean."

"So I hear. I know Claire," I said. "She's in the Drama Club with me."

"'Course." He nodded. "That'd be her kind of thing."

"And he disappeared just before his wedding, I hear?" I said, pulling on my jacket and wrapping the scarf tightly around my neck.

"Aye. I was supposed to go to it. Awful for poor Lisa. Every woman's nightmare, I'd say, being stood up on your wedding day."

"Lisa was his fiancée?"

"Aye, Lisa McCauley as she was. Pretty girl. She used to come and watch us play. Out in all sorts of weather she was. Mad about him. They were together for years."

"God. Did she ever meet anyone else?"

McFadden smiled ruefully. "Would you believe she got married a fortnight ago? Due back from her honeymoon any day now, she is." He added quietly, as if in disbelief, "And now this happens. It'll have to set her back."

I made a face. "What a thing to come home to."

"Aye." McFadden opened the door of the squad car. "Well, maybe we'll have some answers on Monday. Enjoy the rest of the weekend."

I watched McFadden drive away, then walked farther on up the road until I came to an old pedestrian gateway with an ornate iron gate and an arch with a stone cross above it. The snow had settled on the arms of the cross like icing sugar. This was the entrance to the old Whitewater Church graveyard.

The gate whined as I pushed it open and closed it again behind me, and I trod carefully up the path over the immaculate and undisturbed snow. Mine were the first footsteps; the guards must have done all their work here the day before, meaning that I had no way of telling where they thought the body had been buried. It was even difficult to tell where the footpath was in parts, since the snow had drifted a little here and there.

The winter sunshine did nothing to reduce the strange sense of melancholy that comes with walking alone in an old graveyard, but still it was oddly beautiful. The only sounds came from a family of rooks calling to each other high up in the laden yew trees, and the creaking of the snow beneath my feet.

The sea lay in the distance, a patch of blue above the white, the line separating water and sky invisible. I looked around me. The gravestones were simple and weather-beaten, and all the more dignified for that. Some of the gravestones were half-buried, some half-fallen maybe. It was hard to tell with the snow. Others were taller, or on higher ground. These somber gray soldiers cast long shadows across the white. They were covered in lichen, demonstrating, if at all necessary, the purity of the air.

I peered at some of the names, those that weren't yet obscured by time. The family names were familiar – all common to the peninsula: Dohertys, McLaughlins, McDaids – their common nature the very reason for the local reliance on nicknames. As a blow-in I'm still a bit of an amateur at their usage, but I'm getting there. I knew it was two generations since Phyllis Kettle's grandfather had sold pots and pans in the town, but there wasn't a soul who called her Doherty.

Most who were buried here were long dead, twenty-five years ago or more, I noticed. Family plots were the exceptions: new names added to ancient gravestones. I noticed one or two more modern-looking stones, but they had dates from even further back. I wondered if they marked the burial sites of bodies moved from the crypt when the church was deconsecrated. Had the skeleton in the crypt made an eerie journey in the other direction, I asked myself, from the graveyard to the crypt? I looked around, wondering, if so, from where it had departed.

Suddenly, out of nowhere, a huge gull swooped down right in front of me, making me jump, missing me by inches. Heart pounding, I watched as it flew low along the ground for a short while and then rose again to soar off into the distance. I waited until my breathing had calmed down, then continued on my walk.

As I made my way back along the path that meandered through the graves, I thought about my reasons for coming up here. It wasn't just for my clients. A phone call would have sorted that out. But being here, in this peaceful place, gave me space to think.

Inishowen is an easy place to lose yourself, to cut yourself off from the rest of the world. But sometimes the walls you build up don't feel so secure anymore. A familiar ache had been returning gradually to my heart over the past year. I had suppressed it, was afraid of what lay beneath, afraid I would revert to asking the questions I had come to Donegal to forget. The ones I knew would never be answered.

I had told Molloy nothing of my past or my reasons for coming to Inishowen, although recently I had come close. We had begun to spend time together outside of work, to talk about things that weren't work-related, to eat together whenever our jobs kept us in town late. That was, until New Year's Eve, six weeks ago.

I had been out with Maeve, drinking too much, something I have a tendency to do when my unhappiness spills over – usually at major Christian festivals, I have discovered. Stupidly, I stayed out long after Maeve had gone home, despite her attempts to persuade me to leave. Molloy drove by the Oak, saw me standing outside talking to a Scottish cousin of Tony's who was home on holiday, and offered me a lift back to Malin. I took it, his sudden appearance bringing me to my senses.

We stayed sitting in the squad car outside my cottage talking for a long time. The conversation was easy and natural; two friends chatting in the dark, not looking at one another's faces. I came so close to telling him then, to pouring it all out, but I found myself having more fun than I'd had all evening and I didn't want it to end. And then something changed. The car was cold, I asked him in, and he said no. Suddenly I was embarrassed. I wasn't sure exactly what I had intended by my invitation but I felt rejected, foolish.

But then I had been about to get out of the car in hurt silence when he turned to face me, and our eyes met in a way they never had before. Without a word from either of us, a line was crossed and we both knew it. He leaned in close, close enough for me to see the dark flecks in his gray eyes, to breathe in the faintest trace of aftershave. As he reached for me, his phone rang. He pulled back immediately. His eyes scanned the number and his expression changed: it was as if someone had switched off a light. *"I've got to take this."* Matter-of-fact, businesslike, not a trace of apology or regret in his tone. He waited until I was out of the car to return the call – I saw him on the phone as I walked away.

Since that night, neither of us had spoken of it. In fact, until the discovery of the bones in the church, we had spoken very little at all.

And so the position remained the same; no one in Donegal knew who I was or why I had come here. I was beginning to wonder if that was a mistake.

I looked around me, at the snow-covered mounds: graves of people who for the most part, I assumed, had been allowed to die a natural death. Not everyone was so lucky. Even as a teenager I wondered what it was that made people kill. Not in war, that's a different issue – you know there are other factors at play – but what is it that drives one person to end another person's life, to take the most extreme, irreversible action? To look someone in the eyes and take everything away from them? And then continue to exist afterwards. That's the bit that truly gets me, and always has.

Ironic really, the way my life has turned out. That I should have to ask myself that very question; that fate would provide me with enough empirical evidence to have a go at working the answer out for myself.

The muffled sound of a tractor on the road dragged me back to the present. I cast my eyes around to get my bearings and saw that at some point I must have veered off the footpath. I caught sight of the gate again and started to make my way towards it. Suddenly, my right foot sank deeply into a drift and I lost my balance. I put my hand out to steady myself and gripped one of the gravestones.

With difficulty, I managed to extract my soaking foot and regain my balance. As I raised my head again, I saw the inscription on the headstone.

Jack Devitt born February 1, 1950 died August 12, 1987.

There were no details of family. I stood there for a minute rereading the name and dates. Jack Devitt: Conor's father, maybe? Claire had made no mention of her father. I wondered if this Jack Devitt had been fortunate enough to die a natural death. It seemed unlikely, given that he had been only thirty-seven when he died. A young man. Silently, I thanked him for breaking my fall.

Was it possible that the bones in the crypt were this man's son? And if so, how had they ended up in such a strange position? And how had he died? These were questions to which the family deserved answers – but it wasn't my job to find them. That was up to the guards. I had my own issues to resolve.

Chapter 7

ON MY WAY back into town I rang Kelly, but he didn't pick up. I'd try again later. What I wanted to say didn't feel appropriate for a voice message.

When I stopped in the square to buy a newspaper, the town had a busy, bustly Saturday-morning feel about it. I narrowly avoided a head-on collision in the doorway of the shop with a large pink creature laden down with two shopping bags.

"Sorry about that. Always have been a bit on the clumsy side."

"Morning, Phyllis. Not in the book shop this morning?"

She made a face. "I have my nephew doing Saturday mornings for me as a favor to my brother, but he's driving me up the wall. I had to get out of there, but now I'm away I'm convinced he's going to burn the place down."

I grinned. "That seems a bit unlikely, doesn't it?"

"I'm not so sure. Not a difficult thing to do with a book shop, you know, and he's perfectly capable of it. I keep catching him smoking out the back."

"Ah."

"Have you got a second?" she whispered.

I nodded and she beckoned me to the window of the wool shop next door, dumped her bags on the footpath, and let out a long breath.

"You haven't heard anything more about that Whitewater business, have you?" she asked. "If they know whether it's Conor Devitt or not?"

"I haven't. The tests take a few days, I think."

"Oh dear."

"Why?" I asked.

She lowered her voice even further. "Well, it's wee Danny."

"Danny?"

"Danny Devitt, Claire's brother. I've just seen him. He's drunk – and it's not even midday. I don't think he's handling it very well."

I remembered Claire's comments on the beach the day before.

Phyllis looked anxious. "I don't really know him but I wondered if there was something I should do. He's always been a bit odd; he might not welcome any interference."

"How old is he?" I asked.

She gave it some thought before replying. "Thirty-six, give or take a year or two?"

I smiled. "He's an adult, Phyllis, I'm afraid. He's free to have a drink if he wants to. And it's kind of understandable this weekend. Where did you see him?"

"Just going into the Oak."

"Tony'll take care of him. He's not going to serve him if he's in a bad way. He'll probably even drive him home."

"Aye, I suppose you're right. Only I feel a bit helpless."

"I know what you mean. I met Claire on the beach yesterday. What's the story with their father, by the way? She talked about her mother but she didn't mention him."

Phyllis' face fell. "Jack Devitt? Oh, he's dead. He committed suicide years ago – shot himself with his own shotgun. God, it was awfully sad. I think it was wee Danny who found

him in one of the outhouses. Poor kid . . ." She trailed off.
Something was distracting her on the other side of the road.
My eyes followed hers.

"So they're back," she said thoughtfully.

"Who's back?"

She gestured towards a tall, dark-haired man going into the
Oak. "That's Alan Crane. Lisa McCauley's new husband."

I tried to call Raymond Kelly again before I set off for Derry,
but there was still no answer. For the first ten minutes, driving conditions were actually okay. Maeve was right: the
main roads had all been gritted and the temperature had
risen, meaning that the snow was starting to melt anyway.
However, by the time I reached the coast road, the sky had
darkened ominously and it started to sleet. Dirty, icy rain
splashed down on the windscreen quicker than the Mini's
wipers could clear it. I drove along at a snail's pace, struggling to see out through the brown sludge.

I decided to drive via Buncrana on the off chance I could
catch Kelly at his pub. It would save me chasing him on his
mobile all weekend. The rain finally stopped as I arrived and
parked in the main street of Buncrana, a large town about ten
miles from Glendara. For a pub along this stretch, Kelly's was
pretty grand. It looked as if it might once have been an old
bank or public building.

The owners had used the whole premises, all three floors.
There was a fine old mirrored bar downstairs with booths
and leather seating, brass lighting, and an impressive staircase
leading to the upper two floors. A sign on the wall indicated
a restaurant upstairs. A Miles Davis tune played quietly in the
background.

The bar was empty of customers. I looked at my watch. It was early, twelve o'clock. There were two people behind the bar: a young barman of about eighteen with spiky black hair, in black trousers and a white shirt, and a woman. They were having a laugh as they polished glasses and filled the dispensers.

The woman saw me and came over. Her black hair was tied loosely at her neck. She was striking, with heavy dark eyes and a full mouth. Tiny lines under her eyes only served to make her look even more intriguing. She was one of those rare specimens for whom age is not the enemy.

"What can I get you?" she asked.

"Nothing, thanks. This is Raymond Kelly's bar, isn't it?"

"It is. I'm his wife, Alison." She spoke with a hint of an American lilt. I realized it was a similar rounding of consonants that gave her husband's accent its distinctive quality, though I thought his had something extra.

"I've spoken to you on the phone, but we haven't met. I'm Ben O'Keeffe."

The woman gave me a smile, pushing her hair out of her eyes. "You're the solicitor? Ray's mentioned you. This is my son, Trevor."

The boy with the spiky hair shot me a grin. He had his mother's looks. Lucky boy.

"I was wondering if I could have a quick word with Mr. Kelly."

"Sure. He's in the office pretending to do paperwork. No doubt he'll be glad of the interruption."

Alison emerged from behind the bar and led me down the back of the building towards a door marked Private. I liked the feel of the place, even empty. I said so.

"Thanks," Alison replied. "We really wanted this one to work, and it's doing well. It's our third. We also have two pubs in the west, and one in London, too, that I try to check up on a couple of times a year. But I'm sure Ray's told you all that."

"Well, no actually. I've done very little for him so far, to be honest. He just asked me to have a look at a possible remortgage on the church and said he might have some more work for me after that."

She smiled, a knowing sort of smile. "He does that. He's not too happy with the solicitor we've been using in Buncrana so he thought he'd give you a go. Liam recommended you." She put a hand in front of her mouth in a mock whisper. "You're on probation."

I grinned. "Fair enough."

"We've a couple of other properties that Liam is selling for us though. Ray will probably get you to act for him in those." She sighed. "If they ever sell in this financial climate."

"Well, this place looks great."

"I think so." She looked around her. "We brought the bar over from the States, and some of the lighting. And we have the restaurant, of course." She indicated upstairs. "Great chef. You should try it sometime. He's particularly good with fish."

She pushed open the door and led me down a narrow hallway cluttered with drinks crates and cardboard boxes to a second door marked Office. Here, she knocked briefly and without waiting for an answer walked in whilst I hovered outside. Through the gap I could see that her husband was sitting at a desk completely buried in paper, punching numbers into a calculator with some force, an expression of abject misery on his face.

"Visitor for you, Ray," she told him. "I said you'd be very upset to be dragged away from your beloved accounts."

She perched on the desk in front of him and beckoned me in. Kelly peered around her and caught sight of me for the first time. His face registered momentary surprise and then his features clouded again, as if reminded of something unpleasant. I didn't take it personally. Solicitors aren't always welcome. Still, he managed to force a smile and waved his hand in the direction of a seat on the other side of the desk, which I took.

"Sorry to interrupt. I have a bit of news for you," I said.

"Hope it's better than the last news I got."

"It is. I wanted to let you know they've finished with the church for the moment. I've just come from there."

"Nice of them to tell me," he grumbled.

"Well, they only finished this morning. I'm sure you'll get a call later on."

"What have they found out?" he asked.

"Not a lot, I don't think. They're still working on identification."

"So they don't know who it is yet?" That was Alison.

"Not yet," I replied. "There's a possibility it could be a man named Conor Devitt. He disappeared a number of years ago. They're doing DNA testing with his family to make sure one way or the other."

Alison nodded. "We heard that." She shuddered.

"Did you know him?" I asked, surprised.

"Oh, not really. Well, a little," she said quietly. "We knew each other when we were children."

Her husband touched her gently on the arm. "They were school friends."

"I went to Whitewater primary school for a while, that little school on the way up to the church? It's a ruin now, too."

"So you're local?" I asked. "I assumed . . ."

"You're wondering about the accent?" She smiled. "My parents are Irish-American. They came back to Inishowen for a few years when my sister and I were kids. I was the new kid in school, *the Yank* . . ." She looked down. "And Conor was nice to me. Kinda like a big brother. One of those good kids that notices the shy ones, you know? But my parents couldn't make it work in Donegal. They ran a shop, but it closed down."

"Seems neither of them had their daughter's head for business. Kept giving out credit apparently," Kelly added with a grin. "Couldn't see you doing that, eh, Alison?"

Alison ignored him. "They only stayed for a few years and then we all moved back to the States. Broke my heart."

Kelly put his arm around her and kissed her shoulder. "It's just as well you did or you'd never have met me."

"You met each other in the States?" I asked.

"Yeah – Boston. I spent a long time there learning the pub trade," Kelly said. "We came back, what," he looked at Alison, "nine years ago?"

She nodded. "The three of us. We had Trevor in the States."

"I wasn't sure it was such a good idea, but Alison was dead set on it. And as you'll learn, Miss O'Keeffe, my wife always gets what she wants."

"I love that part of the world around Whitewater. It's so beautiful up there. I never forgot it," Alison said.

"It's why I decided to buy the church," Kelly explained. "Not my best business decision, I have to say. We thought we might be able to do something with it, naively as it turned out. Something for the community." He sighed. "And then this happens."

"You didn't know Mr. Devitt yourself, then?"

He shook his head. "Nope. I never met him."

Alison picked up a pen from the desk and started to draw lines on a sheet of paper. "Imagine, they think that might be him – in our church. Weird, isn't it? What on earth was he doing there, I wonder?"

"I have no idea," I said. "Assuming it is him, of course. They don't know that for certain yet. They're still doing tests."

"Is there anything we can do for the family?" she asked.

"I don't think so, to be honest. They just have to wait for the results," I said.

Alison leaned in towards her husband and rested her head on his shoulder. I noticed there was quite an age gap. Kelly was a good ten years older than his wife.

"I'll be sure to let you know if I hear anything more," I added.

"Thank you."

I turned to go then paused at the door. "By the way, do you still want to go ahead with the remortgage now that the sale is off? I had put it on hold when Liam told me you were selling."

Kelly gave me an odd look. I thought I saw a flash of anger but it was gone as quickly as it appeared. "No, it's fine. I'll leave it for the moment. Send the deeds back to the bank."

Chapter 8

I DROVE ON into Derry, following my usual route down the Strand Road, past the row of pubs and nightclubs clustered at the bottom of the hill below Magee University and along the river. The streets were considerably quieter than they usually were on a Saturday afternoon and buried under a filthy layer of slush. A centuries-old shipping town, Derry is now the most westerly port in the United Kingdom. The city centre with its sophisticated riverside restaurants and bars usually gives the impression of being a million miles from the huge old shipyards, but not today. The quayside was a foul-looking industrial brown, and the river battered against the crash barriers, its water level as high as I had ever seen.

Across the river, on the Waterside, the sky was oppressive, the clouds a steely gray looking fit to burst. The huge expanse of housing estates covering the hill seemed to be cowering in anticipation of the coming deluge. I looked over towards the "Peace Bridge," the new pedestrian footbridge connecting the two sides of the city. Those few brave souls who were prepared to risk it were battered mercilessly by the wind as they fought their way across.

I parked in the Foyleside shopping centre and ran onto Shipquay Street, barely halfway there when I was stung by pelting, icy rain. Thirty seconds was all it took for me to get completely soaked. I crossed the road and dived into the covered craft village with its shops and restaurants. Grateful for the warm blast that greeted me, I shook myself off like a dog in the doorway of the Tavern as I scanned the restaurant for Maeve. No sign. I found a table by the window, and ordered a tea. I discovered that there was a radiator running along the wall under my table and surreptitiously removed my shoes to toast my wet, socked feet.

I looked at the menu and realized I was starving. Apparently, a good bracing walk in a graveyard brings on an appetite. I was immersed in semi-delirious thoughts about a piping-hot bowl of seafood chowder when Maeve suddenly appeared in front of me bringing a blast of cold air in with her.

"Jesus Christ, what a dirty day," she said as she took off her jacket and scarf.

"I know. I'm still drying my feet."

She looked under the table and made a face. "Ugh."

"You're late, by the way."

"I nearly didn't make it at all," she retorted. "I could be in the garda station as we speak, or the bloody morgue."

"What happened? Are you all right?" Maeve wasn't usually prone to exaggeration.

"Just about. I was coming through Glendara, out the Derry road, doing no speed at all when Danny Devitt staggered right out in front of me."

"Drunk?" I asked.

"Completely pissed. Out of his head. At one o'clock in the bloody afternoon."

I nodded. "I heard he was drinking."

"I swear, Ben, if I hadn't been driving the jeep with its snow-tyres, he was a goner."

Just at that moment the waitress came over to our table. Maeve wanted an extra minute and I watched the waitress as she ambled gloomily back to the bar. The place was quiet; she had little to do.

"I swerved and nearly ended up in the ditch," Maeve went on. "And your man Devitt kept on going as if he never even saw me."

"Jesus."

"I mean, what if I'd had the kids with me?"

"I know. You have to feel for him though. This must be a hell of a weekend to get through. I think if I was in the same boat I might drink my way through the next forty-eight hours."

"He should be at home, supporting his mother and sister. That's what Conor would be doing if he were still around."

I took the course of least resistance. "You're right. He should."

"Although in fairness, that Danny Devitt has always been better with animals than people." Maeve shook her head. "He doesn't often venture into town. You can see why; it doesn't suit him."

The waitress reappeared and we speed-read the menu then ordered some food.

Maeve leaned back in her chair and crossed her arms. "So the whole peninsula is waiting with bated breath. I hear you were actually there when they found the body?"

"Who told you that?"

She gave me a wry look.

"Okay, fair enough."

"I hope your presence was just a coincidence?"

Molloy is not the only one aware of my tendency to stick my nose in where it's not needed.

I grinned. "Utterly. Nothing to do with me."

"Good." She uncrossed her arms. "So, is it likely to be Conor Devitt, do you think?"

"No idea. He's the only missing person from the area so he's the obvious possibility, I suppose. I had never even heard of him until these bones turned up," I added. "I don't think anyone ever mentioned him to me."

"No, they wouldn't have. People stopped talking about him – I think they were afraid to upset the family. He disappeared the year before you came up here. They'd given up looking for him by the time you arrived. I think everyone just assumed he'd done a runner, taken the boat to England."

"Did you know him?" I asked.

"Oh yeah. Everyone knew him. He was a carpenter – a good one. He did my mother's kitchen. Straightest guy you'd ever meet. We could have done with him by the time it came to do ours. Bloody cowboys."

I let that one go. It could have gone on for a while.

"He worked for Mick Bourke," she continued. "Did his apprenticeship with him, I'd say. I think Bourke was a bit of a father figure to him after what happened to his own dad. Though there was no comparison in terms of what they could do."

"What do you mean?"

"Bourke's pretty average, but Conor was a brilliant craftsman, really talented. He even used to do some wood carving – plaques, figures, that kind of thing. He should have gone to college but he didn't get the chance, he started work so young. We have one of his pieces in the sitting room – over the fireplace. That one was to benefit the Lifeboat service."

I pictured it. I had stared at it more than once, glass of wine in hand. It was a striking abstract piece with angry figures.

"The boys don't like it, for some reason," Maeve said. "They say it's scary. Oh, thank God. Here comes our food."

The waitress arrived at our table with a tray laden with steaming bowls of soup and thick sandwiches. She returned within minutes with an enormous pot of tea. As I poured, the room darkened and a sudden shower of hailstones clattered violently against the window.

I groaned. "Talk about four seasons in one day."

"That's Donegal for you. By the way," Maeve said through a mouthful of sandwich, "do you fancy going to a play at the Millennium next week? We could have something to eat beforehand."

"What's on?"

She grinned. "Thought it might be right up your street. Not that I want to encourage you or anything. It's an Agatha Christie play: *Witness for the Prosecution*."

On Sunday afternoon I was curled up on the couch, with Guinness snoring gently on my knee, surrounded by the Sunday papers. I had combed them for any mention of Whitewater but could find nothing. The discovery of the bones had made the back pages of the national papers on Friday as well as the radio and television news, and the *Derry Journal* on Saturday. But there had been nothing since.

The fire was beginning to have its usual soporific effect, and I could feel myself dozing off. With a huge effort I shook myself awake and summoned the enthusiasm to go into the office for a few hours to make up for the early afternoon I had taken on Friday. To his ill-concealed disgust, I tossed Guinness off my knee and picked up my keys. I drove slowly into town with the window rolled down, hoping the salty air would revive me. The sleet and hailstones had stopped for the time being, but the sky was dull and laden with the promise of a further attack.

My grand plan to work was abandoned the second I felt the freezing temperature in the office. I put my hand on the radiator behind the reception desk. Icy. The heating was off. I checked my watch; the heating was due to come on at this time for an hour each day over the weekend. I peered inside the oil tank in the backyard: empty. What wretched timing, in the middle of the worst weather we'd had all winter! Cursing, I dragged an old electric heater down from the attic to reception, ready to be used on Monday morning, bashing myself on the ankles more than once in the process.

On impulse, I decided to take home the title deeds to Whitewater Church. Even though I knew it was absolutely none of my business, I couldn't shake the feeling that the placing of the bones inside the crypt had to be significant, especially now it appeared that they had been moved there. The placing was so utterly deliberate, the wrapping of the bones in a blanket and the placing of a pillow under the skull such a strange act of kindness. Whitewater Church itself was key in some way; I was convinced it had to be. It was also a possibility — remote, I accepted — that there was something significant in the deeds. And for the moment at any rate, I had them. But I would have to send them back now that the sale was off.

As I was leaving, I caught sight of Claire Devitt. She cut a lonely figure, walking up the hill. I wondered if she was going to look for Danny. I unlocked my car and got in, dumping the deeds on the passenger seat. I was about to pull away when a squad car appeared, speeding past me along the deserted street, McFadden at the wheel, a guard I recognized from Buncrana in the passenger seat. They were headed in the direction of the square, the same as Claire. I hesitated for a second then turned off the engine, locked the deeds in the boot, and set off up the hill after them on foot.

The squad car was parked up on the footpath outside the Oak, blue lights flashing. Alone on the street and feeling conspicuous, I hid in the doorway of the newsagents, closed now for the afternoon. The door of the Oak burst open and I watched as McFadden and the other guard marched a large bearded man out onto the street and hustled him into the back seat of the squad car. The man's head was bowed.

Before McFadden had closed the door of the car, the pub door was flung open again with considerable force and a tall man with dark hair stormed out, shouting and waving his fists. He pressed his face up against the back window of the squad car and shouted something at the man inside. McFadden pulled the dark-haired man away from the window and into the alleyway to the right of the pub. I couldn't see the alley from where I was standing, but shortly afterwards, the man reappeared, followed by McFadden, and went silently back into the pub. As he did so, I caught sight of his profile. It was the man Phyllis had pointed out to me the day before, Lisa McCauley's new husband, Alan Crane. I emerged from the doorway and the squad car drove past me, the bearded man in the back seat gazing expressionlessly out of the window. I waited for a few minutes to see if Claire reappeared, but the street remained deserted.

The sound of Van Morrison greeted me as I pulled open the door of the pub. There were only two people in there, one standing behind the bar and one sitting on a stool drinking a pint of Guinness. Neither of them was Claire. Tony glanced up and gave me a rather odd look and I smiled, feeling a little stupid, knowing I was about to walk straight back out again. Alan Crane spun around on his stool, gave me the briefest of disinterested looks, and returned to his pint.

As I closed the door of the pub behind me, I saw Claire walking very quickly on the other side of the road. She passed the chemist shop, stopped at Eithne's front door, and knocked. I decided to leave her alone.

Back at home I threw some turf on the fire and spread the deeds out in front of me starting with the most recent. The Deed of Conveyance, from December 14, 2005, had transferred ownership of the church, the access lane, and an acre and a half of land to Raymond and Alison Kelly, excluding the graveyard, which was retained by the trustees. They had paid a considerable sum for it, even at a time when property in Ireland was overvalued. Molloy was right – it was a hell of a lot more than they were selling it for now.

The original of the map I had given Paul Doherty was pasted to the back of the 2005 conveyance. The one that had omitted the crypt. It did, however, show the subdivision of the church site from the graveyard and the narrow lane connecting the two. I checked the deed. It contained a clause agreeing that this access was to be closed up; the properties were to be truly separate. The Kellys had been the first buyers since the church was deconsecrated in 1995. The trustees had taken their time in selling it: ten years. I wondered what it was that had made them finally sell. Did they need the money?

The 2005 deed carried over restrictive covenants from a previous deed, the 1995 Deed of Deconsecration. Maybe that had been part of Kelly's difficulty in getting planning permission? I opened the Deed of Deconsecration and smiled to myself as I read it. There was a covenant forbidding the consumption of alcohol on the premises, outside of the celebration of Holy Communion. That shouldn't have caused him any trouble; it was a covenant that was unlikely to be enforceable today.

I looked for some reference to the removal of the bodies from the crypt, but found nothing. I rooted through the contracts, receipts for deposits, and copies of maps scattered throughout the deeds. Eventually, I came across a sheet of paper folded in four. It was a contract between the church trustees and an English company called Nec-Move, dated January 12, 1995, for the removal of the bodies from the crypt and their reburial in the graveyard. That confirmed it: there were no bodies left in the crypt, and hadn't been since before the church was deconsecrated. Which made sense: they'd have had to allow continued public access, if there were.

The deeds prior to the deconsecration were sparse. One by one I unfolded them and laid them out in front of me. The slightly mouldy smell that usually emanates from old paper wafted upwards. There was a Fee Farm Grant from 1890 granting the land to the Catholic Diocesan Trust for the purposes of the erection of a parish church "to serve the sea-faring communities of the townland of Whitewater" and a certified copy of a marriage settlement from 1785. It settled large tracts of land amounting to over a thousand acres from various parts of the peninsula, of which the church and graveyard made up a tiny part, on a certain Louisa May Alringham.

I sat back on the couch and rubbed the nape of my neck. Guinness grabbed his opportunity and leaped up onto my lap. I stroked his fur distractedly as I thought how sad it was that Whitewater Church had served the community of Whitewater for over a century and then, suddenly, just ceased to be a church. I presumed dwindling attendances had meant that it was no longer considered necessary and had therefore simply been deconsecrated.

It was a bleak place now, beautiful and desolate. The houses that were occupied were few and far between, a couple of distant farmhouses. A run-down cottage almost entirely smothered by ivy on the road accessing the church was the closest building. I assumed it was deserted. But at one time Whitewater must have been a vibrant area. Vibrant enough to require the building of a church to serve its community, and a school where Alison Kelly had met Conor as a child, another victim of the death of a community.

Sighing, I bundled the deeds back together and retied the ribbon around them. I had discovered nothing whatsoever to shed any light on why someone would choose the crypt of Whitewater Church to leave a set of human bones wrapped in a blanket. I wondered if I should find someone who knew something of the history of the church, an old warden or caretaker perhaps.

I shook myself. I was trying to find answers again. Answers to questions no one had actually asked me. This was none of my business. I put away the deeds, returned to the Sunday newspapers, and started to think about something to eat.

Chapter 9

PUNCTUALITY HAS NEVER been my strong suit, but I made
it into the office by a quarter to nine the following morning. I badly needed to sort out the heating crisis – the office
was like a fridge. I switched on the heater I'd dragged down
the stairs the day before, managed to find an old blow-heater
that I plugged in upstairs, and made a phone call to Glendara
Fuels. Finally, still wearing my coat and scarf, I sat at my desk,
turned on my computer, and tried to ignore the crackling
noise and rather odd smell coming from the heater at my feet.

I checked work e-mails first. There was nothing that
couldn't wait. Then I Googled the words *Conor Devitt+missing
person+Donegal* and was rewarded with 10,400 results. I
scrolled down. Most of them had absolutely nothing to do
with what I was looking for, but one caught my eye. It was
a website with a link to archive editions of the *Derry Journal*.

I clicked on the link, and the front page of the *Journal* of
July 6, 2007, opened up before me. It was dominated by a
black-and-white photograph of a handsome, smiling man in
a checked shirt, with long dark curly hair and bright eyes.
He had the same nose and firm jaw as his sister. Unfortunately for Claire, they looked better on a male than a female.
The piece underneath the photograph was short, a matter
of a few lines, simply asking for any information regarding

the whereabouts of the missing man. People were asked to contact Glendara garda station or the man's family, and the relevant telephone numbers were supplied.

I stared at the picture for a few minutes and did what I was sure Conor Devitt's family had done countless times. I searched his face for some kind of clue. Some hint in those smiling eyes as to why a young man would leave behind all who loved him and simply disappear. But, of course, there was nothing. I knew all too well the capacity we have to conceal our true intentions.

But then, maybe Conor's family was right. Maybe he hadn't left of his own volition. Maybe the worst *had* happened. Claire, for one, appeared to be utterly convinced that the bones found in the church were her brother's. I looked at my watch and wondered if the DNA and dental-test results were in yet. Wondered if it was too early to ring Molloy. If he'd even tell me anything if I did.

I heard the front door open and Leah's voice call up the stairs. "Jesus, it's freezing in here. What happened?"

I headed downstairs to take the mail from her.

"I forgot to order oil. Sorry. It's done now though. It should be here later this morning. Many appointments today?"

She checked the book. "Only two." She grinned. "Since it's quiet, you could always start preparing for the Law Society audit next week."

I groaned and headed back up the stairs. Before opening the mail, I dialed the garda station, reasoning that it would be common knowledge soon enough.

"Yes?" Molloy sounded weary.

"It's Ben. I wondered if there was any news yet, on the DNA tests?"

He sighed. "Not till this evening."

"Okay. Fair enough."

"And, Ben?"

"Yes?"

"We do have to tell the family first, you know."

I didn't have the nerve to phone Molloy again, so when I arrived at the Oak for the Drama Club meeting that evening, I assumed I had no more information than anyone else there. Again I was the last one in. Tony was behind the bar and Phyllis, Hal, and Eithne were at the table by the fire. Tony poured me a Coke and then followed me back down to join the others.

There was no mention of Claire. Phyllis and Hal were engrossed in discussing possible plays to put on this year. As usual, Tony pushed for a comedy.

"Ach, the town could do with a laugh, so it could. There's so much misery about at the moment," he said.

"We did a comedy last year, if you recall," Hal retorted. "And it wasn't exactly a roaring success."

"I don't know." Tony grinned. "It had its moments."

"If you mean when the backboard started to collapse in the middle of the first act, I'm not sure that's the kind of laughs we should be looking for," Phyllis responded, lips pursed in mock disapproval.

The previous year's play had been a catalogue of disasters from beginning to end. A mouse had run across the stage at one point, studiously ignored by the cast and noticed – we hope – only by a couple of kids sitting in the front row.

"I think it's about time we did one of the old Irish standards," Hal said. "A Sean O'Casey perhaps – *The Plough and the Stars* or *Juno and the Paycock*."

"Ah, Jesus, not one of those bleak civil war plays," Tony groaned. "That's the last thing we need."

"If you want to do a classic play, what about an American one? A Tennessee Williams?" Phyllis suggested. "*Cat on a Hot Tin Roof*? I think I could do a damn fine Maggie the Cat. What do you think?"

She tried her best to strike a screen siren pose, not made any easier by her sizeable figure, nor the fact that she was squashed behind a pub table. "Now who wants to play Brick?" she asked, a mischievous gleam in her eye.

Hal and Tony shifted uncomfortably in their seats, until they saw Phyllis wink in my direction. Eithne seemed distracted. She touched her face nervously as she took her phone out of her bag, checked it, and put it back in again. After a few minutes she got up to go to the bathroom, taking her phone with her.

"Is she all right?" I asked Phyllis, when the two men had left for a minute, Tony to check on the bar and Hal to pay for some more drinks.

Phyllis lowered her voice to a whisper. "She's waiting to hear from Claire with the results of the DNA tests. Claire promised to phone her as soon as she knew."

"God, I'm surprised she's here at all," I said. "We could have put the meeting off again."

"Claire insisted that we go ahead with it. Carry on as normal, she said. So that's what we're trying to do."

"I thought it was a bit odd no one had mentioned it."

"We're trying to keep Eithne's spirits up. She's very anxious about Claire . . . shhh!" Phyllis said suddenly as the door to the toilets opened and Eithne came back in. Phyllis gave her hand a squeeze as she sat down and Eithne smiled wanly at her.

"Nothing yet," she said, the first words she'd said since I came in.

"They probably haven't heard themselves. These things sometimes take longer than expected," I offered.

Eithne nodded and put her phone back in her bag. The two men returned from the bar with a tray of drinks and the conversation resumed.

"I was thinking, what about a play about the Troubles?" Hal said, taking a gulp out of his pint of Guinness, leaving a line of white foam on his upper lip. "We've never done one before."

"Aye," Tony said, raising his considerable eyebrows. "That's not such a bad idea."

"I thought you wanted a comedy?" Phyllis rounded on him. "A play about the Troubles isn't likely to be a barrel of laughs."

"I wouldn't be too sure about that," Tony replied. "There's a fair bit of black humor in a lot of the writing that was done at that time."

"You don't think it's too soon?" Eithne asked. "People are still very sensitive, you know."

"I think we've put enough time behind us to do a play about the Troubles without upsetting people," Hal said.

"Maybe," Phyllis said thoughtfully. "I could have a look and see what I can find in the shop, if you like. I have a good collection of old drama books and scripts in a box upstairs. They don't really sell so I don't display them, but there might be something in there. I know they're mostly Irish play-wrights. Maybe there's one there with a bit of humor in it."

"Good on you," Hal said. "You'll find something – I have the utmost faith in you. Have we that sorted then? A play about the Troubles, if Phyllis can find one we all like?"

Suddenly dance music sounded loudly from the seat beside Eithne. She jumped, knocked her glass over, and spilled her drink across the table. She didn't even notice, so intent was she on scrabbling frantically in her bag. Her panic was infectious. Tony and Hal started messing about with bar mats, trying to mop up the spilled orange juice, and Phyllis grabbed at the glass rolling slowly towards the edge of the table.

It felt like an age before Eithne found her phone lying on the seat, and it seemed impossible that it would not stop ringing before she answered it. But she got it. She managed a muted "Hello" as she moved away from the table and went outside. There was a short pause before Tony finished wiping up the sticky mess and strode over to the bar to get Eithne a replacement juice, muttering that it was at times like these a person needed a good stiff drink and that Pioneers had a lot to answer for, Eithne being a strict non-drinker of the Pioneering, Temperance-preaching type. In her own quiet way.

She was probably gone for all of about three minutes, but it seemed like twenty. Eventually, the door opened and she came back into the pub. She looked shocked. She swayed a little and Hal darted over to help her back to the table. Phyllis put her hand gently on her arm.

"It's not him," Eithne said.

There was an exchange of glances, and then everyone spoke at once.

"But that's good, isn't it?"

"Are they okay?"

Eithne didn't respond; she just kept staring at the phone on her lap as if she couldn't quite believe what it had just told her. In the end, Tony voiced what we had all been thinking.

"So if it's not Conor, then who is it?"

"They don't know."

There was silence for a few seconds.

I broke it. "How are they? How's Claire?"

Eithne shook her head. "They were so sure it was him; they were ready for it. And now they don't know what to think. In a way they should be glad, but if it isn't him . . ."

". . . then who is it . . . and where is he?" Phyllis finished her question.

"So what happens now?" Tony asked.

Four heads turned towards me as if it were the kind of thing I should know. I didn't.

"I presume they will continue to work on identification. And keep looking for Conor Devitt, of course – if they can."

"That's not going to be too easy after six and a half years," Phyllis said. "God, and we were all so sure it was Conor."

"What'll they do with the body," Hal said, "if they can't find out who it is?"

"I suppose they'll have to hold on to it until they do."

"Well, I hope that's soon. Whoever it is, they deserve a decent burial."

Phyllis put her arm around Eithne. "Are you heading up there?" she asked.

Eithne gave the big woman an unexpected glare. "Of course I am. Claire needs me."

Phyllis pulled back. "Okay, pet. Let us know if there is anything we can do."

Chapter 10

THE FOLLOWING MORNING was dark and cold, and the faces that greeted me as I walked from the car to the office were somber. It was as if a shiver had traveled down the town's collective spine. It was obvious that people had derived no comfort from the news that the bones lying on the floor of the damp crypt beneath the disused church were not those of the person they thought.

Whoever it turned out to be, it was still someone with family and friends. More significantly for the people who knew Conor, he was still missing. In most societies there exists a very human need to bury the dead. The closure that Conor's family had expected and needed hadn't come. And there was still to be grief for some other family, as yet unknown. One answer had produced a thousand new questions.

I was standing at the reception desk going through the last of the morning's mail when the sound of the front door opening, followed by a man's heavy tread, made me look up. The narrow hallway was filled by a large male figure, his broad shoulders in silhouette against the dim light coming through the tiny window above the door.

As he came closer, I found myself looking into a pair of intense gray eyes set under thick eyebrows in a bearded face.

The man could have been thirty or fifty, or anywhere in between. His hair was long and unkempt, a mixture of black and gray. There was something wild about him that didn't belong inside. He reminded me of a wounded animal. There was pain, suppressed anger maybe – a slight madness, even, about him. I was disturbed by the feeling that there was something familiar, too.

He spoke gruffly. "You the solicitor?"

There was a smell of stale alcohol on his breath. His eyes were slightly bloodshot.

"I am."

A bearlike hand was offered, black hair visible on the wrist emerging from the sleeve of a heavy dark overcoat. I shook it – his skin was clammy and cold. The man attempted a smile of greeting, but it lacked any real warmth. And there were far too many other things going on in his face that contradicted the smile. I remembered then where I had seen him before. He was the man I had witnessed being ejected from the Oak the Sunday before.

"I'm Danny Devitt," he said.

"Claire's brother?"

He nodded. "Aye."

Now I saw the resemblance to his brother. But the photograph of Conor Devitt in the newspaper had shown a handsome, open face. The man standing in front of me was another illustration of the arbitrary nature of genetics, for the same ingredients arranged slightly differently had produced a freakish opposite. I realized I was staring at him. I recovered quickly.

"Can I just say how sorry I am, Mr. Devitt? I know your family is going through a rough time at the moment—"

He interrupted me. "I want to talk to you."

"Of course. Come on up."

He followed me upstairs, bowing his head to get in the door of the office. He refused the chair I offered, which was becoming a regular occurrence. But unlike Kelly, he didn't pace. He walked to the window and stood there, staring out onto the street, hands rammed into his pockets, as if he needed to be able to see outside to think. I half-expected him to twist the latch, open the window, and lean out to breathe. I stood behind him, unsure of what to do next. He was so broad he blocked whatever feeble winter light was coming in, making the room feel small and cavelike.

"How can I help you, Mr. Devitt?"

He replied, still with his back to me, "My mother said I should come and talk to you."

"Okay."

I waited, but he said nothing. Feeling a need to fill the silence, I spoke again. "I've never met your mother, but I know Claire. I can't imagine how hard it must be for all of you."

Still nothing.

I tried again. "Anything you say to me is completely confidential."

He still didn't respond, or move, so I decided to sit at my desk and let him take his time. After a few seconds he shook his head vigorously, like a dog after a swim, still with his back to me.

"I don't know what happened," he said. "I thought . . . for all those years I thought it was me, that I had . . ." He stopped.

"You thought you had what, Mr. Devitt?"

"It was the cold, that's why I . . ." He shook his head again. "And all the time, all the time . . ." His voice hardened. "You can't trust people, ever."

Suddenly he punched the wall to the right of the window. Hard. I flinched. It must have hurt; it's an outside wall.

I stood up, my voice shaking a little. "I'm going to have to ask you to calm down, please, Mr. Devitt."

I wondered if I should call Leah. B for bouncer – I thought that might be pushing it. As it turned out, I didn't need to. Danny unclenched his fist and his shoulders slumped as he lifted his arm and wiped his sleeve across his face. After a few seconds, he cleared his throat and spoke again, calmly this time.

"I'm sorry."

"That's okay. Maybe you should tell me what's wrong?"

"I don't know what to do."

"You don't know what to do about what, Mr. Devitt?"

He turned to face me. His eyes were shining. "I need to know who it is. Can you find that out?"

"Who *who* is?"

He was silent, as if I should know what he meant.

"Are we talking about the body in the church?"

He nodded. "Can you find that out?" he said again, more urgently this time.

"Well, not really, Mr. Devitt. But I know the guards are working on it at the moment. I'm sure they'll have an answer soon."

His eyes welled.

"Why do you need to know?" I asked. "Do you know something about it?"

Without replying, he turned back towards the window. I stood up and approached him. With trepidation I touched him briefly on the arm.

"Mr. Devitt, what do you know?"

He spun violently around. I leaped back. Shockingly, there were great, glistening tears streaming down his face. He was crying like a child cries, letting the tears fall as if he were powerless to stop them. As if he expected a parent to be there to catch them. I flushed, staring at him, helpless and unsure what to do.

I know I should be better at this by now – after all, there's a reason why solicitors keep tissues in their desks. But I am ashamed to say that I have never been great with people who cry. I freeze in the face of emotion. My old master used to say that even if the work is everyday drudgery to you, most people who come to see a solicitor come at an important or traumatic point in their lives. It isn't everyday drudgery to them. He was right. But grief frightens me. The best I could come up with was to hand Danny the box of tissues I keep in the drawer of my desk.

He grabbed a handful and started clumsily to mop his face. He blew his nose loudly and, at last, he took the seat I had offered him, although I was concerned for its ability to take his weight.

"This was a mistake. I'm sorry." His voice was hoarse.

"Don't be sorry, for God's sake. You've all been through a rough time."

My words sounded limp, one of those useless platitudes that come from the right place but that sound so hollow by the time they leave your mouth.

I tried again. "Talk to me, if you need to. That's what I'm here for. I meant it when I said that anything you say to me is completely confidential."

"I'll sort it out myself. I know what I have to do."

He stood up and faced me with his shoulders back and legs apart, shoving the sodden tissues into the pocket of his coat.

"Do you think the sergeant would be there now? At the station?"

"Molloy? I expect so. Do you want me to ring and check? I can come down with you if you like."

"No, thanks. I'll go down myself after a while. There's something I need to do first."

"Are you sure I can't do anything?"

"Aye, I am. Thanks for your help." He shook my hand.

"Well, I haven't really done anything."

He set off back down the stairs. I heard the front door slam and he was gone.

I went over to the window to watch him leave. He walked across to an old black-and-white sheepdog tied to a street lamp on the other side of the road. The dog looked up adoringly at him as he untied the rope, and the two of them headed off towards the square. One thing was clear: he wasn't going in the direction of the garda station.

What had he wanted to tell me? And why was he so concerned about the bones in the crypt? I spent the next ten minutes twisting a pen in my fingers and staring at the wall, trying to figure out what I should do. But there was nothing I could do – my hands were tied. I just hoped he would talk to Molloy . . .

I was in another world when the phone buzzed.

"Shouldn't you be gone by now?" Leah asked.

"Huh?"

"Court . . ."

I looked at the clock. It was twenty past ten. Court started at half past. I sprang up from my seat.

"Oh, shit!"

"The files are down here. They're all ready."

I barreled across the square towards the courthouse, briefcase in hand, keeping a half-eye out for Danny Devitt. There was no sign of him. I was relieved to see the judge's car drive past the courthouse and turn into the car park at the back as I was walking up the steps. It meant I had five minutes. I jumped when someone grabbed my elbow. I turned around to be greeted by a broad grin on a freckled face.

"Hey, Solicitor."

The Oak's barman, Eddie Kearney, took a deep drag on the cigarette between his fingers. "What's going to happen this morning?" he asked in a bored tone.

"Not much probably, unless you want to plead guilty today to the possession charge."

"Do I fuck? That weed wasn't mine. I told you that."

"Okay. It'll go back to another date then, for the State to have the Certificate of Analysis in court."

The Certificate of Analysis is an essential proof in a drugs case. The prosecution requires a certificate from the Medical Bureau to prove that the substance recovered is a proscribed drug. Without it, there is no case. The difficulty for the State is that the lab is now so overworked that it can take months to produce the Certificate, which inevitably delays the proceedings.

Eddie's grin got broader. "Right, I can head off then, so. I have a shift at eleven." He made to head back down the steps.

"Not so fast," I called after him.

He stopped in his tracks and turned back to face me. "What?"

"You're on bail to appear today. You have to be in court or the judge will issue a warrant for your arrest."

The grin disappeared to be replaced with a look of gloomy resignation, and its wearer shuffled reluctantly into the court-house ahead of me.

I made my way up to the solicitors' benches at the top of the courtroom. Molloy was sitting on the State side with a stack of files in front of him and a queue of guards and solicitors waiting to speak to him. Molloy prosecutes the criminal and road traffic cases for the State. I cursed inwardly. Stupidly, I had forgotten that he would be in court this morning. Not surprising, considering I had forgotten that *I* was supposed to be in court this morning myself. But it meant that Danny Devitt wouldn't be able to get hold of him until court was over. Molloy glanced over at me as I took my seat. I smiled at him. He looked back coldly and returned to what he was doing. Not even a nod.

The court rose for lunch at one o'clock. I knew Molloy was always last to leave, so I feigned great interest in some road traffic charge sheets until I was sure everyone else had gone, leaving him with no choice but to walk out with me.

"You all right?" I asked.

He didn't look at me. "Why wouldn't I be?"

"You look tired."

"Yes." He opened the gate and let me through. I stood and waited for him as he closed it.

"So are you? All right?"

"I'm fine."

"Okay, don't bite my head off."

His face softened a tad. "Sorry. Yes, I'm tired. We got a report of another break-in last night. I was out there till two a.m. Another couple of newlyweds home from their honeymoon to be greeted by an empty house."

"Empty?"

"Yes, empty. The whole place cleared out. Everything taken. Wedding presents, all their new appliances, cooker, fridge, furniture, even light fittings. The thieves must have had a van."

"Jesus, that's a mean sort of a crime, isn't it?"

"Third this month. Second one in three days, the last one was Saturday. They target rural, newly built houses, full of new stuff, no neighbors to disturb them. They wait till after the wedding, when they can be sure that the couples are away for two weeks and they can do the job at their leisure, completely undisturbed."

"So now you have that to deal with on top of the body from the church?"

"Yes."

We walked up the street towards the square. I buttoned my coat and wrapped my scarf tighter around my neck. The wind was like a knife accessing any bit of skin that was even slightly exposed.

"And the bones aren't Conor Devitt's, I hear?" I said.

"No."

"Hard for the family."

"Yes."

"Back to not knowing."

"They were utterly convinced it was him. But there was no real reason to think it would be – they were told that."

"Really?"

Molloy stopped walking for a second.

"Actually, there's a coincidence," he said. "The break-in on Saturday was at the house owned by Lisa and Alan Crane."

"Conor Devitt's ex, Lisa McCauley?"

"Yes. Her new husband is Alan Crane, a plumber from Buncrana."

"I've seen him. God, she's had a tough weekend."

"Mmm."

"So is there any progress on the identification?"

"None."

"Pathologist still in Letterkenny?"

Molloy's eyes narrowed. "Why do you ask?"

I looked down. "No reason. I just wondered. I presume she's still working on the body and doing tests on the blanket, that kind of thing."

There was silence for a minute. Neither of us moved. I bit my lip.

"It's almost a quarter past one. Do you want to get a sandwich in the Oak?" I ventured.

"I haven't time. I have some work I need to do before two." He turned to go.

"Tom?" I said.

He turned back to face me. "Yes?"

"Is there something else bothering you? Have I done something to annoy you?"

"I don't know. Have you?" he asked.

"It just seems as if—"

He interrupted me. "I wish you trusted me, Ben, that's all. I thought you did."

"I do trust you."

I reached my hand out to touch his arm. He looked down at it. His eyes widened as if he was about to say something and then he changed his mind.

"I have to go," he said.

Chapter 11

I WATCHED MOLLOY stride off in the direction of the garda station with a strange, bitter sensation in the pit of my stomach. He knew. I was sure of it now. That pathologist woman had told him who I was. Why would she have done that? More to the point, why hadn't I managed to summon the courage to tell him myself before she got the chance? He had been so distant. I was surprised to find how much it hurt.

I heard a knock on glass and realized Molloy and I had been standing outside Phyllis Kettle's book shop. I wondered how much she had heard. I pushed open the door, causing the bell to tinkle. Phyllis' shop is an Aladdin's cave of books: her practice of giving people discounts on new purchases when they return the books they've read means that the stock keeps growing and growing, with the result that the shop is fit to burst.

Gravity-defying stacks are piled all over the floor and on the stairs; early editions of P. G. Wodehouse rest on top of Jackie Collins paperbacks with no apparent order, but closer inspection shows that all have their prices carefully pencilled on the inside flap in Phyllis' neat hand. For despite the apparent chaos of the place, Phyllis Kettle is a canny businesswoman. Her trade in old and rare books has given her a comfortable living for many years, and allows her to take off to obscure, far-off places for several months every year.

Today she was perched on a high stool behind the counter looking like an enormous kingfisher, clad in bright blues and reds and yellow. I looked down at my black suit and mourned the convention that requires lawyers to wear dark colors.

"So, you got rid of the nephew then?"

She sighed dramatically. "Oh, I did, thank the Lord. He was gone by Saturday evening. What a liability. Anyway, I know you're very busy, but I've managed to unearth a few plays that might fit in with what we were discussing last night." She thrust a couple of paperbacks in my direction. "Take them with you and have a look when you get a chance. They're all written by Derry playwrights, as a matter of fact, and there's a fair bit of black humor in them, which should satisfy Tony"—she winked—"with a bit of misery thrown in to keep Hal happy."

"Great," I replied with a grin.

She looked at my suit. "Are you heading back to court?"

"Not till two. I must try and get a bite before I have to go back."

"Fancy some mushroom soup?" she asked. "I have some warming on the stove upstairs."

Phyllis lives in the cosy flat above the shop. It's like an extension of the shop, full of books and plants, with food and wine thrown in – great food and wine in my experience.

"I was going to have some myself down here at the counter," she said. "It'll save me closing the shop. Not that there's ever anyone about on a Tuesday afternoon anyway. But you know people. They'd be the first to complain if I put the Closed sign up. You're welcome to join me if you want?"

I looked at my watch. I didn't have time now to go back to the office or the Oak for that matter. And I could smell the soup; that was the real deciding factor.

"That would be fabulous, Phyllis. Thank you. I'd love it."

"Excellent. You can sample some of my walnut bread, too."

She climbed the winding wooden staircase leading to the upper floor of the book shop, skirts rustling. I started to flick through the plays. The first one was called *Mary Magdalene*. It had been written in the 1980s. The second was *After the Rain* and had been written more recently. I looked at the Cast of Characters first: both were relatively short. That would suit our little group. And they looked like black comedies. Perfect.

I heard the rustling of skirts above me again and looked up to see Phyllis struggling down the stairs with a laden tray. She cleared some space on the counter and lifted off two steaming bowls of soup, a basket of soft homemade bread, and some butter.

"That smells fantastic, Phyllis."

"Doesn't it! You drag up another stool from behind that shelf, and I'll be back down in a minute with the tea."

The food tasted as good as it smelled. Fifteen minutes later we had finished the soup and were leaning back with cups of tea.

"You haven't seen Claire, by any chance, since last night's revelation?" Phyllis asked.

I shook my head. "You?"

"Nope. Must ask Eithne how she is."

"Eithne seemed very involved in the whole thing. I hadn't realized she and Claire were so close."

"You know Eithne used to be a nun before she trained as a pharmacist?" Phyllis said.

"No!" I exclaimed in surprise.

"Spent some time in Uganda in the missions."

"Really? Any idea why she left?"

"Couldn't take being told what to do, that's what I reckon. She's still big into doing her Christian duty anyway."

"The Devitts are probably glad of her support."

"Hmm, maybe." Phyllis clicked her teeth. "Bit of an anticlimax all the same, wasn't it? I saw Danny again this morning. He'd sobered up since the last time I saw him."

"When did you see him?"

"About eleven o'clock. He drove by the shop with that dog of his sitting up in the passenger seat like a child. Not a man that drives too often, I'd say, by the state of the wreck he was in."

Uneasily, I wondered if I should tell Molloy that Devitt was looking for him when I went back to court, but decided it wasn't my place. Also, things were more than a little weird between us at the moment.

"Any other possibilities for the body in the crypt?" I asked. "Conor Devitt seemed to be the only name mentioned."

"I have absolutely no idea. I suppose he was the obvious one." Phyllis gestured at the books I had left on the window-sill. "So what do you think of the plays?"

"Great. I'll have a better look at them tonight, but they seem to be just what we were after."

She picked up the first one I had looked at and said, "I'm not sure we should do this Feargus O'Connor one, to be honest."

I looked at it again. "Why not?"

"It was written in Long Kesh – and there's nothing wrong with that; it was a long time ago and he served his sentence. But he's back in the Midlands Prison, convicted of member-ship of one of those dissident groups a couple of years ago. And all sorts of other nasty stuff."

"Fair enough. Maybe a step too far."

"But I do think Tony's right. We should do one of the Derry plays. To hell with people's sensitivities, it's about time we got over ourselves. More tea?"

She sloshed a hot drop into my cup before I had a chance to reply.

"Was Inishowen much affected by the Troubles?" I asked.

"Aye, a bit. Nowhere was completely immune. We were too close to avoid the odd sideswipe. And, of course, there was the *Sadie*."

"The *Sadie*?"

She widened her eyes in surprise. "You've never heard of the *Sadie*?"

"No. Tell me what happened."

"It was a cargo ship that was blown up by the IRA in 1985."

"Where?"

"Along the Foyle. They hijacked the pilot boat at Whitewater and got aboard that way."

"What's a pilot boat?"

Phyllis laughed. "How long have you been in Inishowen?"

"I know. I'm still learning."

"When a large ship enters an estuary, a local pilot is taken out to the ship in a small boat. The pilot then takes over from the captain and directs the boat up the estuary and into the harbor. There used to be a pilot station down at Whitewater, just below the church. I can't believe you've never heard about the *Sadie*. Sure, that's what happened to the Devitts."

I was confused. "I thought . . . ?"

At that moment my phone rang. I reached over to get it, checking the time before I answered it. I stood up quickly, nearly knocking my cup over. It was 2:05 p.m.

"Ben, where are you?" It was Leah. "You've three clients waiting for you outside the courthouse and the judge has started already. He's having a fit."

"Tell them I'm on my way." I drained my cup and replaced it on the saucer.

"Sorry, Phyllis, I have to go. I'm late. That's the second time I've done that today. Can we continue this conversation later? I want to hear the rest of that story."

I gathered my things together and shot out the door, calling over my shoulder, "Oh, and thanks for the soup!"

I was in court till six o'clock. I had just managed to get out of the office at quarter to seven and was heading to the car when my mobile rang. It was Maeve. As usual she was trying to make herself heard above a racket; this time it was dogs barking. She must have been still in the clinic.

"Hiya. You free this evening?"

"What's left of it. What did you expect I'd be doing?"

"Oh, I don't know. You could have some secret lover, for all I know. Anyway, you're free?"

"I'm free."

"Do you want to go and see that play I mentioned to you? I've checked and there are seats available tonight and none for the rest of the week."

"The Agatha Christie?"

"Yep."

"Sure. Sounds good."

"Great. I'll book the tickets. It's at half eight. I'll see you at the Millennium at a quarter to and we can have a drink?"

"Great."

* * *

An hour and a half later I was sitting on my own with a glass of wine in the cavernous stainless-steel bar of the Millennium Theatre in Derry waiting for Maeve. She came blustering in the door as the final call was sounding, red-faced and breathing heavily.

"Sorry. Had to operate on a dog. Twisted gut. Nasty."

"Spare me the details. Come on, we have to go in. Do you have the tickets?"

She produced them triumphantly as we joined the queue to enter the theatre. We found our seats and she looked around her with interest while I examined the program. Suddenly, she nudged me and I looked up.

"Hey," she whispered, nodding in the direction of a seat about three rows in front of us. "Isn't that . . . ?"

I looked.

"I didn't think this would be his kind of thing," she muttered.

At least I think that's what she said. I wasn't really listening. My stomach was doing flips. Three rows ahead of us was Molloy: I would have known the back of his head anywhere. But that wasn't the problem. Sitting beside him was the pathologist. What the hell were they doing together in a theatre? Were they friends or something? Or worse? My face started to heat up.

"Who is that with him?" Maeve asked.

Suddenly, I found it hard to breathe. The first time I'd seen her in the garda station had been a shock, but I'd handled it. I'd only seen her for a second, after all. This was different. I was forced to stare at the back of her head – at her neat blond bob and her narrow shoulders, exactly as I had done eight years ago as she had walked out of that awful courtroom.

Unbidden, memories started to flood back. She had given her evidence that day in a cold professional manner, just as you would have expected, appearing utterly unaffected by the pain her words would cause, the nightmares that would follow for years to come, and the pain she would inflict on my parents – a pain from which they would never recover. But I knew that was unfair; she was only doing her job. Without her, there wouldn't have been a conviction at all, for murder or manslaughter. The manslaughter of my little sister.

God, I couldn't relive those scenes here, in a theatre, in public. My head felt as if it was about to explode. I could feel the wine coming back up my throat. I gripped the seat rests, swallowed hard, and finally the urge to vomit receded. But my head was still swimming.

Maeve looked at me, her eyes widened in alarm. "Jesus, Ben, are you all right? You look awful."

I swallowed again, hard, struggling to get the words out.

"I'm fine." I closed my eyes.

"You looked as if you were about to throw up."

I took a deep breath, and another.

She produced a plastic bottle from her bag. "Do you want some water?"

I took the bottle from her and drank from it slowly. Gradually my head stopped swimming and I began to feel better.

"It must have been something I ate. I'm all right now," I said.

"Do you want to leave?"

"No. I'm fine."

She looked at me doubtfully. "Okay, if you're sure."

"I am."

We sat in silence for a minute or two while I gathered the courage to speak. "I think that's the pathologist with Molloy."

"Ooh." She looked at them with renewed interest. "The pathologist who . . ."

"Yes. The one who was examining the body from the church."

"And are they, you know – she and Molloy? Or are they just friends?"

"I've no idea."

"They're sitting awfully close."

Amongst the overwhelming horror of the memories that seeing that woman evoked, I was dimly aware of another feeling. I felt hurt that Molloy was with her. I took another gulp of water while I stared at the stage, willing the curtains to open and the play to begin.

I have absolutely no memory of *Witness for the Prosecution*. Maeve tells me it was great. At the intermission I spent as long as I possibly could in the Ladies while she chatted to a farmer she knew. I slipped into my seat moments before the start of the second act and managed to avoid the encounter I dreaded.

Now at least I knew why she had told Molloy. It wasn't simply random gossip. They knew each other outside of work. How much had she told him? Had it made him see me differently? And again, why the hell hadn't I told him my-self? But I hadn't told anyone in Inishowen. Maeve thought I had left Dublin to recover from a broken relationship. Tell a lie as close to the truth as you can and you're less likely to be found out, isn't that what they say?

In any case, telling people would have defeated the whole point of moving here: to escape. Here I could pretend it had never happened. I could disappear, use my mother's maiden name and a shortened version of my middle one. It was the only way I could have carried on. I ran away, simple as that, and it had worked, to a limited extent. Until now.

When the play was over, I turned down Maeve's suggestion of a last drink on the basis that I had an early appointment in the morning, and drove home alone. I doubt she believed me, but she didn't push it. Twice I found myself veering dangerously towards the edge of the road. Thankfully, the roads were dry. Had they been the way they were a few days before, I would have ended up in the sea. After my second fright, I forced myself to haul my mind back from the dark corner it was trying to clamber into and focus on my driving. But as soon as I turned the key in the lock of the front door of my cottage, that churning, panicky feeling returned. I poured myself a very large whiskey.

Chapter 12

I WOKE THE next morning sweating profusely, with stabbing sunlight in my eyes and a cat on my stomach. My neck hurt like hell. When I finally managed to shift Guinness off my ribs and raise myself into something resembling an upright position, I realized I was still on the couch. Apparently, I hadn't made it to bed but had somehow managed to let Guinness in to join the party during the night. And I'd turned the heating up. I had no memory of either. The house was like a sauna.

The whiskey had done its job of stifling my memory; it was a pity it had less pleasant aftereffects. My mouth was sour and dry, and my head felt like it had a meat cleaver stuck in it. As I came to, the memories that I had been trying so hard to block last night started to trickle back into my consciousness, like a faulty tap with its insistent, insanity-inducing drip.

I reached for my watch. With a degree of relief, I saw that it was 8:05 a.m. I had an hour to pull myself together and get into work. I had just lain my head back down on a cushion when Guinness leaped off the couch and trotted purposefully off in the direction of the kitchen. With a huge effort, I heaved myself off the couch and dragged myself after him.

It's amazing what a pot of coffee and a shower can do. By five to nine, I was driving along the coast road on my way to the office. The sunlight that had woken me so cruelly an hour earlier had been a false indicator of the day ahead, for the sky was gray and turbulent and the sea unappealing and murky. Rain was on its way again. As I drove, I tried to push away the sense of dread that was threatening to engulf me and to fill my mind instead with everyday things so there was no room for other, darker, thoughts. It wasn't working. I turned on the radio.

I had driven across the old stone bridge halfway between Malin and Glendara when I noticed something flashing in the distance on the coastal side of the road. A couple of sharp bends later and I came to an abrupt and unexpected halt about a mile out of the town. A line of cars snaked ahead of me.

Glendara is not known for its traffic jams, so I craned my neck out of the window and spotted a blue and white garda sign in the middle of the road some way ahead. One side of the road was completely closed off. It was an odd time for a checkpoint, just before nine. Finally, the traffic started to crawl. As I got closer, luminous yellow garda jackets and traffic cones came into view. With a sinking feeling, it occurred to me that the squad car with its flashing lights must be blocking the scene of an accident.

Eventually, I reached the front of the line of cars. The guard directing the traffic was McFadden. I stopped the car and rolled down the window. He was ashen-faced.

"Andy, what's going on?" I asked.

"There's been an accident."

"So I see. Was anyone hurt?"

He leaned in the window. "It's Danny Devitt."

My breath caught. I looked towards the ditch and caught a glimpse of the rear of a blue Opel Vectra. The back wheels were off the ground. I couldn't see the front, but it looked as if the bonnet was in the ditch.

I swallowed. "Is he all right?"

McFadden shook his head. "He didn't look good. He had some shocking-looking head injuries."

An image of a big bear of a man standing in my office with tears running down his face jumped into my mind.

"What happened?"

"It looks as if he drove his car into the ditch. He must have been going at some speed as the car's a total write-off. The ambulance took him to Letterkenny about two hours ago. I haven't heard anything since. I've just been standing here doing this."

"When did it happen?"

"We're not sure. He could have been here a while. I came across him about half six. He was unconscious at that stage."

"Was there anyone else involved?"

"We don't think so – he was on his own in the car." Mc-Fadden paused. "He has been drinking a lot lately."

I swallowed, suddenly conscious of the taste of stale whiskey in my mouth as I stared at the crashed car. "Do you think he was drunk?"

He shrugged. "Maybe."

I felt a lump in my throat. I caught sight of Molloy emerging from behind the squad car and I rolled the window back up and drove on.

Leah looked grim.

"Did you see the accident?"

"I did. Drove past it just now – it looked awful. I hope he'll be okay."

"Yes. And him only in with us yesterday morning, poor man."

I hung up my coat. "He was really distressed about something yesterday but he wouldn't tell me what it was."

She handed me the mail. "Danny? How do you mean?"

"I'm not sure. He wasn't making much sense. And I saw him in town on Sunday being taken out of the Oak and bundled into the squad car."

Leah rested her chin on her hands. "Poor Danny. He was always a little odd. All his life. Bit impulsive."

"You knew him? When you were kids?"

"Oh aye. When we were teenagers. He came to school here in Glendara. A bunch of them came down from Whitewater when it closed, but school didn't really suit him. He was always skipping school and getting into trouble."

"A wild kind of a kid."

She smiled. "He sure was. Of course, his father was gone when he was still very young, so that can't have helped. There was talk that he was the one that found his father's body. Maybe he was traumatized by that. You know how his father died?"

I nodded.

"Conor was the eldest so he kind of took over as the man of the house. Though Conor was only thirteen or fourteen himself when his father died. It can't have been easy on him. Although that probably wasn't too easy on Danny, either."

"What do you mean?"

"I always got the feeling he resented his brother telling him what to do. Especially when he was a teenager. Conor had a bit of a Daddy complex, if you know what I mean. He always had to be in charge."

Unbidden memories of my own teenage squabbles came into my head. It must have shown on my face. I pushed them away.

"No family of his own then, Danny?" I said. "Wife, children?"

Leah grinned. "Not unless you count Fred."

"Who's he?"

"His dog – a mangy-looking thing. They're always together. God, Fred wasn't in the car, was he?"

"I don't think so. So there's no girlfriend or anything?"

"I doubt if any female would be willing to live the way he does. He lives in that cottage up by Whitewater. You know the one. It's on the road on the way up to the church, covered in ivy."

"God, I thought that was derelict."

"Not far off. I don't think he has electricity or running water."

"What does he live on?"

"I don't know, the dole? I suppose he shoots birds and rabbits and so on." Leah smiled to herself again.

"What?" I asked.

"I've just remembered he had a big thing for Lisa McCauley in school. I'm trying to imagine her living like that, in that old cottage. She's a real glamour puss."

"The same Lisa who was engaged to Conor?"

"That's right."

"God, so the two brothers loved the same girl?" I knew better than most how jealousy and resentment could destroy a sibling relationship, often outliving the desire for the prize itself.

But Leah waved her hand dismissively. "Ah, no. Conor was a long, long time after that. And anyway, it's not as if Danny and Lisa ever went out. They were just friends. In school, like."

I took the mail upstairs and tried to start putting together some contracts for the sale of a pub in Malin Head, but I couldn't concentrate. The words swam in front of my eyes. I walked to the window and leaned my cheek against the cool glass while I gazed out onto the street. The wind was rising, the trees in the square swaying. A few spatters of rain hit the windowpane and made my head hurt more than it should have. I needed some painkillers. I muttered something to Leah about needing pen cartridges, grabbed my coat, and took off out the door.

The square was deserted; anyone with an ounce of sense was inside, out of the wet. I, on the other hand, found the wind and rain oddly soothing. I've always loved storms. Sometimes it helps to have a reminder that nature is the one with the real power and we're merely going with the flow. I suppose in a way that's what people get from religion. The comfort of thinking that someone else is in charge, that it's all someone else's responsibility.

I fought my way across the square towards the chemist shop. Opening the door wasn't difficult; it swung violently inwards as soon as I turned the handle. Closing it was a different story. I was still wrestling with it when Eithne suddenly materialized beside me and helped me push. She was a lot stronger than she looked. I gazed at her in surprise. Eventually, it clicked shut.

"Thanks, Eithne. Jesus!"

"I'm going to have to get something done about that."

"I don't think it's the door. It's wild out there."

She made her way back in behind the counter, which seemed to diminish her. It was almost as if, after her valiant battle with the door, she had shrunk back to her original size. I definitely needed painkillers; I was beginning to hallucinate.

"Isn't it awful about Danny Devitt?" she said, putting her hands to her face.

I nodded.

"He's a drinker, you know," she said in her tragic little whisper. "We all try our best to help him, but it never does any good."

I leaned back a little, hoping she couldn't smell the stale whiskey on my breath.

"I suppose he must have been drunk when he crashed?" she said, her eyes searching my face for some nugget of information.

"No idea, Eithne. It's awful for the Devitts though, isn't it? This week of all weeks."

"It's cruel. So cruel, what some people have to go through in their lives. When others have so much and squander it." She shook her head sadly.

"Yes, I suppose."

"What can I get you?"

"Just some painkillers, please. I have a bit of a headache, probably the weather."

I felt like a child lying to a teacher. Eithne wasn't the kind of pharmacist you'd want to buy condoms from if you were eighteen. Or fifty-five, come to think of it. Still, she wasn't about to cross-examine me. Business was business. She turned towards the shelves of tablets behind her, selected a packet of painkillers, and placed them on the counter.

"These should do."

As she was ringing the price up on the till, the door opened and a blast of cold air hit the back of my neck.

A loud voice came from the doorway. "Fuck!"

I turned around to see a large, heavyset man with a sandy-colored comb-over standing straight up on his head shoving the door closed behind him, almost knocking down a large Valentine's Day makeup display in the process.

He turned towards us, red-faced. "Sorry, Eithne."

She nodded piously, conferring forgiveness.

"I have them ready," she said. She knelt down behind the counter and stood up with a small paper bag, which she handed to the man. He was on his way towards the door again when he stopped and turned.

"Should I . . . ?"

"No, don't worry. Claire said she'd settle up later on."

"Grand. I'll see you later on up at the house." And he left.

"Sorry about that. Where were we?" Eithne asked, turning her attention back to me.

"He looks familiar," I said.

"That's Mick, my brother. The carpenter, Mick Bourke? Conor Devitt used to work for him." Her eyelids fluttered shut in that irritating manner of hers. "He's been very good to Mrs. Devitt through all this."

I was buffeted across the square and almost fell in the door of the office, colliding with the postman on his way out. He didn't seem in the mood to chat, which wasn't like him. I said as much to Leah. Her expression darkened.

"It's Danny Devitt. He died about an hour ago. In the hospital."

"Ah, no." I sank onto one of the seats in the waiting room.

Leah stood in the open doorway. "He hadn't a hope, apparently. The postman just told me."

"Jesus. What a week that family is having."

"I know. Expecting one funeral and getting another."

Now I had no choice. I had to face him.

"Did Danny Devitt come and see you yesterday?" I asked.

"No," Molloy said. "Why?"

He looked as if he hadn't slept in days. I felt an unexpected surge of sympathy for him, which made me lose my train of thought for a second. Then I pulled myself together.

"He wanted to talk to you about something."

"Oh?"

"He came to see me at the office and said he was going to come and talk to you after. I thought you should know."

McFadden looked up from his computer.

"Do you know what he wanted to talk to me about?" Molloy asked.

"I don't, I'm afraid. He was a bit cryptic."

"That was his style all right," Molloy said heavily.

McFadden cleared his throat. "Em, Sergeant?"

Molloy turned. "What?"

"She's right. He did want to speak to you. He came down to the station last night after you went off duty."

"Why the hell didn't you tell me?"

McFadden reddened. "I forgot. You were off duty and I was going to tell you this morning. Then with everything that happened . . . well, I meant to."

Molloy sighed. "Come in here for a minute, will you?" he said, picking up some papers and walking towards the interview room. I followed him. He shut the door behind us and put the papers on the desk.

"Traces of Danny Devitt's DNA were found on the blanket and the pillow from Whitewater Church," he announced.

"You're kidding."

"Nope. We had his DNA from the samples we took on Friday. If Danny Devitt wasn't dead, we'd have been taking him in for questioning this morning."

I struggled to absorb this new information.

"I'm only telling you this because it appears you would have been representing him if he were still alive. It's not common knowledge. I'm trusting your discretion."

I looked at the ground, trying to make up my mind.

"Was there something else?" Molloy asked. "Ben?"

I swallowed. "He asked me if I could find out the identity of the bones in the church."

"Really?" Molloy said slowly. "And what did you tell him?"

"I said you were working on it." I whistled. "God, Danny, what did you do?"

"That's exactly what I want to know," Molloy replied. "And now we can't ask him."

"He seemed so distressed."

"And he gave you no idea what was upsetting him?"

"None really, other than what I've told you."

Molloy frowned. "What the hell was he doing up there?"

"He really didn't strike me as someone who'd kill some-one," I said, although even as I uttered the words, I pictured him punching the wall in my office.

There was silence between us for a few seconds.

"Still no identification?" I asked.

"Not yet. We're waiting for some DNA comparisons."

"Oh?"

Molloy gave me a look. No more information for me.

"Will there be a postmortem on Danny?"

"Yes. The pathologist is going to stay and do it this afternoon."

"Busy lady."

Molloy crossed his arms and leaned against the door. His tone changed as he said, "So, did you enjoy the play last night?"

"You saw me?" I stumbled.

"Yes. I didn't know you could run so fast."

I couldn't look him in the eye. I said the first idiotic thing that came into my head. "I thought you might want some privacy."

"Why would you think that?"

"I don't know. Maeve wondered if you might be on a date."

"Oh, did she now?" Molloy perched on the desk and studied my face.

Why couldn't I remember her name? Suddenly it became absolutely essential that I did. So I asked.

"Dr. Callan. Laura," he replied.

Laura Callan. Of course. How could I have forgotten? Another example of the mental firewall I'd created.

"You obviously know her?" I stuttered. "More than just professionally, I mean."

"I've known her for a long time. We were in college together. Before I joined the guards."

"Oh." I stared down at my feet. I knew Molloy had come to the guards late. That he had studied science before switching lanes.

"It wasn't a date."

I looked up. His eyes were creased at the edges, his brow furrowed with concern. Suddenly, I understood that Molloy was never going to ask me the questions I dreaded. It wasn't his way. He would wait until I was ready to tell him myself. If I ever was.

"So will that answer Maeve's questions, I wonder?" He smiled gently.

Chapter 13

LEAH RANG AS I was leaving the station.

"Tony from the pub called in."

"Is he still there? I'm just walking up the hill."

"He didn't want to wait. Said he needed to get back. He told me to tell you that Danny Devitt is being waked this evening in his mother's house. He thought you'd want to know."

"Thanks, Leah. I'll go tonight."

"Tony said the cortège should be back from the hospital about seven, if they release the body about half five, like they say they will."

I dialed Maeve's mobile and left a message. She rang back in seconds, farmyard noises in the background.

"Where are you?" I asked.

"Malin Head. Testing. What's up?"

"Have you heard about Danny Devitt?"

"Just this minute. Dreadful news."

"I'm going to the wake this evening. You coming?"

"Aye, I'll have to. I probably won't get to the funeral. I'll drive if you like. Pick you up at the office about half seven?"

The afternoon was quiet. I've noticed that fatal accidents do that. They subdue a town. It is as if people feel a sense of guilt for going about their normal business so they postpone things, at least for a day or two.

Maeve was bang on time and we turned into the narrow lane leading to the Devitts' farm about quarter to eight. After the afternoon storm the temperature had plummeted again. The night was pitch black, but despite the frost, there wasn't a single star visible.

"Where are we? I'm not familiar with this part of the world at all," I said, rubbing condensation from the window of Maeve's jeep. We had taken a route I had never been on. Inishowen is a warren of back roads and shortcuts, and Maeve, being a vet, uses them all.

"Really?" she asked.

"I lost you at Malin."

"You'd recognize it in daylight." She inclined her head towards the left. "Whitewater is over there. About half a mile as the crow flies, across the fields. The old pilot station is just down the hill."

"Oh right. I had no idea the shore was this close."

"On a clear day you could probably see the church from here."

I thought about that for a minute. "Was Conor Devitt still living at home when he disappeared, do you think?"

"I'd say so. He would have moved into the new house he built in Glendara with Lisa after the wedding. She'd have wanted to live in the town."

"I can see now why the family thought the body in the church might be him. Claire said he used to go up there sometimes."

"Oh, aye, it would have been only across the fields for him."

"You'd think they would have looked there when they were searching for him, wouldn't you?"

"I'm sure somebody did. But they probably only searched the grounds, not the crypt," Maeve said. "Although to be honest, I don't remember there being a large-scale search for him. It wasn't as if he was a child."

We slowed down as the lane became gradually narrower and came to a stop at the back of a line of cars parked along the ditch.

"We won't get any further," Maeve said, pulling in as tight as she could to the hedge. "We'll have a bit of a walk. It's another half-mile or so."

Maeve took a torch from the glove compartment and we set off up the muddy lane, joining at least a dozen other people heading in the same direction. Ice was forming on the potholes, crunchy now underfoot. A murmur of voices surrounded us. Although it was hard to see faces in the darkness, some silhouettes are difficult to mistake. Phyllis' distinctive shape appeared just ahead, and as we got closer, I could hear Tony Craig's deep tones.

"Poor Danny," Phyllis sighed, after we caught up and fell into step with them.

She was carrying a large casserole dish and had a plastic bag with loaves of bread hooked around her fingers. Tony was carrying a cardboard box, which, if the noise emanating from it was anything to go by, was full of bottles.

"Funny place to have an accident, wasn't it?" he said. "I mean, it's a good straight road, there coming into the town. And it's not as if it was icy last night. That road was salted yesterday morning – I saw them doing it."

"He must have been going very fast," Phyllis said.

"Or he was drunk." Maeve voiced what I assumed everyone was thinking.

"Although, there was a terrible accident along there a few years ago during the summer. That exact same stretch. Do you remember? That young fella from Derry," Phyllis said.

"That was a while back," Tony replied. "The roads are better now – I'd bet on it."

"No, it wasn't that long ago," Phyllis argued. "Six or seven years at the most. Hal did the burial. I remember because I was doing a bit of office work for him at the time. Poor Hal, can't add to save his life, he needed help. That young fella's father was from up here originally; his mother was dead, I think. So, they wanted him buried in the family plot. Now, what was his name . . . McFerry or something."

"What happened to him?" I asked.

"He was blind drunk and driving like a boy racer," Tony said. "Should have had more sense, he wasn't a kid."

Maeve threw him a look. "Danny Devitt wasn't a kid either."

"Now, we don't know for sure that Danny was drunk," Tony said.

"Hmm," Maeve said doubtfully.

"Anyway, drunk or not, Danny Devitt had lots of good qualities," Tony went on. "I was fond of him."

"He was certainly bloody good with animals," Maeve conceded.

"Liked 'em better than people, from what I knew of him," Tony said.

"Not always such a bad policy," Phyllis added.

"He had his own remedies, didn't he, made from wild flowers and herbs and things? I heard him talking in the pub about it," Tony said.

Maeve nodded. "Some of the other vets didn't like him interfering, but from what I saw, he had a fair idea of what he was doing. He made his own poultices. I saw him cure a really nasty abscess on a horse's leg once, when no amount of antibiotics had any effect on it. I don't know what was in his potion, and it stank to high heaven, but by Jesus it worked."

"What'll happen to his dog?" I asked.

Phyllis made a small sound in the back of her throat, like a whimper.

"Oh, don't worry, Phyllis. Fred will be okay," Maeve said cheerfully. "I'd say Danny's mother will take him. Here we are."

We arrived into a yard flooded with light and packed full of cars. The Devitts' home was a small, uneven, whitewashed farmhouse with a porch. As we made our way inside, we passed through a group of men clustered around the outside step, smoking. One of them was Mick Bourke. He gave me a brief nod of recognition.

The porch led into a narrow, low-ceilinged hallway that ran to the right of the stairs. It was hot and gloomily lit, and crowded. There were people standing the length of it, leaning against the wall, sipping cups of tea or drinks, talking to each other in hushed, respectful tones.

A woman in an apron emerging from a door at the end of the hallway, carrying a tray of sandwiches, resulted in an impasse. While we huddled at the foot of the stairs to let her by, I heard someone quietly direct Maeve towards a doorway to the right.

"I'm going to take this into the kitchen," Tony whispered, nodding at the cardboard box he was carrying.

Phyllis was behind him. "Me, too. We'll catch up with you two in a minute, Ben."

There was a steady stream of traffic in and out of the room Maeve and I were shown into. A rarely used dining room that probably hadn't changed in a couple of decades, it had the same low ceiling as the hall, with a dresser along one wall, full of elaborately patterned china. A large oval-shaped dining table dominated the space. The chairs, which were occupied mostly by women of a certain age, had been moved away and lined up against the wall as if in preparation for a dance. An old sideboard rested against the back wall. The mirror that hung above it had been covered with a black cloth, and the clock on the opposite wall was stopped. Despite the cold, one window was open.

I forced myself to look at the table and its burden. An open coffin. Seated next to the coffin was a woman with white hair and a small, tired face. She gazed silently at the floor, something set and determined, almost stoic about her expression as if she was willing this all to be over. I followed her eyes to the floor. She was wearing moss-green shoes.

Maeve approached the coffin first. I watched as she leaned forward and whispered a prayer, blessed herself and moved aside. Now it was my turn. My throat tightening, I gazed down at the face framed by the folds of white satin and remembered the man's awful sadness at the office. How different he looked now, his complexion an unnatural shade of beige, his hair neatly combed, his beard trimmed. I suspected Hal had done a hell of a job to conceal his injuries. He was dressed in a navy suit, although even in death he didn't look like a man who would have had much call for a suit. A set of rosary beads fell from his clasped fingers. I wondered if the religion had been thrust upon him, too.

Conscious of being watched, I racked my brains to come up with some words of prayer, and failed. Silently, I moved away.

Chapter 14

WE PASSED PHYLLIS in the doorway on our way out.

"Claire's in the kitchen," she said.

I noticed some unusual paintings in the hall, abstract oils in vibrant colors with no frames. Incongruous against the beige, flowered wallpaper. I would have liked to have taken a better look but it seemed a bit crass to ask people to move so I could admire pictures at a wake.

The kitchen was large and bright with a high ceiling, modern cabinets, and shiny new appliances. Harsh fluorescent tubes made me blink after the yellow gloom that bathed the rest of the house. I thought I detected a faint smell of fresh paint. The room was a hive of industry: teapots being filled, surfaces being cleaned. Two women at the counter buttered bread for sandwiches and two at the sink washed up. By the wall on one of the lower cabinets, Tony had set up a bar. Maeve and I stood in the middle of the floor unsure of what to do next.

"Should we offer to help, do you think?"

"Looks like they're pretty much sorted."

I lowered my tone to a whisper. "I presume that was Danny's mother sitting by the coffin?"

She nodded. "Mary Devitt."

I hadn't spoken to Mrs. Devitt in the other room. I was relieved when I saw that she was surrounded by people as I moved away from the coffin, but knew I must at least speak to Claire before leaving. I scanned the room for her, but there was no sign. A door to the left looked as if it might lead into a back kitchen of some sort. Tony appeared at my shoulder, glass in hand, as if reading my mind.

"Looking for Claire?" He gestured at the door I had been contemplating. "She's in there talking to Eithne. You could rescue her."

I opened the door and peered into a small room containing a washing machine and freezer. Claire was standing with her back against the wall beside a tiered vegetable basket full of carrots and potatoes, eyes downcast and clutching a stringy-looking tissue in one hand. Eithne, dressed in a long brown skirt and lilac cardigan, was stroking her other hand while talking to her in a low urgent tone. At the sound of the door opening, Claire looked up, startled, and immediately pulled her hand back from Eithne's grasp.

"Ben," she breathed.

Eithne turned to face me, as if irritated at being interrupted. Claire walked past her and ushered me back into the kitchen. She looked flushed and untidy.

"Have you had some tea? Or a drink?" Her voice was shrill.

I shook my head. "I'm fine."

Eithne followed us into the kitchen and stood observing, hand resting on the counter.

Claire pushed me towards the table. "Come and sit down for a minute, anyway."

There was nowhere to sit. All of the kitchen chairs were occupied. Claire's eyes darted frantically around the room as if her life depended on finding me a seat. She flew out of the room and reappeared, followed by Mick Bourke carrying two chairs. She instructed him to place them at the table, dismissed him unceremoniously, and sat down. I looked for Maeve, saw her chatting to Tony, and sat, too. Claire shoved a loaded plate towards me.

"Cake?"

"No, thanks."

"I wish you would. We've enough cake to feed the entire French peasantry." She gave a slightly hysterical giggle. "I don't know if you know Lisa and Alan."

I glanced at the deeply tanned couple across from us.

"They're just back from their honeymoon. The Maldives."

The man I had seen twice in the past week. The woman was blond and slim, heavily made up, eyes lined with black kohl. She wore a black formal jacket with some kind of silk top underneath. I realized I recognized her, too. I struggled for a second to place her before it came to me; she worked in one of the banks in Buncrana.

This was the couple who had been burgled while they were on their honeymoon. I wondered how they were coping. The woman's perfume lingered heavily in the air above us, her arm linked with that of her husband. He was dark-suited and unshaven. Not Danny Devitt unshaven, more George Michael. He smiled a tight, uncomfortable smile, showing slightly discolored teeth. Claire introduced us.

Lisa's eyes were glistening. "We were sharing memories of Danny when he was a kid. We were all in school together." She had a twitch above her left eye, which the makeup did nothing to conceal.

"What was he like?"

"He didn't like being inside, that's for sure. Always wanted to be out with the animals – cattle, sheep, pigs, didn't matter. Skipped school constantly to help on the farm, didn't he, Claire?"

But Claire wasn't listening. She was staring at something by the sink. I followed her gaze, but I couldn't see anything out of the ordinary, merely the continuing conveyer belt of dish-washing. Eithne seemed to have vacated her post.

"Claire?" Lisa said again.

"Sorry?" Claire sniffed loudly and returned her attention to the table.

"Danny. He ran the farm himself for a while, didn't he?"

"Oh aye. Mam used to say he was half-goat." She sniffed again. I wished I had a fresh tissue to offer her. "Never happier than when he was covered in muck."

"Do you still have a farm here?" I asked. I got the feeling the shiny new kitchen I was sitting in hadn't seen much farm life lately.

Claire shook her head. "The land's been sold." Abruptly, she stood up and walked out of the room, slamming the door behind her.

I swallowed, feeling uncomfortable, as if I'd asked a particularly intrusive question.

There was a low whine as Alan pushed his chair back, too. "I'm just going out for a smoke . . ."

Lisa looked up at him in alarm and grabbed his arm. He leaned over and gave her a brief kiss on the lips. "I'll be back in five minutes." Her jaw tightened as she watched him leave the room.

Before I had a chance to say anything, the door reopened. I looked up. Standing in the doorway, wearing a dark coat and red velvet scarf, looking startlingly exotic in the hive of domestic activity, like some aristocratic lady come to visit below stairs, was Alison Kelly. She glanced quickly around the room and approached our table, her eyes fixed on Lisa. Lisa's expression changed in an instant from one of alarm to one of utter hostility.

Alison didn't seem to notice. "Ah, Lisa, how are you!" she exclaimed. "What a sad occasion to have to meet."

Lisa glared at her.

Alison took Alan's seat. "Where are the family?" she said. "I must talk to poor Mrs. Devitt."

Lisa looked away as if she hadn't heard.

"Claire's gone that way," I said, indicating the door Alison had come through. "And Mrs. Devitt is in the front room."

I'm never sure how to respond when I meet clients out of context. If the only way I know them is professionally, I usually let them take the lead, as I did now. Alison nodded a curt thank-you but gave no indication that she knew me. After she left the room, the uncomfortable silence resumed. Lisa sat staring at her hands, her mouth fixed in a thin line.

I struggled to come up with something to say. "Sounds like Danny and Conor were very different?" I said.

Lisa's eyes flashed. A look not of grief, it struck me, but of anger, crossed her face again, but it passed quickly. She looked towards the door as if she wanted desperately to follow her husband. Suddenly it burst open again and Claire came back into the room. She had changed her clothes and was wearing a bright red dress, high-heeled sandals, and big gold hoop ear-rings. I caught Maeve's sideways glance from across the room.

"Sorry. Lots of people. All over the place," Claire said breathlessly. "So many people to speak to." She sank back down into the chair she had vacated earlier and began to play with her hair coquettishly. "Now what were we saying?"

"I was asking if Danny and Conor were very different."

Claire smiled. "Not when they were kids. They both loved being outside. Danny was crazy about animals and Conor was always down by the shore. He was dead keen on the big ships; he used to go down at all hours of the day and night to watch them coming in." Her eyes widened and she put her hand to her mouth as if suddenly frightened. She stuttered, "N-not that I remember really; I was too small."

"You're the youngest?" I said.

She nodded. "It was Conor, Danny, and then me. Conor used to boss us around like mad."

"I wouldn't say Danny took a blind bit of notice of him," Lisa said with a weak smile.

"Oh, he hated it. Danny hated being told what to do, but Conor sure loved telling us. Just because he was the eldest. The good boy." Claire's tone was resentful, like a sulky child. "But Danny was going to be Conor's best man. He'd have had to do what Conor said that day – he wouldn't have liked that."

I shifted, ill at ease. There was something deliberately care-less about the way she mentioned the wedding; almost cruel. Lisa stared into her cup.

"He got very peculiar after that – after Conor disappeared," Claire went on. "Did you notice, Lisa?"

"I didn't see much of him, to be honest."

"You weren't the only one. He took off up to that cottage of his, and we never saw him from one end of the year to the next, even though he was only across the fields."

"That must have been hard on your mother," I said.

Claire's voice was angry. "She was better off without him. Danny was a drunk."

I caught sight of Eithne watching us from across the kitchen. She had resumed her position at the counter, was standing there silently, arms crossed, lips pursed.

"I don't think he could help it, Claire. He had a problem," Lisa said softly. "He wasn't always a drunk."

"Of course he could help it! He could have given it up. And now look what's happened. He goes and drives his car into a ditch." Claire's lips trembled. "Stupid, stupid, *stupid* man. As good as killed himself. As if we haven't enough to cope with."

Her face crumpled and she started to cry. Immediately, Eithne appeared, glass of water and fresh tissue in hand. She knelt beside Claire, put her arms around her, and started to talk to her in a low murmuring voice, like a mother talking to a baby. Lisa pushed her chair back, stood up, and left the room, shutting the door behind her with a quiet click while I looked away, embarrassed. Maeve caught my eye and looked pointedly at her watch.

I cleared my throat. "We have to go, Claire, I'm sorry," I said.

Claire lifted her head. "Thanks for coming." Tears spilled from her eyes and down her cheeks. "The funeral is on Friday, after eleven o'clock Mass."

"I'll be there."

I crossed the kitchen.

Tony whispered in my ear, "Looks like Phyllis is going to be here for the duration, and I have to get back to the pub. Any chance of a lift into town?"

* * *

After a complicated series of maneuvers in the narrow lane, Maeve finally managed to get the jeep pointing in the right direction.

"Jesus, that was some bit of drama from Claire at the end." Tony rubbed the windscreen with a yellow cloth from the dashboard on Maeve's request. "Never one to shy away from being the center of attention, that one."

"That's a bit harsh, Tony, isn't it?" I said.

"Eithne needs to stop giving her those damn pills for a start, I reckon. They're doing her more harm than good."

"What pills?" I leaned forward from the back seat.

He shook his head. "Ah, nothing."

Maeve turned the jeep onto the main road. "Why did she change her clothes like that?"

"God knows," Tony said. "She looked like a bloody flamenco dancer."

"It was a bit odd," I agreed. "Still, she has just lost her brother. Maybe two brothers." I paused. "What do you think happened, Tony? Do you think Danny was drunk?"

He sighed. "Sure, what do I know? All I can say is that when he was in with me last night, he was drinking orange juice."

"Seriously? In the pub?"

"Aye, in the pub. Now I'm not saying he didn't get a drink in somewhere else after that, but he didn't get it from me, that's for sure."

"What kind of form was he in?"

"He was quiet. As if he had something he needed to think through. Never seen him like that. But then I've never seen him in the pub drinking orange juice either."

I wondered when it would become common knowledge that Danny's DNA was in the crypt.

"What happened with him and Alan Crane on Sunday?" I asked.

Tony threw a look at me over his shoulder. "What's this? *Twenty Questions?*"

I ignored him. "Did they argue?"

"There is such a thing as barman's confidentiality, you know."

I grinned. "It's pretty selective though, isn't it?"

"Well, I'm giving you no details, but in my opinion Danny was behaving like someone who wanted to get himself arrested."

"You don't think he might have driven himself into the ditch on purpose . . . ?" Maeve's question trailed off.

"Not after the father," Tony said firmly. He paused. "God, I'd hope not anyway. Jack had his reasons. He never recovered from what happened to the *Sadie*."

"What had Jack Devitt to do with the *Sadie*?" I asked. "Phyllis started to tell me about it but didn't get finished."

"Jack was one of the crew of the *Sadie*," Tony explained. "Ach, the whole thing was grim. It was a night in December – a real clear winter's night, like tonight. The Whitewater pilot boat was hijacked and taken out to the *Sadie*. But before that, the pilot on duty was shot dead, just outside the pilot station."

"Jesus."

Tony nodded in agreement. "I know. Brutal. God knows why they did it – always seemed strange to me, that. Seemed so bloody unnecessary. Those operations were usually fairly tight."

"What do you mean?"

"They can't have *wanted* to kill him. You'd think they'd have taken him with them. But it looked like he was trying to make a run for it. Someone must have screwed up – taken their eye off the ball, I'd say. And after they shot him, they just left him lying there on the shore, took the pilot boat and used it to board the *Sadie*. They set the crew afloat on life rafts before they blew it up."

"And Jack?"

"Jack Devitt was luckier than others. He survived – physically, at least."

"When you say luckier . . . ?"

"Two crewmen from the *Sadie* were killed – they were still on the ship when it was blown up. I don't think they were meant to die either; something went wrong there, too, I reckon. They were probably hiding. It's possible the hijackers didn't know they were there." He said somberly, "They were locals from Whitewater, too, neighbors of Jack Devitt."

"Most of the men from Whitewater were employed on the ships at that time," Maeve explained.

"God." I ran my hands through my hair in horror.

"Aye, it was awful," Tony said. "The pilot they shot was a friend of Jack's, too – Eamonn McCauley, Lisa's father. Jack was never the same again. He couldn't get over seeing the boat blown up with men still on board. His mind went. He never worked a day after that. Couldn't manage the farm, even. Just wandered about in a daze."

"So that's what they meant when they said Conor had to take over as the man of the house, when he was young."

"Aye. Poor Jack Devitt was dead long before his heart stopped pumping. Shot himself with his own gun. In one of the outhouses."

"Christ."

"The kids were teenagers at the time, I think, or even younger. Danny, poor kid, was the one that found him. Must have affected him. That's when Conor went off and got his apprenticeship with Bourke and started to support the family. His mother was lucky to have him. So were his brother and sister. Although Danny worked hard, too, on the farm when he was still only a youngster."

He clicked his teeth in disapproval. "But that Claire one, she hasn't had a job since that stint she did for Eithne about ten years ago. Spoiled wee thing, in my opinion. Lazy as sin. Sees herself as some class of artist. I've never seen any bloody paintings. Not by her anyway."

"I thought she was looking after her mother."

He laughed. "Who told you that?"

Maeve left Tony at the Oak, then dropped me off at my car. My head was beginning to ache again. I looked for the painkillers in my bag, but I'd left them in the office. Maybe I deserved to suffer a little.

As I approached the site of the accident, I pulled the car in and got out to have a look, leaving the headlights on. There was nothing to see now, other than some broken bushes. The car had been removed and the road cleared of glass and debris. I looked down the road towards Malin, the direction Danny had come from less than twenty-four hours earlier. Tony was right. This stretch of road was straight and even, and the night before had been mild and frost-free. The state I'd been in, I'd probably have come a cropper myself, if the roads hadn't been in decent shape.

I stood for a moment and looked across the water to the lights on the other shore. If the results of the blood samples confirmed Danny Devitt's sobriety, then surely there had to have been something odd about his accident? If it was an accident at all. And still no one knew what had happened to Conor Devitt – the man everyone had expected to be waking this evening.

Chapter 15

I ARRIVED EARLY at the office the next morning to find the estate agent Liam McLaughlin waiting for me on the doorstep. He looked surprisingly chipper.

"Morning," I said, as I turned the key in the lock. "You're about bright and early."

"Good news will always get me up and about," he said with a grin, as he stubbed his cigarette out on the wall and followed me inside.

I dumped my keys and bag on the counter. "Go on, tell me. I could do with hearing it. Not much good news about at the moment."

He frowned. "Aye, you're right."

"So what is it? I'm listening."

"You know that English couple?"

"You're going to have to be a bit more specific."

"The English couple who were going to buy Whitewater Church," he said impatiently.

"Oh, yes."

"They're back on board!"

"Back on board?" My brain was particularly sluggish this morning. Sleep had eluded me again the night before.

"They want to buy the church again."

"You're kidding." Not what I was expecting.

"Nope. It looks like they've managed to get over their squeamishness and they're still interested. Same price, the works."

I crossed my arms. "Wow. That's great news. Kelly will be delighted."

"Sure he will. I don't know if they still want to live in it, but who cares? That won't matter to Kelly. The important thing is that they want to buy it. I've just thought – I'll have to get Paul Doherty up there again."

"Yes, I don't think he managed to get his survey finished the last time. He was sort of interrupted."

"Maybe I'll ask him not to be so thorough the next time," Liam said wryly. "In case he turns up something else."

I smiled. "I don't think he's going to be too thrilled to have to go back up there at all, to be honest."

"Wouldn't blame him. I'm not too keen on the place my-self." Liam turned to go.

"Do you want me to phone him?" I asked.

"That'd be great. Just wait till I call Kelly. I'll give you a shout when I get him."

Half an hour later, I was going through the mail at the desk when the front door opened again. The smell of perfume hit me long before I saw the source. It was Lisa Crane. I was sur-prised to see her. I didn't think she had particularly warmed to me the night before. Ignoring Leah, she addressed herself directly to me. "Would you have a minute? I don't have an appointment."

Leah opened the diary, a smile playing at the corners of her mouth.

"Your first appointment isn't till ten," she informed me.

* * *

Lisa arranged herself carefully on the seat. She made me feel unpolished and scruffy despite my suit. She was wearing sky-scraper heels, a cobalt-blue woolen dress with the top button opened to give a hint of tanned cleavage, and she carried a chic-looking green coat, which she laid across her knees. If I were asked to bet, I would have said that both the dress and coat were cashmere. She was heavily made up, as she had been last night. I wondered what her salary was at the bank. She would have been an expensive lady to dress.

"What can I do for you, Miss McCauley?" I asked.

"Crane," she said.

"I'm sorry. Mrs. Crane."

"It's fine. I've never dealt with you before. We've always used Keavney's," she said, referring to the other solicitor's firm in the town. "But Alan thought, after we met you last night . . . in the circumstances, since you weren't around when he went missing, well, that maybe you might be the one to talk to."

"I presume we're talking about Conor?"

She nodded. "I know the Devitts use Keavney's, too. And what with everything that's happened, I wanted to be dis-creet. I have no wish to be insensitive."

"What is it that you want?" I asked.

She appeared to choose her words carefully. "I want to know when he can be declared legally dead."

I leaned back in my seat to gather my thoughts. "Okay," I said, "under the law here, a missing person is presumed alive for seven years. After seven years he is presumed dead."

"That's what I thought," she said. "So, we're nearly there."

"When did you last see him?"

"The fifteenth of June, seven years ago this summer. The day before our wedding."

I took out an attendance sheet and wrote down the date.

"So, I can do it this summer? Have him declared dead?"

"In theory, yes. But it's not quite as simple as that. I'll have to look into it but I think it can be quite complicated, in fact. It involves an application to the High Court."

She sat forward. "Yes?"

"Probably with an affidavit. And even though you were his fiancée, you may not be able to do it on your own. We may need a relative – a blood relative." I paused. "So you may need to involve the Devitts, whether you want to or not."

Her face fell.

"Is there any particular reason why you want to do it?"

She delivered her response like a well-rehearsed answer to a question in an oral exam. "Conor and I built a house. It's in our joint names, and I need to have his name taken off it."

"Very well." I returned to the attendance sheet and started to take some notes. "How were you registered, can you re-member? What type of joint ownership?"

"Joint tenants. I'm sure of it. We were asked what way we wanted it."

I was surprised. It's not a question clients can usually an-swer so easily. I said as much.

She shrugged. "I'm in charge of mortgages at the bank."

"So, if Conor is declared presumed dead, you will inherit."

A look of displeasure crossed her face. "That's not why I want it done."

I put down my pen. "I'm sorry. Why is it you want it done, then?"

Her face hardened. It made her look older. "I want him out of my life. It's been over for a long time, and I don't want to have to think about him anymore. I want to stop getting letters from the bank addressed to Conor Devitt and Lisa McCauley, letters from the Revenue Commissioners about property tax, letters about God knows what." Her accent seemed to get stronger as her voice grew louder. "I'm blue in the face asking them to change it, but they haven't a notion of doing it while they can't be sure if he's dead or alive. I can't live in limbo any longer. This whole thing's been going on for long enough."

"I understand," I said.

"I want it over and done with. He's gone and that should be it."

"Especially now that you're married to someone else."

"Alan's got nothing to do with it. I was full sure I was going to do something about it when I came home from the holiday, but then when that body was found and everyone seemed to think it might be him, I thought maybe it would be over and done with that way. And what with the break-in and all, I didn't feel like doing anything about it, anyway. But then when it wasn't him . . ."

I interrupted her. "Did you think it might be?"

"I didn't know," she said firmly.

"So, you're not hopeful of him being found alive, then?"

A look of fury flashed across her face. It was the same look I had seen the night before.

"Hopeful? You are joking, aren't you? If that man is alive, he's downright humiliated me. Have you any idea of what it's like to be stood up on your wedding day? To have relatives over from America and England and God knows where, spending everything you have on your dream wedding only for the groom not to bother turning up?"

"No, I don't," I said quietly.

"Well, then." She sat back in her seat.

"Have you talked to his family about what you're intending doing? Claire, or his mother?"

She shook her head.

"They might have some feelings about it, you know. They've just lost Danny."

"I know that."

"Well, as I said, you may need them for the application. But even if you don't, I still think you should discuss it with them."

Lisa sighed.

"You never know," I said gently, "they may be in agreement with you. I understand they're convinced something must have happened to him. They don't believe that he left of his own accord."

"They wouldn't believe he put a foot wrong, so they wouldn't," she muttered. "Claire thought the sun shone out of his arse. Did anything he told her to do. And his mother was the same."

"What do *you* think happened?"

She sighed again. "To be truthful, I don't know. Things weren't right for a while, I know that much."

"Between the two of you?"

She shot me a warning look. "It's not something I want said, mind."

"Of course. Anything you say to me is confidential."

She hesitated. "He was behaving a wee bit off. I don't know what was going on, but he'd disappear for hours on end, turning his phone off so I couldn't get him."

"What do you think it was?"

She looked at me. "You're thinking he was cheating on me?"

"No, I . . ."

"Well, maybe you're right. I've no proof, but maybe you're right. Conor Devitt was the kind of man women like, if you know what I mean?"

I knew exactly what she meant.

"Even my mother liked him," she said. "My grandmother used to flirt with him and she's eighty-two." She smiled for the first time since she'd come in. "That should have been a warning sign. My grandmother's a right old battleaxe. She didn't even mind that he didn't go to Mass."

It was my turn to smile.

Her expression became sad. "We were together for a long time, you know? He was the first serious boyfriend I had. A few years older than me, good job, great football player. Sure, I was mad about him. But I never really trusted him. Strange, that."

"Why not?"

"I don't know. He was too good to be true. Handsome and sensible. You don't get that combination in one fella. Especially not in his twenties. There had to be something wrong."

"How long were you with him?" I tried to calculate in my head.

"Nine years," she said. "All the years when I should have been having a family." Her eyes welled. She shook the tears away impatiently.

"I'm sorry," I said.

She looked down at her hands. A large solitaire diamond, a wedding ring, nails bitten to the quick. "I don't know why I waited so long. I think in my heart I knew he didn't want to get married. But I never thought he'd do that to me, just not turn up. That was cruel."

I was beginning to feel sympathy for her when her voice hardened again, as if she regretted her show of emotion.

"The dress, the flowers, the hotel, the band, the photographer." She counted them all off on her fingers. "The best of everything we had. I wouldn't have any crap. A video man down from Derry. Doves, for Christ's sake."

I tried not to smile.

"All paid for. And the morning of my wedding I'm being driven round and round the town like a tool for a full hour." Her eyes watered again. "He broke my heart. At first I was worried, then when he didn't appear in the days after that . . ."

"Then?" I prompted.

She clammed up. "Nothing."

"Are you saying you don't think he is dead?"

"Like I said, I don't know," she answered sullenly.

"If you have any reason to believe he's still alive, Mrs. Crane, you'll have to tell me. It may cause a difficulty in obtaining a declaration of presumed death," I warned her. "Everything will have to go into the affidavit."

"I don't. I don't know what happened to him and that's the truth," she said firmly. Her expression didn't change as she leaned forward, fixed me with a resolute gaze, and said, "So, are you going to help me get rid of the bastard or not?"

Chapter 16

I OPENED THE door to clear the cloud of perfume lingering in the air. It was way too cold to open a window. There was something about Lisa Crane I couldn't warm to. Something cloying, a bit like her scent. Strange, because when I had heard the story of her fiancé's disappearance before their wedding, I had felt sorry for her. But she was hard to like. I wondered if that was intentional on her part. I'm a woman, and Lisa Crane was a man's woman. Or at least she wanted to be.

There was a brittle quality to her that she covered with aggression. I thought about how thin the line is between love and hate, how quickly one can turn to the other when someone's trust is betrayed. What was it that she wasn't telling me, I wondered.

The morning passed in a series of appointments. At one o'clock, after a message from Liam, I thought I'd call Raymond Kelly to confirm his instructions about the sale and get Paul Doherty back up to Whitewater Church to finish the survey. I was halfway through dialing Kelly's number when it occurred to me that I should talk to Molloy first to ensure that we had access. I dialed the garda station and got McFadden.

"Is the sergeant there, Andy?"

"No. Can I help you with something?"

"Maybe. I wanted to make sure your crime scene people are completely finished up at the church. We need access."

"Aye, I think so. I believe they finished last week. Why do you need access?"

"Well, it looks as if the buyers are going ahead after all and we need to get the place surveyed again."

He whistled. "Jesus. They're brave wee souls. There's no accounting for taste."

"It is a beautiful setting," I said.

"Well, you couldn't pay me to live there."

"I know what you mean. Anyway, you're all finished with it?"

"Just to make sure, I'll give them a call up in Letterkenny and I'll ring you back before two o'clock. That do you?"

"That'd be great, Andy. Thanks." I hesitated. "Where's Molloy, by the way?"

I could hear the mischief in his voice when he replied, "He's gone off to have lunch with his lady friend."

"She's still here?" I could feel the pins and needles traveling slowly up my neck again.

"Aye, she stayed an extra day to do the postmortem on poor Danny yesterday afternoon. I think she's heading back tonight."

I hung up the phone and stared at the wall. I couldn't figure out what was making me so bloody uncomfortable – the identity of this pathologist Laura Callan and her place in my past, or the fact that Molloy was spending so much time with her, and in such a fashion that McFadden was calling her his lady friend.

Whatever it was, I hated it. Every time her name was mentioned, I started to think about things I didn't *want* to think about. I wished her gone – far away from here.

I couldn't face a sandwich. So I stayed at my desk over lunch. Stewing.

Leah arrived back at a quarter to two as I was making myself a quick coffee. She shoved her bag under her desk, asking, "So, how did you get on with our Lisa?"

"Okay. I met her last night at the wake."

She smiled.

I rested my mug on the counter. "You seem to have a view on her. Spit it out."

She shook her head. "Ach, it's nothing really."

"Go on."

"She's just a bit possessive, always has been – every woman's a threat, if you know what I mean."

"You sound like you're talking from experience."

She looked embarrassed. "Maybe. Anyway, it looks as if she's met her match. Her husband came in after her and waited for her down here the whole time she was in with you."

"Alan?"

"Yes. Walked her out the door by the arm. Very proprietorial. Oh, and by the way, I ran into Mick Bourke in the town. He wants to know if he can see you tomorrow afternoon after the funeral."

"That's fine. Give him a call back and stick him in wherever there's a window. Did he say what it's about?"

"No, but he was a bit jittery. As if he didn't want anyone to see him talking to me."

Leah took a slip of paper out of her bag and picked up the phone to dial. She stopped halfway through and placed the phone to her chest.

"Oh, I nearly forgot to tell you."

"Something else? You've had a busy time."

"There's been another break-in. Paul Doherty – his office."

"Oh no! When?"

"Last night or this morning. Two computers and some engineering equipment were stolen – mobile phone, too, I think. The postman told me."

"No cash or anything?"

"No. But Paul's furious."

"I bet. I hope he's insured."

I didn't like the apprehensive feeling I had walking in the door of the garda station. I wasn't used to it. This was my turf; I had walked through these doors hundreds of times. I resented the fact that I felt uncomfortable now and I resented the person who was making me feel that way.

Luckily, she wasn't there. Molloy and McFadden were on their own, squabbling about something. The atmosphere was tense. I had to add to it, of course.

"How was your lunch?" I asked.

Molloy gave McFadden a glare. McFadden reddened and stared intently at the statement he was typing. Immediately, I felt guilty.

"Fine. How was yours?" Molloy replied, approaching the desk.

"I didn't have any."

The words hadn't sounded sulky when I formulated them in my head, but when they came out of my mouth I realized

I sounded like a five-year-old. Molloy gave no indication that he'd noticed.

"Andy tells me that your buyers are back and you want to have the church surveyed again."

I nodded.

"That's fine. All the evidence has been collected according to the Garda Technical Bureau. It's a matter of carrying out the tests now, and that's going to take some time."

"No cause of death yet?"

"Still up in the air."

The door opened behind me. It was Paul Doherty, stubbing out a cigarette. The burglary had obviously induced his emergency smoking again.

"I'm here to give you that statement," he said.

"Andy, can you?" Molloy nodded at McFadden.

"Sorry to hear about the break-in, Paul," I said.

"Thanks. Could have done without it, that's for sure."

I looked at Molloy. "Could I have a quick chat with you?" I asked.

"Fine."

I followed him into the interview room. He shut the door behind us.

"Any idea yet why Danny Devitt's DNA was on the blanket?"

He crossed his arms. "Well, we've searched his cottage and it appears both the blanket and pillow came from there. So it does look as though he was the one who wrapped the bones."

"Right." I took a few seconds to digest this. "So where did the bones come from? Do you still think they were moved into the crypt from somewhere else?"

"We're not sure," Molloy said slowly.

"What about the soil samples?"

"They match the soil in the old graveyard, which is no indicator of anything," he said. "The traces were minimal and soil is pretty similar throughout this area."

"What about the disturbed soil in the graveyard? Under the trees?"

Molloy raised his eyebrows.

"Andy told me. Could they have come from there? A shallow grave?"

Molloy didn't reply. Was I imagining it, or was he avoiding my gaze?

"Could Danny have dug them up and moved them into the crypt?" I asked.

Molloy shook his head. "Unlikely. The bones were fairly fragile. It's not as if they would have held together."

"I don't know if it's relevant, but he had some knowledge of anatomy, I think. Animals, anyway. He was a bit of an unqualified vet."

"So I believe. To be honest, even wrapping the bones in the blanket would have been difficult. The pathologist believes that was done relatively recently. Moving a skeleton and having the bones remain intact would have been virtually impossible."

It was a macabre image: Danny Devitt in a darkened crypt beneath a deserted church, carefully wrapping a human skeleton in a blanket and placing a pillow beneath the skull. Maybe with his dog in tow. A picture of Fred running away with one of the bones in his mouth crept into my head. I chased it away.

"Why on earth would he do something like that?"

"God knows."

"And why were the bones there in the first place?" I said again. "I just can't imagine Danny Devitt killing someone."

Molloy looked away. There was something he wasn't telling me, I could sense it. But I knew better than to push him. Molloy was like a set of tangled Christmas tree lights. The harder you tried to find a way in, the more inaccessible he became. I tried a different approach.

"You know I told you that he was anxious to know if the bones had been identified?"

Molloy nodded.

"Something was confusing him. Something didn't make sense to him. He said he wanted to talk to me about it and then he changed his mind. Then he wanted to talk to you, but he said there was something he needed to do first. I don't know what that was."

Molloy scratched his chin thoughtfully.

"Tom?"

Molloy looked up.

"Was there anything strange about his death?" I asked. "Are we sure it was an accident?"

Molloy was unfazed. "Impossible to tell. He crashed into a ditch. We can't be a hundred percent sure, but there was no other car involved as far as we could see. There were no skid marks, other than his own."

"His body was released very quickly."

"Yes. The postmortem didn't take long. Cause of death was very straightforward. Head injury caused by the impact of the crash."

I said nothing.

Molloy frowned. "Are you implying that something was missed?"

"No, of course not."

"He died in hospital, remember?"

"I know, I know."

He raised his eyebrows. "So?"

I sighed. "It's just it's a bit of a coincidence, don't you think? The bones in the church turn out not to be Conor Devitt despite everybody's expectations to the contrary, and within forty-eight hours his brother is dead, killed in a car accident."

"Yes, I do. But I also think that we can't rule out suicide as a possibility."

I didn't like to think about that.

"How about the blood alcohol tests?"

"There was no alcohol in his system when he died. He was sober when he crashed."

Chapter 17

Now I was hungry. I had just enough time to grab a sandwich and take it back to my desk. I was standing at the bar in the Oak waiting impatiently for Eddie to finish his spat with the espresso machine when I heard someone call my name. I turned to see Alison Kelly sitting by the fire with her son Trevor, the remains of sandwiches and soup on the table in front of them.

"I was about to call your husband," I said.

"We've saved you a phone call, then. We've just been dropping some food up to the wake – stuff from the restaurant."

"I'm sure that'll be appreciated."

"Well, you do what you can, don't you? Ray and I felt bad for them. We couldn't help feeling we were part of it in some way, with that whole business with the church."

"It's hardly your fault."

"I know, but we felt one of us should go last night, to show our sympathy. Ray would have been there, too, but he's a bit under the weather. I didn't know too many people there though, I was surprised. Apart from you, of course."

"And Lisa – you knew Lisa?"

"Oh yeah," she said dismissively. "I know Lisa from the bank in Buncrana. But I thought I might know some people from years back, from when I used to live there."

"And you didn't?"

"No." She looked wistful. "Though I suppose I was just a child then. Funny how you can get caught up with these sentimental notions about a place. I was so homesick for Whitewater when we went back to the States that I built it up into some kind of Utopia in my mind. Stupid really, the way you can allow yourself to be swept away by something, when it's the here and now that's important."

"I know what you mean."

"It was one of the reasons we bought the church – stupid sentimentality." She smiled ruefully. "Or rather, it's one of the reasons I persuaded Ray to buy the church." She gestured at the empty seat next to her. "Sit down, join us."

"Thanks, but . . ."

"Go up and order us a couple of coffees, would you, Trevor?"

"No, really I can't, I'm afraid," I told them. "I have to head back to the office."

Alison looked disappointed. "Okay, if you're sure. Just one then, Trevor, could you?"

Her son nodded amicably and sauntered up to the bar.

"What did you want to talk to Ray about?" Alison asked. "I can give him a message."

"Well, it was both of you really. It's the church. Liam tells me the buyers are going ahead with it."

Her face brightened. "Yes, so I believe."

There was a hoot of laughter from the bar. I looked up to see Eddie and Trevor bent double over the bar with tears running down their faces.

Alison smiled. "Pair of idiots. I'm not sure which one of them is a worse influence."

Her son strode over, handed her a cup of black coffee, and returned to the bar. I decided to keep my opinion to myself on this occasion.

"Not much I can say though; I had some wild moments myself when I was younger," she said as she produced some diet sweeteners from her bag and dropped two into her cup. "I've had my fun."

"Anyway," I said, "I've checked with the guards and they've finished what they had to do up there, so we can get Paul Doherty back in and start the ball rolling again as soon as possible, if you want."

"Great. The sooner we get that place off our hands, the better I'll like it, I can tell you."

My name was called, and I turned to see Eddie waving a small brown package and takeaway cup at me and putting it on the counter.

"My food's ready," I said. "I'll give you a shout after I talk to Paul."

I didn't get a chance to touch my sandwich. Leah was on the phone as I got back in the door of the office.

"Hold on, she's here," she said, putting the call on hold. "Ben," she told me. "It's your mother."

I could feel my limbs freeze.

"Ben?" Leah gave me a curious look.

"Sorry. Put her through. I'll take it upstairs."

My legs felt like lead as I climbed the stairs. I sat at my desk and pressed the incoming call button.

"Sarah?"

"Ben, Mum."

"Sorry. I keep forgetting. I know you don't use your first name anymore." There was a shake in her voice. I had heard that shake before. I felt a sudden chill.

"What's wrong?"

"It's your dad."

"Is he sick? What's happened?"

"He's not very well. I'm not saying he's in any danger or anything, but he's had a bad fall and he's in the hospital. He's very down."

"What do you mean by 'bad fall'?"

"He was on the roof."

"What was he doing on the roof, for God's sake?"

"He was cleaning out the gutters."

"Ah, Mum, surely you can get someone in to do that kind of thing?"

"He likes to keep busy," she said quietly. "Helps to keep his mind off things. He'd love to see you."

"Has he said that?"

"No, but I know your father. Would you think about it?"

"I'm very busy at work at the moment, Mum."

"It's been a long time, Sarah. A long time."

"I know, Mum."

"Two years. You used to come more often."

I hesitated. "I think it's better this way, don't you? Less painful all round. For everyone."

"No, I don't. Anyway, he's coming home on Friday if you'd like to come for the weekend, maybe? Or even just the night. You wouldn't need to go to the hospital."

"I'll think about it."

* * *

I hung up, stared at the phone for a second, and immediately dialed again. Nature hates a vacuum. I needed to fill my mind with work.

Paul groaned when he heard my voice. "This is the phone call I've been dreading, isn't it?"

"Very possibly."

"I met Liam in the square. He told me the church buyers are back on board." His tone was resigned.

"Then yes, it is the phone call you were dreading. How soon can you get up there?"

"Saturday morning?"

"Great."

"And it'll be first thing. There's no way I'm going back up there close to dark. I'm beginning to feel that the place is cursed. I've had nothing but bad luck since I was up there."

"You sound like Kelly. Any news on your break-in?"

"What do you think?"

I was about to hang up when I had an idea.

"Paul? This might sound a bit odd, but would you have any objection to me coming with you on Saturday?"

I could hear the smile in his voice.

"Absolutely none. You're a complete bloody weirdo, but none."

"That's settled then. I'll meet you up there about nine?"

"You're on."

Leah appeared in the doorway with something in her hand.

"You left your sandwich downstairs. Do you want it?"

"No thanks, Leah. I'm not hungry anymore. You can throw it out."

"You must be joking. In this weather? There's some pretty hungry-looking robins out the back that'll be glad of it."

"Grand."

She didn't move from her position in the doorway.

"Anything else?" I asked.

"Is everything okay?"

"Yeah, grand. My dad had a fall, so he's in hospital. He's all right though."

She said carefully, "You don't get to see them very often, do you? Your family."

"No."

"Suppose it's not easy, living this far away."

"No."

"Donegal's kind of a long way from anywhere."

"Yes." *I for Interrogator* sprang to mind.

Thankfully, the front door opened, and I was rescued when Leah bounded downstairs. Phyllis' voice sounded up the stairs and my muscles relaxed. I couldn't help but smile when I saw her. Today she was in highly patterned orange, from top to toe. She looked more African queen than Donegal bookseller.

"Great outfit, Phyllis."

She beamed. "Thanks. Kampala, about ten years ago. I thought it might cheer things up a bit. Everything is so bleak at the moment."

"I know what you mean."

"Actually, that's why I'm here. We were thinking of getting a wreath for the funeral tomorrow, from the drama group. What do you think?"

"Good idea. Count me in."

Phyllis leaned her large bosom on the reception desk and showed no sign of leaving. It didn't escape me that she could have phoned about the wreath. I took the hint.

"Tea, Phyllis?"

"Lovely. It would be nice to take the weight off the old bones," she said.

"Leah?" I asked. She nodded, handing me over her empty mug with a grin. "Yes, please."

I went into the little kitchen at the back of the waiting room and Phyllis trailed in behind me.

"So what do you think of this whole business?" she said.

"You mean Danny Devitt?"

"The whole lot, the bones in the church last week and now Danny this week."

"Do you think the two are connected?" I asked.

"Don't you?" She looked at me as if trying to read my face.

"I'm not sure," I said slowly, filling mugs with tea and rooting in the cupboard for some biscuits. I knew it wasn't yet public knowledge that Danny's DNA had been found in the crypt. Molloy had told me that they had decided not to release that information until after the funeral, out of consideration for the family. "What makes you think so?"

"Well." She lowered her voice. "There's something I've been wanting to tell you."

"Go on." I handed her a mug.

"Do you remember that weekend after the body was found, before we knew it wasn't Conor, I said I had seen Danny in the town and he was very drunk?"

I nodded.

"Well, he was saying some very queer things."

"What kind of queer things?"

Before Phyllis had a chance to reply, I heard the front door open, followed by voices.

"Let's go into the front room," I said.

I put Leah's tea on her desk and left her to deal with making an appointment for the young couple at reception while Phyllis and I went into the front office, Phyllis taking the chair while I perched on the desk. Despite the radiator, the room was not warm, and judging from the noise outside, the wind was gathering force again.

"Jesus, it's freezing in here." Never one to suffer in silence, Phyllis gripped her mug with both hands.

"Sorry, it needs insulation, this room. Where was it you were talking to Danny Devitt?"

"On the street. After I talked to you."

I looked at her suspiciously. "I thought when I met you, you said you had seen Danny going into the Oak?"

A stubborn look flickered across her face for a second and was gone. "Okay, okay. I went in after him. I wanted to see if he was all right. I was worried about him. I used Claire as an excuse. Asked him how she was."

"What did he say?"

"He was kind of rambling. He kept talking about the cold, the cold ground. That it would all be grand now, now everyone would know, that it would all be out in the open."

"Everyone would know what?"

She shook her head. "I don't know. He was very drunk, mind, he was probably raving. I thought maybe he was talking about Conor's body in the cold crypt. At that stage we still thought it was Conor."

She blew on her tea. Her brow was furrowed, and she looked as if she was trying to make her mind up about something.

"Was there something else?" I asked.

She bit her bottom lip. "It's just that it reminded me of a conversation I overheard at Christmas. That's what bothered me."

"Christmas?"

"Christmas Eve just gone. You'll think I'm a right busybody, eavesdropping on other people's conversations. But it was in the pub. I was up at the bar; the place was packed – you couldn't help hearing what other people were saying."

"Of course you couldn't."

She leaned forward. "I overheard Lisa telling Danny that she was getting married to Alan Crane. I'm sure it wasn't easy for her to tell him, what with Conor and everything, and Danny did seem really upset. He didn't approve of her choice of husband."

"Not surprising, I suppose. Apart from her relationship with Conor, Leah said Danny had feelings for Lisa himself." I took a gulp of my tea. Phyllis was right. It was the only thing keeping the chill out.

She nodded. "I think everyone knew that. No, it was what he said after that was so strange. I didn't think much of it at the time – I just thought it was Danny being his usual odd self. But then last week he said exactly the same thing."

"Go on."

"He went off on a kind of rant about the cold ground. Just the same as he did last week. He wasn't making any sense. Poor Lisa just stood there, didn't know what to do. I felt so sorry for her. I'm sure she was only trying to do the right thing, telling Danny that she was getting married. And she certainly had no reason to feel guilty, not after six and a half years. When he'd finished his rant, he just left. Full pint on the bar, walked out of the pub. Left her standing there."

"And that was – what? Six weeks before the bones were found?"

"At least. It was Christmas Eve." Phyllis sighed. "Oh, maybe you'll say I'm imagining all kinds of things because of what's happened, but he had a sort of haunted look about him, if you know what I mean."

I pictured Danny's face at the office the last time I had seen him. I knew exactly what she meant.

She put her mug on the desk. "You don't think he could have done something bad, do you? Killed someone? And then driven himself into that ditch on purpose – out of guilt?"

"I don't know, Phyllis. I just have no idea."

The old wooden windowframes rattled suddenly, and we both jumped. The chill in the room made the conversation we were having feel even more bleak.

Phyllis straightened herself, cleared her throat, and made a valiant attempt to change the subject.

"So, did you get around to having a look at those plays?"

Chapter 18

MICK BOURKE WAS sitting in the waiting room when I arrived in the next morning.

"I thought he was coming in this afternoon after the funeral," I whispered.

"He asked if you'd mind seeing him now instead," Leah explained. "You don't have anything else on. I cleared your diary for the funeral."

I checked my watch. "Okay, give me two minutes to get myself organized and then send him up."

Bourke was formally dressed for the funeral in black suit and tie, which did nothing to camouflage his ruddy, outdoorsy complexion. He took the seat I offered him and immediately started to deliver what sounded like a prepared speech, concentrating hard on the desk in front of him as he did so.

"I'm sorry for coming early. When I thought on it again, I realized I wouldn't be in the humor for doing this after the funeral. I thought I'd be better doing it when I'd made up my mind to."

I wasn't sure if he meant that he would be drinking after the funeral or that the funeral would weaken his resolve.

"What is it that you have decided to do, Mr. Bourke?"

He sat up in his seat. "I've decided to try and get my money back."

"What money would that be?"

He looked me in the eye for the first time. "Lisa said she was going to come and see you yesterday."

"I'm sorry, Mr. Bourke, I don't follow. You'll have to explain things to me. Start at the beginning."

He took a deep breath. "It's Conor Devitt, you see."

"Yes?"

"Conor was taking money from me for a long time. I didn't know it until after he disappeared, but he was. A lot of money."

"I see. How do you know?"

"Well, he was working for me for years. Since he was a schoolboy. I took him on after his father died. And the wife, well, she always did the books, you see."

"Your wife?"

"Aye. Until her sight got bad there a few years back. She had to have a cataract removed y'see. Wild nasty things, cataracts. Three months she was, on a waiting list to get them removed in Letterkenny. Bloody health service."

My patience was wearing a little thin.

"Conor, Mr. Bourke?"

"Oh, aye. Well, when she couldn't do the books no more, I got Eithne to do them."

"Eithne?"

"Aye, Eithne. The chemist. She volunteered, you see. Eithne's my sister."

"Oh yes, she said that."

"Well, she does her own books and she said it'd be no trouble to do mine, too. So, when she got a look at them, didn't she discover that there was money missing. That money had been taken for years."

"By Conor?"

"It had to be. He was the only one working for me apart from the wife." He smiled. "And it wouldn't do her much good to take it. She'd be stealing from herself. There'd be no more meals out, so there wouldn't. Or shopping trips to Derry. Or foreign holidays."

"Okay, Mr. Bourke. So, you didn't get a chance to challenge him about it? Conor, I mean."

"I didn't find out about it until a good while after he was gone. A few months, I think it was."

"Did you tell anyone else about it?"

"Not at the time. I didn't want to upset the family. I knew I'd be able to sort it out eventually, some way or other. Then I told Lisa."

"When did you tell Lisa?"

"Ah, not so long ago. I thought she might know what to do."

No wonder Lisa had given me the impression that she thought Conor had left of his own accord, if she knew he had been taking money from his employer. What else had she not told me? But I could think of only one reason that Bourke would tell Lisa about the missing money. I voiced it.

"Did you think maybe she might pay you back herself, Mr. Bourke, out of guilt?"

He shook his head vehemently. "No, no. I wouldn't have wanted that. Poor wee girl, she's been through enough."

"Or maybe you thought she might have access to his bank accounts, working in the bank?"

His eyes widened. "Nothing like that, I swear. I wanted it all above board, so I did. She told me what she was going to do, that she wanted to have him declared legally dead. And I wondered if maybe there was some way of getting my money back – from his estate or something."

"I see."

"So, what do you think?" He screwed his eyes up as if he were looking at the sun.

"Well, Mr. Bourke. I really think it's something you should go to the guards with. Probably something you should have gone to the guards with a long time ago, as a matter of fact. It could be relevant to his disappearance, you know."

"No. I don't want to involve the guards. I wouldn't want to upset his poor mother. That'd be a terrible thing to do."

"Well, I think you might have to – if you want to have any chance at all of getting your money back."

Bourke's expression changed to one of alarm. He got up out of his seat and started to back out through the door, as if he was afraid that I might be tempted to call the guards any second myself.

"I'll think about it and get back to you. Is that all right?"

"That's fine, Mr. Bourke."

At a quarter to eleven we closed the office, and Leah and I made our way across the square to the church. February or not, spring still felt a hell of a long way off this morning. Despite my boots and heavy socks, my toes were numb, and I pulled my coat tighter around me as we walked up the steps to the churchyard. A crowd had gathered at the entrance of the church, huddled together for warmth like penguins, their faces contorted against the stabbing cold. There was very little chat, as if it was too cold for people to think of anything to say, or make the effort to say it.

Phyllis was closest to the door. She was whispering into the ear of a tall man in an anorak and woolly hat. It took me a few seconds to recognize McFadden out of uniform. Lisa Crane stood a few feet away from Phyllis, clinging as usual to her husband's hand.

A car's engine sounded faintly in the distance, barely audible above the wail of the wind. A few seconds later, Hal's large black hearse came into view, proceding in dignified fashion up the driveway, followed closely by a second large black car. The hearse came to a halt in front of the church door. Hal walked slowly towards the back of the hearse, opened the door, and stood there silently, hands clasped, eyes downcast.

The second car drove around the side of the church and parked there. The driver's door opened and Mick Bourke emerged wearing a heavy black coat and scarf. He opened one of the rear doors and Claire climbed out, followed by her mother. Mick took one of Mrs. Devitt's arms and Claire the other, and they made their way slowly towards the hearse. The crowd watched silently as the coffin was carefully unloaded and carried into the church. The pallbearers were Bourke, Tony Craig, and two other men I had never seen before.

"Cousins," Leah whispered.

Claire and her mother walked behind carrying wreaths, supporting each other. With Bourke carrying the coffin, they looked very alone. The absence of the one remaining brother and son seemed unnecessarily cruel. As Leah and I joined the crowd and followed the procession inside, grateful at last for the warmth of the church, I noticed Eithne playing the organ in the gallery. By the time we found seats, the church was almost full – and Glendara is a huge church.

An hour later we emerged from the church to driving icy rain.

"I'll go back and open up the office," Leah said, as we huddled on the porch along with about forty other people.

"Don't you want to come to the burial?"

She shook her head. "No. I'll leave it, I think. That'll take a while. He'll be buried up at Whitewater. The family plot is in the old graveyard up there."

I had a flashback of seeing Jack Devitt's grave after I had stumbled in the snowdrift on Saturday morning. As I watched Leah make a dash for it down the steps, Phyllis appeared beside me.

"Going up to the graveyard?" she asked.

"I think so."

"Any chance of a lift? No point in both of us driving."

"'Course," I said, wondering how on earth Phyllis was going to fit in the Mini's tiny passenger seat.

I can't pretend it was easy; the top of her head grazed the roof, and there were some interesting contortions required to allow me to reach the gearstick, but we managed it.

"God, he didn't get very far really, did he, poor man?" Phyllis said sadly as she rubbed vigorously at the condensation on the passenger window. "When you think he was born less than a mile from here, and he lived most of his life just there."

We were passing Danny's cottage. It was tiny, probably only three rooms. I imagined that whatever happened with the church, this old cottage's chances of revival, now that Danny Devitt was gone, were pretty slim.

"It's lonely up here, isn't it?" I said.

"Wasn't always, you know," Phyllis told me. "You go back twenty-five years or so and this was a vibrant little community. There was the church and the primary school and a community hall, and a shop. I think there was even a post office in the shop. And the pilot station, of course. There were a good few families living up here once upon a time."

"Did they just die out? Or emigrate?"

"Work dried up; people had to leave. A few things happened that didn't help, of course."

"That ship being blown up?"

She nodded. "If you asked me, I'd say the *Sadie* was the final nail in the coffin for Whitewater as a community. Not only were there men lost, but the big cargo ships stopped coming this way after that. They're back now, of course, but it came too late for Whitewater. The pilot station hasn't been used since."

I pulled into the narrow road leading to Whitewater Church.

"It had a big effect on employment at the time – the men had to go elsewhere. It meant there were women left on their own up here with small children, and I dare say it became too remote for them. Some of them didn't even drive. They all moved into town eventually."

"Wouldn't Danny's mother have been one of them?"

"She would, I suppose," Phyllis agreed. "Jack was as much a victim of that day as if he had been blown up with the ship. He was nothing but a wreck of a man after it."

"But she stuck it out, stayed here even though she was left alone with three children?"

"She did."

"It must have been awful for her."

"Aye." Phyllis tutted at the memory. "But Mary had two big strapping sons – Conor to bring in a wage and Danny to keep the wee farm going. She was lucky in that way."

The car bumped along the last couple of yards as Whitewater Church came into view. It made a striking sight, its dark gray shape silhouetted against the turbulent sky.

"Was that why the church was deconsecrated and sold, because nearly everyone left?"

"I suppose so. There weren't enough people to justify keeping it going. Sad, I always thought. I liked coming here. I used to come up here the odd time when that bloody priest in Glendara was driving me nuts." She shot me a sly grin.

I pulled in tight behind the line of cars outside the graveyard, and we wrapped up and made our way in through the gate. Thankfully, it had stopped raining, but the wind-chill factor on this exposed hill was ratcheted up to the highest level. I was pathetically grateful for the woolly hat Phyllis found in my glove compartment when she was doing her usual nosy ferreting about.

Walking along the narrow pathway towards the Devitt family plot, I noticed an area that had been cordoned off and covered with a waterproof sheet a little to the left of the path, underneath the trees. I wondered if this was where the soil samples had been taken. I hadn't noticed it before when I had been along this section of path, but of course the ground had been covered in snow then.

I tore my eyes away and followed Phyllis. The group gathered around the grave was small and the few words from the priest were mercifully short. When he had finished, a little queue formed to pay condolences to Claire and her mother, who were standing beside the grave. Bourke had moved next to a woman with dyed blond hair in a heavy, fur-collared brown coat.

Claire's high-pitched voice carried on the wind as she greeted people. Mrs. Devitt looked particularly frail beside her. I wondered if it would be so awful if the two women were excused this ritual just this once. I recalled my own graveside experience, and I don't remember it helping much. But then everyone is different. For some, rituals are part of the healing.

I found myself in the queue behind Lisa Crane and her husband. Neither acknowledged me. When I reached Claire, I thought she looked exhausted. In fact, she stumbled as she took a step towards me. I caught her arm, noticing that her eyes were glassy.

"You're wonderful to come," she said. "Do you know my mother?"

I looked at the woman standing beside her. There was no way around it this time. I had to face her. Mary Devitt looked at the ground as I delivered the standard platitudes about how sorry I was, and she thanked me graciously. I was about to move away when I realized that I was the last in the line; people were leaving the graveyard. If I walked away, I would have left her alone. Claire had moved into a huddle with Phyllis and Eithne. It was clear she hadn't noticed that her mother was on her own, with only me for company.

Chapter 19

I HOVERED UNCOMFORTABLY, with nowhere to go and nothing to say now that I had delivered my one useless-sounding line. Mary Devitt looked up at me and acknowledged my discomfort with a pale smile and a strong, lucid gaze. Immediately, I got the impression that she was in charge.

There was a strength of character visible in that single look that flipped all the assumptions I had made about Mary Devitt on their heads. Here before me was a woman who had been through a lot. She had lost her husband while she was still very young, first of all to mental illness and then to suicide. She had brought up three children on her own and now she was having to cope with burying one son while the other was still missing. There had to be a resilience about her, for her to have survived at all. This was a woman who was used to having to recover quickly, to pick herself up and carry on in the face of unbearable tragedy.

It was a resilience that was absent in Claire. I saw now that what I had witnessed earlier was mother supporting daughter, not the other way around. Maybe it was a generational thing, this stoic acceptance. Our generation has given that up; we rail against bad fortune, refuse to accept it if things don't go our way. And it never makes one damn bit of difference, since so much is out of our control.

Mary Devitt's eyes were rimmed with red, but bright and alert like a bird's. They darted around, taking in the scene. At first, all I had seen when I looked at her was an old lady in a black coat and black hat. On closer inspection I could see that the hat was a rather quirky, hand-knitted beret with an odd pattern on the side and an old cameo brooch pinned to it. The little flourish struck me as a tiny act of rebellion, of defiance against age and tragedy. I remembered her green shoes from the wake. Another little flourish.

She seemed content to stand beside me without conversation, for a while at least. The priest was talking quietly to the gravediggers, who were standing patiently by, waiting for the stragglers to leave so they could get on with their job and then go home to something warm to eat. Claire was still deep in conversation with Phyllis and Eithne.

"So, how did you know Danny?" Mary asked after a minute, when it became clear that her daughter's conversation was going to carry on for some time.

"I didn't know him very well, I'm afraid. I only met him once."

"We hadn't seen very much of him ourselves lately, sadly. He liked his own company."

"Yes, so I believe."

"And that of his animals, of course." She paused for a moment. "I'm sorry, what did you say your name was again?"

"I'm Ben O'Keeffe."

"Ah." She looked at me with interest. "The solicitor, O'Keeffe?"

"Yes."

She lowered her voice. "Danny was going to come and see you."

"Yes."

She linked my arm and steered me slowly away from the grave, out of earshot of everyone else.

"Did he talk to you?" she asked urgently.

"Well, I can't—"

"Oh, don't give me any of that confidentiality nonsense," she snapped. "I was the one who told him to go and talk to you."

"He mentioned that."

"Well?"

"He didn't tell me anything, I'm afraid. Although he was clearly distressed about something."

Her narrow shoulders slumped in disappointment.

"Did you know what he wanted to speak to me about?" I asked.

"I thought it might have had something to do with Conor," she said.

"Why was that?"

She shook her head. "Something he told me that I'm not certain I want to share with you yet. I'm sure a person like you would understand."

I assumed she was simply referring to my profession, but there was something about this little woman that unnerved me.

"I was so afraid for him, you see. I was afraid he might go and do something stupid."

I tried not to, but I found myself looking towards the grave. "Do you think that's what happened to him?"

She followed my gaze and exclaimed. "Suicide? God, no! That's not what I meant. None of them would try anything like that. Not after their father."

I bowed my head. "I'm sorry. I did hear what happened to your husband."

She waved her hand dismissively. "It was a very long time ago. My concern now is for my two boys. I'm afraid Danny might be everyone's scapegoat now that he's gone. It'll be very easy to blame him for things that have occurred, now that he's not here to defend himself. But I'm not going to let that happen." There was an edge of determination in her voice.

She gripped my hands with both of hers. "Danny was a kind boy, Miss O'Keeffe, but he was never the same after Conor disappeared."

"Claire said he disappeared himself for a while?"

She looked away. "Yes. He was gone for a few weeks. I have no idea where he went. He never told me and I didn't ask."

"I see."

"It was as if he had some kind of a breakdown. And when he came back, he moved into that wee cottage by the church and we never saw him. It wasn't even habitable really; he used to use it as a work-shed before that. But it was as if he didn't want to be around us. It was then that he started drinking, I'm afraid."

She sighed. "Danny's father left the farm to him, and he made a real go of it. But after Conor disappeared, he lost all interest in that, too. I have no idea why. And then one day, he sold it. Stock, land, machinery – the lot. Of course there was nothing wrong with that – it belonged to him, after all. Still, it did surprise me. He just landed down at the house one morning with a lot of money from the sale and insisted I take it all."

I couldn't quite figure out why I was being told all of this. But I paid attention. It felt like a client handing me something for safekeeping.

"I put it away for Conor and Claire. I didn't need it, and Danny swore he didn't want a cent of it. As I said, he was a kind boy, Miss O'Keeffe. But he had his problems, I do know that. I'm under no illusions." She looked up at me. "I don't know if there's anything you can do to help me protect his memory somehow, but I'd be grateful if there was."

"I'll do anything I can, Mrs. Devitt."

I realized that Phyllis and Claire were looking curiously in our direction. Mrs. Devitt saw, too, and took my arm again, walking me a little farther along the path. Her grip was surprisingly strong for someone who looked like a bird. She lowered her voice almost to a whisper.

"I know Danny's DNA was found with that body in the basement of the church."

I wasn't sure how to react. "How do you know that?"

"Andrew McFadden told me. That's between ourselves, mind. I know he shouldn't have said anything, but he thought he was doing the right thing. He wanted to warn me. He's known the family a long time."

What the hell was McFadden doing? Molloy would kill him.

"Now, Miss O'Keeffe, I don't know who that poor wee boy in the church is, but I did know my youngest son. And I know there was no way in God's name he would ever have hurt anyone. I've seen him with animals. I've seen him take rabbits out of traps and fix their legs. It just wouldn't have been in him to do it."

"I don't think anyone is suggesting that he—"

She interrupted me. "No, but they will. It's too convenient. I know human nature – I've seen the way it works. Danny had a bit of a drink problem certainly and he had his peculiarities but he was never anything like . . ." She straightened her hat. "I think it's far more likely he was trying to be kind, to do the right thing."

I felt a tap on my shoulder, and Phyllis appeared beside me. She gave Mrs. Devitt a huge hug, almost drowning her in colorful fabric in the process.

"I think Claire's about ready to go, Mrs. D, if you are?" she said.

"Thank you, dear." She gave me a final meaningful look and hastened back to her daughter's side.

"What about you?" Phyllis said. "Are you ready to go?"

I nodded.

"That looked like a fairly intense chat you were having."

"Oh, you know . . ."

My mind was going round in circles. I had a clear but uneasy impression that something had been asked of me, that I had agreed to it, and that now something was expected of me. But what? Phyllis seemed to sense my mood and for once resisted the temptation to ask questions. She was silent the whole journey back to Glendara. I dropped her off outside the book shop and carried on to the office where I found Eddie Kearney grinning up at me through the door of the waiting room when I walked in.

"Sorry," Leah mouthed to me. "He says he's away to Dublin for the weekend and has to see you before he goes."

"All right." I stuck my head in the door. "Come on in to the front room with me, Eddie."

* * *

Eddie plonked himself down on the seat and sat facing me with his knees apart, still grinning, through a strange collection of misshapen teeth.

"What's up, Eddie?" I asked. "I've no Cert of Analysis in yet. Still waiting for it. I should have it by Monday."

"Aye, that's grand. No harm. That's not what I'm in about."

"What is it, then?"

His grin became slightly sheepish. "I have another few for you."

He leaned forward, rummaged in the back pocket of his jeans, and pulled out a sheaf of papers, which he dumped on the desk. I smoothed them out carefully. They were charge sheets; I counted five of them, all for possession of cannabis. I checked them again. I was right – they were all Section 3 charges, simple possession. None for Section 15: intent to supply, but all listed for the following Tuesday's court. I looked up at him. His expression was that of a little boy who had been caught breaking a window with a football.

I sighed. "All someone else's again, Eddie?"

"Aye, of course. That guard McFadden, he won't leave me alone. He's picking on me. I'm doing nothing wrong, but everywhere I fucking go, he searches me."

I checked the dates of the charge sheets. There were five different dates. "And always finds something, by the look of things."

"Aye, well," he said sulkily. "I'm a bit unlucky, that's all."

"You do know if you get convicted of these, you could get a sentence."

His mouth opened wide. "You're joking, aren't you? I thought it was just a fine. It's only weed, it's not fucking heroin."

"Doesn't matter. The fine is only for a first offense. On your third you become liable to a prison sentence. And if you get convicted of all of these" — I leafed through the charge sheets again — "that's five separate offenses, six including the existing one; you'll definitely be in jeopardy."

I emerged from the front office with my head banging, showed Eddie to the door, and went back to the reception desk.

"Oh Jesus, that young fella makes my head hurt," I said.

"I know what you mean." Leah looked up from the computer, her eyes bleary. "How was the burial?"

"Cold. Not many there. You look wrecked, too. What are you at?" I asked.

"Preparing for the Law Society audit next week," she said.

"Oh God, I'd forgotten about that. What day is it?"

"Monday. And he's definitely coming. I had a phone call from him while you were at the burial."

"Do I need to do anything?"

"No." She sighed. "I have it all under control, I think. You'll have to answer all the queries when he gets here though, and do that spot-check thing with the files."

"Is it really two years since the last time we had that done?" I asked. "Doesn't feel that long ago."

"It's three," she said firmly.

I groaned. The last guy had been a right stickler. Though we had passed with flying colors, as it happened. Thanks to Leah's bookkeeping.

"Same guy again?" I asked.

"I don't think so." She checked her note. "I don't recognize the name."

Chapter 20

IT WAS THREE o'clock by the time I got the chance to have something to eat. I ran to the Spar across the road and bought a cheese sandwich and a Coke to have at my desk. The afternoon slipped by in a haze of drafting contracts and probate documents, not exactly riveting stuff but the kind of work that keeps a country solicitor's practice alive.

I also found time to check out the procedure involved in an application for a declaration of presumed death and discovered that, as I had feared, it should include an affidavit from a relative. A barrister friend of mine e-mailed me up a precedent set of papers. It felt in bad taste to phone Lisa on the day of Danny's funeral, so I dictated a letter to her that would go out in the evening's mail – although after my encounter with Mrs. Devitt earlier on, I suspected an affidavit from her would not be forthcoming. My mind kept returning to our conversation in the graveyard. What exactly did she want me to do? And like Lisa Crane, what wasn't she telling me?

Something else was causing an undertow of anxiety as I worked through the afternoon. The funeral had brought back memories of another graveside eight years before. Mum, Dad, and me, just like Mary and Claire Devitt: parents burying a child and sibling burying a sibling. All wrong for the parents and premature for the sibling. However badly I was failing to cope, it was beginning to dawn on me how truly horrific it must have been for my parents. I realized I had a decision to make.

I had started out by seeing them once a year. A quick visit to check in: always short enough to avoid any difficult conversations. Lately it had been even less than that. Two years had passed since my last visit, as my mother had pointed out. I had thought I was doing them a favor, saving them from having to face me all the time and be reminded of everything. But maybe I was only making it easier on myself. I replayed in my mind the telephone conversation I'd had with my mother. *Coward*, I thought. *You bloody coward.*

I left the office at seven o'clock and walked out into a beautiful moonlit night. The wind had eased and there was frost in the air. The sky was clear, and even with the streetlights shining, a couple of stars were visible. The Mini's windscreen was completely opaque. I couldn't face going back into the office to heat up some water, so I sat there with the engine switched on and waited for it to clear, my hands tucked under me to warm them. I was feeling bleak. The prospect of a Friday evening at home alone did not appeal, even with Guinness, and there was no guarantee he'd be there. Tomcats have notoriously flaky personalities. A better offer, and he'd be off like a flash. He was perfectly capable of having ingratiated himself with some other family and be contentedly curled up by someone else's fire, with not an ounce of guilt.

Eventually, the lower half of the windscreen cleared and I drove reluctantly out of the car park. I turned left towards

Malin and past the garda station. To my surprise, the lights were still on. I wondered if Molloy was there. On impulse, I did a U-turn and drove back. I slowed down and was about to pull in, in front of the station, when I saw that the two spaces were occupied. I parked the car across the road instead and killed the engine. This was my opportunity. It was time I told Molloy. He knew everything anyway, I was sure of it. Maybe the pathologist had done me a favor.

I sat staring at the door of the garda station, looking at the shaft of lemon light coming through the barred window. The minutes ticked by. I took the keys out of the ignition. *Move, damn it*, I thought. *What's wrong with you?* Eventually I took a deep breath and made to open the driver's door.

As the handle clicked, the door of the station opened and light flooded the steps. Two figures emerged. I ducked down quickly behind the steering wheel, holding the door shut. Feeling faintly idiotic, I peered over the steering wheel and saw the unmistakable shape of Molloy, deep in conversation with someone. My heart sank. It was the bloody pathologist. Again. What the hell was she still doing here? Tonight? In Glendara? I thought her work here was finished.

I continued to peer at them over the steering wheel, well aware of how ridiculous I looked. Thank God I had parked across the road. I watched as Molloy walked the woman to her car. When they got there, she turned towards him and gave him a hug. My stomach clenched. What was the hug for? I knew they were old college friends, but that was completely uncharacteristic of Molloy. A car accident I'd been involved in a few years before had merited nothing more than a gruff pat. The only time he had ever put his arm around me was to help me walk to an ambulance. The man was not the touchy-feely type, not by any stretch of the imagination. Even our near miss on New Year's Eve had involved zero physical contact.

I sat up straight, closed the door of the car as quietly as I could, and put the key back in the ignition. My need to bare my soul to Molloy had passed, well and truly. I started the engine and drove back out onto the Malin Road, not allowing myself even the briefest of glances back in the direction of the garda station.

My head was buzzing as I drove the couple of miles along the coast road. I felt irrationally angry with Molloy. Logically, I knew I had no reason to be annoyed with him for being unavailable at the very moment I had finally deigned to talk to him. But knowing that didn't help. I was still furious.

The moon hung in the sky ahead of me; it was nearly full. I needed to clear my head. Dark or not, I decided to go for a swim. I knew it would be bloody cold, but at least there was no wind. And I wouldn't be long – a quick dip, that was all I needed.

When I arrived back at the house, Guinness was sitting waiting for me on the doorstep, tail curled around him. The cat hadn't managed to get a better offer today, apparently. I knew how he felt. I poured out some dried food and milk for him in the kitchen and went off in search of togs, towel, and wash-bag. Unfortunately he wasn't hungry, which meant he followed me around from room to room as I searched for what I needed.

As usual, the cat seemed to sense my mood. I've noticed he gets under my feet twice as much as he normally does if I'm in a temper. I stormed about the house, working myself up into a complete snit. I had just finished throwing everything together and was looking for a bag to put it in, when there was a knock on the door. Cursing, I went to answer it, tripping over Guinness for the umpteenth time in the process. I opened the door with a scowl on my face.

"Do you always greet your callers with such a lovely expression?"

Molloy was standing on the doorstep dressed in jeans and a leather jacket. I stood there like an idiot, without a word, possibly even with my mouth open.

"Well?" he said.

"Off-duty, for a change?" I replied eventually. Nothing like stating the obvious when you're stuck for something to say.

"Mmm."

"What's up?" I could feel my cheeks redden as I realized he might be here because he had seen me watching him outside the garda station.

"I wanted to talk to you about Whitewater."

I hoped the relief didn't show on my face. "So, not entirely off-duty, then."

"No."

"Come on in." I opened the door fully, and he walked in ahead of me into my tiny sitting room. The couch was strewn with towels and swimming togs.

"Sorry. Had a big plan to go swimming."

"Ah. I can catch you later if you like."

"No, don't worry. I wasn't that keen on the idea anyway. Coffee? Or something stronger?"

"Coffee, please."

"We could go into the kitchen, if you like? I know it's a bit chilly in here. Although it's not much better in the kitchen."

The cat emerged from the kitchen as I spoke, as if to confirm the point.

"Want me to light the fire while you make the coffee? If you're definitely not going to head out?"

"Great."

I smiled as I heard Molloy chatting to Guinness as he piled up logs and turf in the fireplace. I came back in to a crackling fire.

"Looks good."

"Should warm up soon."

Molloy had taken his jacket off and was sitting on the couch with Guinness curled up beside him. Guinness is not the friendliest of cats but he has always liked Molloy. I poured the coffee and curled up myself on the armchair.

"Well, what's happened?" I prompted.

Molloy took a sip of his coffee and leaned back, shaking his head as if in disbelief at what he was about to say.

"It looks as if we won't be opening a murder investigation in relation to the bones found in the crypt, after all."

"How come?" I asked. "Last time I was talking to you, there was still no cause of death."

"That wasn't entirely true," Molloy admitted. "We'd established that the body had head injuries and a broken neck, which were probably the cause of death. We now know they were fatal injuries incurred as a result of a car accident."

I was confused. That sounded uncannily like Danny Devitt's injuries and circumstances of death.

"Are you sure?" I said.

"Yes."

"But how can you possibly know that? The car accident bit?"

"Because we have identified the body. We know who it is."

"Who is it?" I asked, amazed.

"His name is Stephen McFerry."

Stephen McFerry, I thought. Where had I heard that name before?

"How do you know it's this Stephen McFerry?"

"Because his DNA turned up on a DNA database in Derry. We couldn't find a match in the south so we sent the samples in to Derry. He was killed in a car accident on the Malin Road into Glendara a few years ago."

That's where I had heard his name. Phyllis had mentioned a young guy killed in a car accident on the same stretch of road as Danny Devitt.

"Luckily for us he had a bit of a record for petty offenses across the border, so he turned up on their database."

Molloy sat patiently, taking a gulp from his coffee, watching me closely as my mind struggled to catch up. I tried to recall what Phyllis had said. Something about his mother being dead and him being buried with his father's people in Inishowen, even though he had grown up in Derry. Something wasn't adding up.

"Hang on. So this kid was properly buried at some stage – in a coffin."

"Yes."

"Where?"

"Whitewater. The old graveyard."

I paused. "Would he not have been embalmed then, or whatever it is that undertakers do? Orifices blocked up, that sort of thing."

"Yes."

"Could the pathologist not tell? I mean, I know the body was completely skeletonized but still?"

"Well yes, she could. She did."

My head was swimming. "So are you saying that you never thought the bones were those of Conor Devitt at all? You knew all along that they belonged to someone who had been buried?"

"Yes, and no," Molloy said slowly. "Yes, we knew early on that the bones belonged to someone who had been buried. But we didn't know for sure it wasn't Conor. We didn't know who it was. The family were so absolutely convinced it was him, we had to eliminate him. I told them the pathologist thought it was unlikely to be him, but we couldn't tell them why. We still have no idea what happened to Conor Devitt, and it wasn't possible to say with certainty, without the DNA tests, that it wasn't him."

I was silent. I could see the reasoning, but I didn't like it. I took a sip of my coffee and stared into the fire. Molloy must have seen the expression on my face.

"It's just as well we did do those tests, as it turned out," he said. "If we hadn't, we'd never have identified Danny Devitt's DNA on the blanket and pillow."

"I suppose. So what on earth was this Stephen McFerry doing wrapped in a blanket in the crypt of Whitewater Church, then?"

"Good question," Molloy said. "We were under the impression that he was buried in the graveyard. We presume his poor father was under the same impression." He sighed. "We're going to have to exhume his coffin. And see who, if anyone, is in there. Because it definitely isn't Stephen McFerry."

"Jesus," I said.

"Yes. Jesus," Molloy said.

Chapter 21

I struggled to absorb what Molloy had just told me. Why on earth would someone have taken Stephen McFerry's body from his coffin in the graveyard at Whitewater and placed it in the crypt of Whitewater Church? And in particular, why would Danny Devitt have done that? Did he even know Stephen McFerry?

I realized I had been silent for a few minutes. I glanced over at Molloy, who was staring into the fire, absently stroking Guinness' fur, clearly absorbed in his own thoughts, probably not dissimilar to mine. The firelight cast a warm glow on his face, his firm jawline, his eyes alert. He looked good out of uniform, a confusing thought I batted away.

"What about the soil samples?" I asked.

"As I said, they were minuscule. Whoever moved Stephen McFerry's body must have rested it on the ground at some stage and the soil was picked up that way. A dead body isn't easy to carry. They're pretty heavy."

"So you're assuming the body was moved not long after he died?"

"Yes."

"When are you going to exhume the coffin?"

"Tomorrow morning, as soon as it's light, to try to attract as little attention as possible. We only got this latest information this evening."

"Right."

"Did Danny Devitt ever mention Stephen McFerry to you?" Molloy asked.

I shook my head. "I was just thinking about that. No, he didn't. But even if he did know him, why in God's name would he steal his dead body?"

"He was always a little peculiar," Molloy said.

"But it seems to be completely motiveless."

"Yes, it does," Molloy conceded. "It's a mess. But at least it's not a murder investigation. That's something to be grateful for."

"True. Unless . . ."

"Don't say it." Molloy sighed. "Unless someone else's body is in Stephen McFerry's coffin."

"Exactly. And what if it's . . . ?"

Molloy finished my question. "Conor Devitt. I know. Believe me, the thought had occurred. Let's wait till the morning when we see what the exhumation throws up."

There was a brief silence as we both sat staring into the flames.

"So, what did you want to talk to me about?" Molloy asked.

"Sorry?"

"I'm assuming you wanted to talk to me. I saw you outside the station."

I could feel my toes curl in embarrassment. Had he seen me scrunched down behind the steering wheel? His face showed nothing but concern, pure and simple.

"I just wondered if there had been any developments," I lied. "But you've filled me in."

"Are you sure that's all it was?"

I nodded, looked away. He didn't push it.

"Okay, it's time I got going."

He lifted Guinness gently off his knee and stood up. As he pulled on his jacket, a voice in my head told me to suggest food, but the words never reached my mouth. I walked him to the door and stood there for a second with my hand on the doorknob. Procrastinating.

"Are you all right?" he asked.

I stared at the ground. "Look, I know you know some things about me now. Things I never told you. I expect that pathologist woman, Laura, has told you everything."

"She has told me very little, Ben. Only that she recognized you, and from where."

I looked up. Molloy's expression was kind.

"I did want to talk to you about it sometime, it wasn't that I didn't," I said. "I haven't talked to anyone about it. Not even Maeve. There are things I haven't told anyone."

"I understand. Talk to me about it when you're ready. There's no rush. I'm not going anywhere."

"It's just . . ."

"Yes?"

"My mother rang today. My father's had an accident. Not a serious one, but she wants me to go down. I haven't seen them in a while. Usually I see them once a year, a quick visit, so that I don't give them time to talk about anything."

It came out all in a rush. My voice sounded as if it were coming from very far away.

Molloy responded with one word. "Go."

"You think?"

"Yes. These things get harder, Ben, the longer you leave them. You'd advise anyone else in exactly the same way. Go visit your parents."

"Maybe."

He looked into my eyes. "What are you afraid of?"

"That I'll remind them. That they'll remind me."

"It doesn't look like you need reminding. I'm sure they don't either."

"That they blame me, then. If they did, they'd be right to. There are things I haven't told even them."

I could feel a painful lump in my throat. *Don't cry, for God's sake,* I thought.

Molloy touched me gently on the shoulder. I could smell faint traces of aftershave mixed with leather. The same aftershave as on New Year's Eve.

"They want to see you, Ben. Just go. As soon as you can."

I nodded. I didn't trust myself to speak.

"Do you want me to stay a bit longer?" Molloy asked.

I shook my head. "No, I'm fine. Honestly. I have some packing to do, apparently." I smiled weakly at him.

He smiled back at me. "I'm glad."

I opened the door to let him out, realizing as I did so that I really didn't want him to go.

Oddly, I slept well. Early the following morning, I phoned Paul Doherty to tell him I wouldn't be accompanying him on the survey at Whitewater, after all. He took it reasonably well. I guess the prospect of the crypt was less awful in the early morning with a solid number of hours of daylight ahead. He might even have some company not too far away, if the exhumation was still going on. Not that he would know that.

I threw enough clothes for the weekend into an overnight bag and sent my mother a brief text to tell her I was coming and what time I'd be leaving home. I stood in my bedroom staring at the bag on the bed, wondering if it had been Molloy's complete conviction that it was the right thing to do that had finally persuaded me to make the trip.

It had been a relief to talk about it; it was so long since I had confided in anyone. And Molloy cared about me, I knew that. But I sensed there was something holding him back, something I knew nothing about. I wondered if it had to do with the pathologist, his old college mate. I hoped not. Whatever it was, today I was simply happy to have his friendship back.

I thought about the rest of our previous night's conversation as I drank a coffee at the sink. They would be exhuming Stephen McFerry's coffin this morning. Maybe I should stay until the exhumation and then set off. I'd still have plenty of time to get to my parents by early afternoon.

The seagulls were putting on an impressive display, diving and swooping over the mud flats as I drove up along the coast road. It was a beautiful crisp winter morning, with a bright blue sky. I drove past the entrance to the church, and as I approached the wall of the graveyard, I could see a small crowd of maybe five or six people gathered outside the gate, all huddled together in winter coats, like funeral-goers awaiting the arrival of the hearse. They were facing in towards the graveyard. So much for not attracting attention.

There was white and red garda tape across the entrance, preventing public access to the graveyard. No wonder they hadn't succeeded in keeping things quiet. Although I guessed it would be hard to keep something like the exhumation of a grave quiet in a place the size of Whitewater. I slowed down as I approached, looking over the gate towards the graveyard. The top of some kind of bright orange mechanical digger or crane loomed up.

I pulled in, feeling as much of a rubbernecker as anyone else. The first person I recognized was Phyllis, highly visible as usual. I tapped her lightly on the shoulder, and she whirled around, hand on her chest.

"Oh Jesus, it's you, Ben. You gave me a fright."

"Sorry."

"It's not your fault. It's all this." She pointed towards the graveyard. "It's all a bit creepy, this, don't you think?"

"What's happening?" I said, feigning ignorance. It didn't work. She peered at me closely.

"They're digging up that poor McFerry kid's coffin. Apparently, it was him that was buried in the crypt. Did you not hear?" she said.

"No, I did," I admitted. "How far on are they?"

"I think they're about to start now."

An effort had been made to cordon off the grave from public view, but the height of the graveyard meant it was possible to see a lot of what was going on. We watched as the digger slowly cleared the topsoil from the grave.

Molloy and McFadden were standing close together dressed in white boiler suits. Phyllis gestured towards a hunched man on the other side of the grave also wearing a boiler suit, but a mask and gloves, too.

"Poor Hal," she said. "He's terrified he did something wrong." She lowered her voice. "Like bury the wrong man." She turned to me. "You don't think that's where Conor Devitt is, do you?"

"God knows. Who is that man beside him?" I asked.

"That's Pat McFerry, the young fella's dad."

"God, this must be rough on him."

"Horrific. Imagine spending years visiting a grave and all the while your son is lying on the other side of the wood in a cold crypt." She shuddered. "The other man is the Environmental Health Officer – standard requirement for an exhumation, I'm told."

We watched as the man who had been operating the digger climbed down and started to clear the remains of the soil with a shovel. He was joined by three other men. Using ropes, they slowly lifted a long black coffin from the grave. Soil fell from it as it rose, its sheen reflected brightly in the winter sunshine as if it had been freshly polished for the occasion. There was a general hush as it was lowered slowly to the ground.

Molloy guided Hal towards the coffin. Hal knelt on the ground, Pat McFerry hovering beside him looking as if he, too, didn't know quite where to put himself. Hal started fiddling with the clasp on the lid of the coffin; this seemed to go on for an age. It was as if the crowd around me were holding their collective breath. I certainly was. Finally, something clicked and Hal lifted the lid.

Chapter 22

THE NEWS FILTERED through to the crowd at the gate. The coffin was empty. There was a hum of disbelief. Phyllis and I looked at each other.

"God," she exhaled deeply. "An empty coffin. Buried for all these years. Imagine. How on earth could that have happened?"

"I suppose we don't know how long it's been empty," I said.

"Poor man," she said, looking at the hunched figure of Pat McFerry. "Hal will blame himself, I know he will."

"I'm sure Hal did nothing wrong. It probably happened long after he had done his job."

"He won't see it like that," Phyllis said, shaking her head.

She rubbed her hands together against the cold. "Anyway, that's over. Have you time for a cup of tea? The Oak should be open by now. I could do with something to warm me up before I go back to the shop."

I looked at my watch. "Sorry, Phyllis. There's somewhere I have to be. I'll talk to you after the weekend."

I turned the car around and drove back in the direction from which I had come. I was driving past the church when something struck me – something Phyllis had said. Paul's jeep was parked at the entrance to the church. The gate was open so I squeezed through and made my way up, a considerably easier job than the last time, since the brambles had been cleared to allow the authorities through. It seemed that one advantage to having a body found on your property is that you get the gardai to tidy up your garden. I wondered if I should point this out to Kelly.

Paul was examining the outside wall of the church with some kind of handheld electronic device.

"Morning."

He looked up in surprise. "Thought you weren't coming."

"I'm not really here. I just wanted to check something."

"Help yourself. Do you need me?"

"You haven't a copy of that map I gave you, by any chance?"

"Yep." He took it from his pocket and handed it to me. "I need it back though, it's the only one I have."

"Sure. Five minutes is all I need."

I walked around to the front of the church and stood there for a second, trying to get my bearings. The graveyard was over to the east, I calculated, towards the sea. I opened up the map. The lane connecting the graveyard to the church referred to on the deeds was marked with an X–Y. I followed the angle from the gable end of the church and walked diagonally across to where I thought it should be. There was a line of ancient, overgrown yew trees in front of me that the Garda Technical Bureau gardeners obviously hadn't got to. This must be what Phyllis had referred to as "the wood." She said that Stephen McFerry's father had been visiting an empty grave while all the time his son was in a cold crypt "on the other side of the wood." It occurred to me for the first time that the guards should probably have requested a copy of this map, if they had known that it existed.

I shielded my eyes with my hands as I fought my way in through the undergrowth. Eventually I emerged at a clearing and an old stone wall covered in moss. Facing me was an old-fashioned stile. It had been clumsily blocked up with wooden planks horizontally nailed together, green and slimy and ice cold to the touch. I felt movement beneath my hand; something was loose. Putting the map in my pocket, I pushed at the timber, harder this time and with both hands. The middle section shifted forward and fell away onto the ground on the far side. I ran my fingers along the edges of what remained. The fallen section had been sawn away and fitted back together. The passage had been used since it had been blocked up, although someone was trying to disguise the fact. Not used recently though, I thought; the cut was not fresh.

I climbed through the gap and found myself on an overgrown pathway leading through more yew trees. I followed it for a short while until I heard voices, one of them Molloy's. I had reached the graveyard. I turned back.

I drove along the coast road towards Derry deep in thought, trying to disentangle the latest developments. I had a good four-hour journey ahead of me and I wanted to postpone thinking about where I was going and why for as long as possible. Four hours of thinking about my own situation and what was ahead of me and I knew I wouldn't make it the whole way. I'd lose courage and turn back.

So Stephen McFerry's coffin was empty. Presumably Hal would be able to confirm that it hadn't always been that way, that he *had* placed the body in the coffin in the first instance. So when had Stephen's body been taken, I wondered. Molloy said the pathologist seemed to think it had been done soon enough after burial. Had it been removed from its coffin and carried along the path through the woods? But why? That was the mystery.

I crossed the Foyle Bridge and joined the road for Dublin, driving for about an hour before stopping for petrol in Omagh. As I was heading into the station to pay, my mobile rang. I was surprised to see it was Molloy. Surprised and pleased.

"Just checking up on you. You okay after last night?" he asked.

I could feel a lump forming in my throat again. Jesus, what was wrong with me? That was twice in twenty-four hours and both provoked by Molloy. I swallowed hard.

"Grand," I said. "I'm driving south, as a matter of fact. I took your advice."

I could almost hear the smile in his voice. "Good."

"I'm still not entirely sure you're right, but I'll probably regret it if I don't."

"Fair enough."

"I stopped up by Whitewater on the way through earlier and drove past the graveyard."

"Ah. I thought you might. So you heard then?"

"I did. Empty coffin, eh?"

Molloy made a small noise in the back of his throat but said nothing.

My curiosity rose. "Tom?"

There was something he wasn't telling me.

"Tom?" I said again. "It was empty, wasn't it?"

"Well . . ." I could sense him coming to a decision. "It was empty to the extent that there was no body in it. That is certainly true."

"What do you mean?" I asked. "What *was* in the coffin, for God's sake?"

"Clothes."

"Clothes?"

"The clothes Stephen McFerry was wearing when he was buried, according to his unfortunate father who had the job of identifying them. Jeans, runners, a T-shirt, even a chain with a cross that he used to wear. The clothes are little more than a pile of rags now, of course, but they are still recognizable."

"So someone didn't want the bones identified too easily."

"Looks like it."

I shuddered. I tried to push away the image that was forming in my mind. The image of Danny Devitt, the man I had had in my office only days before, undressing a dead boy. It just didn't fit.

"We'll test the clothing for DNA, of course," Molloy went on.

I leaned against the car and cast my mind back to my conversation with Mary Devitt at her son's graveside. I know that mothers are frequently delusional about their sons, but could she really have been so wrong about Danny? I was more and more convinced that I needed to finish my conversation with her.

"Ben? You still there?" Molloy said.

"Hmm?"

The car behind me in the queue for the pumps was beeping loudly. I had phased out for a bit. I waved an apology and got back into the car to move it out of the way.

"Sorry, Tom. I'm going to have to go."

"Okay. Good luck with everything."

"Thanks. Oh, by the way, there's a pathway connecting the graveyard to the church that maybe you should have a look at. I'm not sure exactly what it means, but there's something strange about it."

I heard the surprise in Molloy's voice. "I didn't know there was a connecting path. We've been tramping along the road between the two gates."

"It was on the deeds, but the stile has been blocked up. And reopened. I tried to put the wood back where I found it, but it may not be perfect."

"Okay, thanks, we'll have a look."

"And, Tom, thanks for calling."

"Let me know how it goes."

As I queued at the cash register, I turned over in my mind everything Molloy had said. I knew what local opinion would be when it was revealed that Danny Devitt's DNA had been on the blanket. It meant that Mary Devitt was going to have to cope with some fairly heavy innuendo. I decided to go and see her after the weekend.

As the cashier was checking the reading on the pump for my petrol, I caught sight of a small stand of books on the counter, picked one up, and had a quick flick through it. It was a paperback, a history of Inishowen, one of those local publications you find all around the country, published with aid from the local County Council.

"I'll take one of these, too," I said to the cashier.

I threw the book onto the passenger seat and drove out of the garage.

Chapter 23

MY ANXIETY LEVELS ratcheted up a little more with every mile of the journey to Dublin. By the time I was half an hour away from my parents' house, it was all I could do to keep the car on the road, traveling in the same direction. I came very close on a couple of occasions to turning around and driving the whole way back up to Inishowen, four hours or not.

But I kept going. By two o'clock I had reached the walls of the Phoenix Park, and shortly afterwards I drove in through the narrow gate of my parents' 1940s semi-detached in Chapelizod, the house I had grown up in. I pulled in behind their car, or at least what I presumed was their car. It was the only one there.

There was no opportunity to calm my thoughts before my mother came running out, as she always did. Some things don't change. We gave each other an awkward hug. She opened with her usual line, which hadn't changed in two years either.

"You made good time."

I provided the predicted response. "I did. Very little traffic on a Saturday."

Playing it safe. We can pretend that everything is normal if we just say our lines. So this was how it was going to be.

Maybe it was for the best. Taking my bag out of the car, I followed her inside.

I took off my coat and scarf and looked around me. I saw the same old kitchen cabinets, the same electric cooker with the ring on the left-hand side at the back that I had no memory of ever working, the same dim lighting. But the room didn't have the warmth it used to have. I supposed that was understandable.

My mother stood there for a second as if unsure what to do next. Her expression of discomfort was temporarily relieved when she took my coat and scarf and disappeared with them into the back kitchen. Through the open door I could see the row of hangers with their stacks of coats. Coats that couldn't possibly all belong to the two people who now lived in the house. I knew there were still coats on those hangers that had belonged to us when we were children. Faye and me.

My mother reemerged and closed the door behind her.

"You got rid of the solid fuel," I said.

"Oh, yes. The old Stanley. It was getting too much for us, dragging in fuel every day to heat the place. We have oil-fired central heating now. Much easier. And much cleaner."

Clean had always been important to my mother. She swiped your cup and plate out from under you to wash it before you were finished eating.

"Great. I'm sure you're thrilled with it."

She nodded.

"How's Dad?"

"Good. Better. He's a bit grumpy though, not being able to swim."

I smiled. "I bet."

"He's in the sitting room. Do you want to see him?"

"Of course."

"You go on in and I'll put the kettle on. I'll join you in a minute with the tea."

My father was lying on the couch, his head propped up on pillows and his leg raised on a footstool. It was in plaster. A set of crutches rested against an armchair beside him. The television was on with the volume turned down and he looked up at the sound of the door. His face broke into a smile when he saw me, and a surge of emotion made me fear tears.

"That looks nasty," I said in a choked voice.

I sat in the armchair beside him. There were lines around his eyes and mouth that hadn't been there the last time I saw him. For some reason I hadn't expected him to have aged. Stupid really. I hadn't seen him in two years. But my mother looked the same and I had thought he would, too.

"Ah, sure I'm an eejit. It was my own fault. What am I doing climbing ladders at my age?"

I smiled. "Well, I did think that you could have got someone in to do the job for you. Most people do that, surely?"

"I like to keep busy." He gave me a wry look. "Still, if it managed to get you down here to see us, maybe it was worth it, eh?"

I looked down.

"I know. I'm sorry. I thought it would be easier on you and Mum if you didn't see me for a while, but maybe I was being easier on myself. And then the time just passed." My words came tumbling out.

"Hush now, let's not talk about it. We have all weekend." He looked up at me anxiously. "You *are* staying for the weekend, aren't you? You're not going to take off again any minute?"

"No, Dad," I promised him with another smile. "I'm here till tomorrow evening."

"You can't stay till Monday?"

"Sorry. Work calls. Can't do anything about that, I'm afraid."

"Oh well, that'll have to do, then. Here comes your mother with the tea."

I stood up to clear a space on the coffee table for the tray of tea, sandwiches, and cakes my mother had managed to whip up. I suspected she had been baking all morning.

"Looks great, Mum."

I gathered up the newspapers that were strewn across the table and couch and went to put them on the dining table. As I walked past the piano, saying some nonsense about how hungry I was, my eyes fell on the old school photograph in the wooden frame on top and my voice faded. Two little girls with curly brown hair sitting at a desk with an atlas open in front of them. Totally posed. I remembered the teacher dragging a wire brush through our unruly tangles before the picture was taken. I remembered how it hurt. Looking at the picture now, I could see it hadn't made a blind bit of difference. Faye and me, two bushy-headed little kids, one much prettier than the other . . .

The room had gone silent. Both parents were looking up at me, two old faces full of concern. Guilt hit me like a ten-ton truck.

"It's okay, sit down and have something to eat," my mother said gently.

* * *

The evening continued as if nothing were wrong, as if the years hadn't passed, as if I had been there the previous weekend, as if I were their only child and always had been. Perhaps they thought that was what I needed. They were parents; they put their children's needs before their own, always and forever. Faye was everywhere in that house. Not only in her photographs, and there were plenty of those dotted about the living room and hallway. Her presence showed that what they probably needed was to talk about her. But they did what they thought *I* needed. And I, coward to the end, let them.

There were childhood snaps at the beach and poses in Irish dancing costumes. Many of the pictures included a slightly older, slightly less attractive version of the same kid standing beside her. Had I known at that stage, or had that come later? As I drank my tea, I noticed her graduation photograph. I certainly knew then that I couldn't compete. Faye was undeniably beautiful, with long brown shiny hair she had learned to straighten, and that wild reckless expression, the laughing look of devilment in her face that meant she was ready to try anything. Those black eyes that men were unable to resist. Some of those men appeared in the pictures – with one notable exception.

Later we watched a film on television, the three of us, around the fire. I think it was *The Wedding Singer*, though it passed in a bit of a blur. And at eleven my mother started to make noises about going to bed. Dad was sleeping on the couch until he was more mobile. I helped fold it out into a bed for him.

As I walked along the landing towards my old childhood room, I passed Faye's door. We used to be able to knock on the wall in between to each other, our own private Morse code. I got a jolt when I saw that the hand-painted tiles my father had brought back for us from some business trip abroad were still fixed to the doors. *Sarah's Room. Faye's Room.* Even then the cartoon depiction of an imaginary Faye was pretty in a long dress. Mine was a scruffy tomboy.

My room hadn't changed. I suspected Faye's hadn't either, but I hadn't had the courage to go in there since her death. I unpacked my bag and toiletry bag and sat on the bed. Was this really any better than us not seeing each other? This artificiality?

I finally managed to get to sleep about three and woke four hours later. At eight, I heard my mother on the landing, and got up.

My father and mother were deep in conversation at the kitchen table with a pot of tea and a mound of toast between them. My mother leaped to her feet when she noticed my presence in the doorway.

"No need to stop talking because I come into the room."

"We weren't – I mean, would you like some tea?"

"Sit down, Mum. I'll get it. I presume the cups are in the same place."

I found a cup and joined them at the table.

"Everything all right?" I asked.

Dad opened his mouth as if he was about to say something. Mum cut him off with a look.

"Of course," she said, her voice slightly more high-pitched than usual.

"What were you talking about?"

"We were just saying . . ." my father said. My mother tried to interrupt, but he ignored her and carried on. "We were saying that there's no need for you to feel guilty because of what happened to your sister, you know."

My stomach clenched.

"Because you're the one that's left behind," he continued.

"Where's this coming from, Dad?"

He looked at my mother. "Your mother has made a new friend at her book club – she's a counselor, and she said that sometimes happens when a sibling dies and another is left behind. We thought maybe that was why you didn't like to visit."

"I don't, Dad, honestly. It's not that."

"And you can't blame yourself for introducing that animal to Faye. We know you do, but you can't have known what he was like. If you had, you wouldn't have been so hurt when . . ."

Dad's voice trailed off. They looked at me with scrutinizing concern. I felt as if my head were about to explode.

"I met the pathologist," I blurted out. "In Inishowen." Immediately I wished I could take it back.

My father's tone grew icy. "The woman who said that Faye was the author of her own misfortune?"

"She didn't exactly say that, Dad."

"She said she took drugs with him. Faye would never have taken drugs."

I knew for a fact that wasn't true, but I couldn't say it. I also knew the bastard I had introduced her to could have given her bloody rat poison.

"That pathologist woman helped him get away with it," my mother said quietly.

"He didn't get away with it, Mum. He got ten years."

"Ten years for murder. I thought it was supposed to be life for murder," she muttered under her breath.

"It was manslaughter, Mum, not murder."

I couldn't believe I was having the same conversation again after eight years. I had lost count of the number of times I had explained this to my mother.

"She's dead and he killed her. That's murder in my book," she said stubbornly, staring into her teacup.

I sighed. "It's not quite as simple as that."

Her eyes welled. "And he had sex with her. When she was in that state. That's rape."

"They couldn't charge him with rape, Mum. There was no evidence of lack of consent."

"Only because she wasn't there to give that evidence. And she wasn't there because he killed her."

I couldn't bear it. The same conversation. Either I told them the whole story, or I left. But I honestly didn't think they could take the full truth. I'd be doing it for me, not them. A clearing of conscience. I stood up and went over to the bread bin on the pretense of making fresh toast I didn't want. I stared at the old tiles on the wall above the sink. But the pretense was unbearable, too. I switched on the radio and the sound of Martha and the Vandellas filled the room.

It was six o'clock by the time I reached the roundabout at Burt, about twenty miles from Glendara. The Sunday papers had helped bridge the gap between the morning's painful conversation and my mother's roast chicken lunch, and enabled us to revert to a fragile peace. I left immediately after lunch, feeling wired.

It was turning into a thoroughly nasty night, with that bleak midwinter Sunday-evening feel about it, spitting rain and howling wind. There were few cars on the road. I set off up the hill towards the Station Inn in the direction of the coast road and Glendara. The Station Inn was a depressing-looking sight, long since closed down, boarded up and battered, having gone the same way as the railway in this part of Ireland.

As I drove up the hill, I saw movement out of the corner of my eye in front of the old building. At first I thought I must have imagined it. The trees at the front of the inn were thrashing ferociously, like whirling dervishes; it was hard to see anything clearly. I peered in closer as I drove past and noticed two cars parked in the shadows under the trees in front of the boarded-up building.

There was a figure standing by one of the cars – a woman, her dark hair flapping wildly about her face. She was talking to a man, gesticulating furiously. I wondered if I should stop; she looked as if she could be in trouble. I pulled in a little way ahead, killed the lights and the engine, and watched in my mirror. I couldn't see the man's face – he had his back to me. But the couple looked as if they were having a row. And then, all of a sudden, she was embracing him. I watched as she turned to open the driver's door of one of the cars and the interior light came on. For a brief second I caught a glimpse of her face. It was Alison Kelly.

What was she doing here? And who was the man? It didn't look like Raymond Kelly, but I couldn't be sure. The man stood there for a minute as if he expected Alison to change her mind about leaving and get back out of the car. But she didn't. Eventually he climbed into the driver's seat of the other car and they both drove off, heading in the direction of Buncrana. On impulse I turned the Mini around and set off after them.

I followed the two cars for about a mile up the road, until we came to a crossroads. One car turned right and the other went straight on in the direction of Buncrana. I hesitated for a second and then followed the car heading to Buncrana.

Ten minutes later we arrived in the town. I followed the car up the main street where it pulled in on the footpath outside Kelly's bar. I stopped a few yards behind on the other side of the road and watched as Alison Kelly got out of the car and walked into the pub. I had chosen the wrong car to follow.

Chapter 24

I woke at seven, my body stiff from the drive the night before. It was still dark outside so I reached over and turned on the radio and listened to the news for five minutes before dragging myself out of bed.

I made it into the office by half eight, remembering, with no pleasure, that this morning involved facing the long-dreaded Law Society audit. Leah was already in, eyes glued to the computer.

"Wow, you've beaten me in. I'm impressed," I said.

"I usually beat you in."

"True, but I'm not usually in by half past eight. What time is this guy coming?"

"Not till this afternoon. He's driving up from Dublin. Doing three practices up this part of the country this week, apparently."

"Good. That means he'll be in a rush to move on, hopefully. What do you want me to do?"

"Nothing. I have all the books ready. At least, I will have by the time he arrives. You just need to meet him and do that spot-check test on the files with him when he wants you to."

"Grand."

She looked up at me, chin resting on her hand. "I hear they dug up that kid from Derry's coffin on Saturday morning?"

"Yes."

"And it was him that was found in the crypt in Whitewater?"

"Yep."

"Weird."

"Mmm."

I started to tackle the stack of files on my desk. There were no interruptions for a full hour. At twenty to ten Leah buzzed me.

"Eddie Kearney's here. He wants to know if you can see him. He doesn't have an appointment."

I groaned. He had probably picked up a whole raft of new drugs charges over the weekend.

"All right," I said. "Send him up."

He walked into the office with a swagger, more exaggerated than usual. He wore a pair of jeans at least three sizes too big for him, which were dragged down to a dangerous level by hands that were rammed into the front pockets. His blond hair was sprayed and combed towards the right-hand side of his head, making him look as if he had been caught in a heavy wind. He leaned against the doorframe in a pose that came straight out of an episode of *The Wire*.

"Yes, Eddie, what can I do for you?"

He was chewing gum with his arms crossed.

"I think this time, it's what I can do for you," he said.

I wondered if he was aware that his pose had switched to *OK Corral*. I tried not to laugh.

"Right," I said slowly. "Why don't you come in and have a seat and tell me what you mean."

He strutted over to the seat I offered him, the jeans travelling southwards ever so slightly with each step. I doubted he would be able to maintain the swagger if they landed down around his ankles. Luckily for both of us, he reached the seat in the nick of time.

"I'm listening," I said.

"I want to do a deal." More chewing.

"A deal with whom?" I asked, though I knew what was coming.

"The cops."

I leaned back in my seat. "Would you like to explain what you mean exactly?"

"I want to get them charges dropped. In exchange for some information."

"What kind of information?"

"Valuable information."

"What information, Eddie?" There was an edge to my voice. I was aware I sounded a bit like a schoolteacher. He picked up on it and responded accordingly, like a teenager in trouble. Sulkily.

"I can't tell you. Unless I know the charges are gonna be dropped."

I sighed. He had clearly picked up this idea during his weekend in Dublin, along with his new hairstyle. The Eddie Kearney I knew sure as hell hadn't the gumption to come up with an idea like this on his own.

"Well, I can't advise you unless you tell me everything. I'm your solicitor, Eddie. Anything you tell me is in confidence."

He regarded me doubtfully. I said nothing for a few seconds.

Eventually he cleared his throat. "All right. It's about what happened last Tuesday night. To that Devitt fella. The drunk fella."

That's rich, I thought. Coming from Mr. Stonehead.

"Go on," I said.

"Well, I was there."

I sat upright. "You were where, exactly?"

"I was walking along the Malin Road. Coming from a party. It was about six o'clock in the morning."

"And?"

"I saw two cars coming flying along the road. At first I thought it was two lads having a race. It was pitch black so I couldn't see properly. But then I copped that one of them was chasing the other, trying to drive it off the road. They nearly ran me over. Never saw me. I had to fucking leap into the ditch. Mental driving."

I ignored the self-righteous tone. "Why do you think this has something to do with Danny Devitt?"

"Because a few seconds later I heard a loud fucking bang, like the cars had hit something. And I thought, serves them right, driving like that."

I sat forward. "Go on."

"Well, by the time I walked the rest of the way up that road – took me half an hour, fucking long road that, I hate it, especially in the dark."

"Eddie." It was all I could do not to grab him by the scruff of the neck.

"All right, I'm getting to it. There he was in the ditch. Your man Danny, in his car, slumped over the steering wheel. Didn't look too healthy."

"And what about the other car?"

"No sign. The cops were there though. That cop who keeps stopping me all the time."

"McFadden."

"Aye, him. And the ambulance and all was there, too."

"And why didn't you say anything to the guard about what you saw, for God's sake?"

The sulky expression returned. "I couldn't."

"Why not?"

"I just couldn't. It would not have been convenient at that very moment." He dragged out the words like a rap.

"You had drugs on you."

"I might have." He looked up again with the hint of a grin. I didn't return it.

He looked down at his lap. "They might have searched me. I did a runner."

I stood up. "You're coming down to the garda station with me straight away."

"Wha'? What about my deal?"

"I'll be struggling to get you a deal that involves you not being charged with impeding the investigation of a murder, you idiot. This is extremely bloody serious. What the hell were you thinking?"

His face fell. For the first time since he'd entered the room, the cocky grin disappeared.

It wasn't exactly a question of my taking Eddie Kearney by the ear and marching him down to the garda station, but it was pretty close. He slouched down the hill beside me, his demeanor very different from what it had been half an hour beforehand.

Molloy was at the front desk. He looked up when I walked in, his air of expectation turning to surprise when he saw Kearney in my wake.

"Mr. Kearney here has something he wants to tell you. Some information," I announced tersely. "And he is sorry it has taken him this long to come down – isn't that right, Eddie?"

Eddie nodded grumpily.

Molloy looked bemused. He led us into the interview room at the back.

In fairness to Molloy, he didn't ask the obvious question about why it had taken Kearney five days to tell what he had seen. His face was grim while he heard what Eddie had to say, and he thanked him for his assistance when he was finished. I suspected it was the first time that Kearney had heard an expression of gratitude from a member of the Garda Siochana. He even began to look quite pleased with himself again, to the extent that he had to be reined in a little as he warmed to his subject and started to exaggerate. Molloy was capable of managing that well enough.

My mind was racing all through the interview. My instinct had been correct. Danny Devitt's death wasn't an accident. Someone had forced him off the road. But who on earth would want to murder a man like Danny Devitt? A man who lived an almost entirely solitary life – until the last ten days, at least. Maeve had said that he rarely came into town. But he had ventured in when the remains at the church had been found, and he had been in town for days after that. Had he known something that someone else did not want revealed? Had he said the wrong thing to the wrong person?

By the time he left the garda station, Eddie Kearney's swagger had almost entirely come back. It appeared he wasn't fussy which side he was on as long as he got the kudos he thought he deserved. I stood at the front desk with Molloy as we watched him leave, his jeans back to their precarious, low-slung position.

"Thanks for that," Molloy said. "I'm assuming there was a little gentle persuasion involved there?"

"Maybe," I said, duty towards client returning. "Although, since he has been so helpful, is there any chance you might consider treating him a little more leniently in relation to some other matters?"

Molloy arched his eyebrows. "We'll see."

"Thanks."

"It would have been a hell of a lot more helpful if he'd fronted up earlier. Although I suspect there was a reason for that."

I avoided his eye. "So what's your thinking? It doesn't exactly sound like an accident now, does it?"

He sighed. "No, it doesn't. As long as your man Kearney wasn't completely stoned when he saw what he says he did, it looks as if we're going to have to open a murder investigation. I'd better give the garage a call. We'll need to have a closer look at Danny Devitt's car."

I called back into the office to suggest an early lunch. As I walked up the street with Leah, I made up my mind to continue my chat with Danny's mother as soon as I got the opportunity. Distracted, I hadn't noticed that Leah was steering me away from the square.

"What are you doing?" I asked. "I thought we were going to the Oak?"

"I thought we could duck through the mart. I'm trying to avoid Eithne," she said, her eyes darting about. "She's bloody well collecting for something again. She was in the office earlier, and I told her you'd be gone for a few hours."

I grinned. "Should we not just give her something? Wouldn't that be easier?"

Leah quickened her pace. "I donated half the petty cash last week after she gave me a lecture on my engagement ring. Said it was a sin to be spending so much money on a piece of jewelry with people starving in the world."

I looked across the square just in time to catch sight of Eithne's familiar figure disappearing into Phyllis' book shop. "Come on, I think we're safe enough now for a bit."

The pub was surprisingly busy for a Monday. The fire crackling in the grate and the hum of voices gave the place an almost festive feel, but there was a distinctly agricultural air about the clientele. The weekly cattle mart was on. We ordered sandwiches and coffee and took seats by the door, the only ones free.

"Paul rang," Leah said, taking off her coat and draping it over the back of her chair. "Said he'll have his report on the church in to us tomorrow, so we can start putting together the contracts."

"Good," I said. "I must give Raymond Kelly a shout then. We need to get details of any planning applications and that kind of thing from the County Council. I know he was refused the full development he'd intended, but there's a change of use permission knocking about somewhere, I think."

"I'll organize that. I'll call into the County Council offices later on in the week."

"That'd be great."

". . . Ben?"

I realized I'd missed what Leah had just said. I'd been watching McFadden at the bar collecting a sandwich and coffee. I stood up.

"Sorry, I'll be back in a minute. I just need to speak to . . ."

McFadden had walked back down the length of the pub and had raised his hand to open the door by the time I caught up with him.

"Andy?"

He turned. "Hiya."

"Have you a minute?"

"Sure."

"Outside?"

We stood on the footpath, McFadden's face full of curiosity.

"What's up?" he asked.

"Andy, did you tell Mrs. Devitt about Danny's DNA being found on the blanket and pillow in the crypt?"

His face froze. "Who told you that?"

"She did. It's all right – client confidentiality. I won't be passing it on."

He looked defeated. "Probably won't make any difference. I'm going to have to tell Molloy anyway, now that it looks like Danny's death wasn't an accident."

"Why?"

"Because there's more to it."

"What do you mean?"

He looked uncomfortable.

"She said you did it to warn her," I prompted.

He shrugged. "In a way."

"She's asked me to help her, Andy. She's afraid Danny is going to be blamed for something he didn't do. I'm not sure what she means, to be honest, but she said he could be an easy scapegoat."

He sighed, turned his back on me, and walked over to the squad car, parked on the footpath as usual. *Damn it*, I thought, *I've overstepped the mark.* I should have kept my mouth shut. But he opened the passenger door.

"Here, sit inside for a minute."

He took a gulp from his coffee before he spoke, the heat steaming up the windscreen. "I'm going to tell Molloy all of this as soon as I get back to the station."

"Fair enough." I waited.

He gave in. "It appears that Danny was making a bit of a nuisance of himself."

"You mean the drinking in town? I saw you taking him out of the Oak a couple of days before the accident."

"No," he said slowly. "Although that, too. It was more in the weeks and months before he died. Danny's always been a little on the . . . *nocturnal* side, but lately he'd taken to creeping around."

"Creeping around?"

"Creeping around people's houses at night. Sort of spying on them. Watching them." He shook his head. "People around here have always been pretty tolerant of Danny, allowed him his oddities, but this was different. It was intrusive and threatening and they didn't like it."

"I can understand that."

"We had complaints. Or at least *I* had complaints. And I didn't exactly share them with the sergeant." He gave me a sheepish look.

"Who were the complaints from?"

"Lisa Crane and her husband. Well, Alan really, first of all at any rate. He said Danny was hassling Lisa, wouldn't leave her alone. Waiting for her outside the bank in the evening when she finished work. Hanging around outside their house at night."

"That's odd. She gave me the impression that she was pretty fond of him when I was talking to her at the wake."

"I think she was, but he was certainly pushing it."

"Are you sure?"

"Aye. I saw him myself a couple of times sitting in that battered-up car of his outside their house. I had to tell him to go home."

"Was that what the row was about, that afternoon in the Oak? Between Danny and Alan?"

"Not really. According to Alan, Danny insisted he knew who had burgled their house but he wouldn't tell him who it was. He was winding him up about it. Alan was convinced it was Danny himself. Still is."

"But you don't think so?"

"No, I don't. He'd have needed a van for a start. And Paul Doherty's place was done the night after Danny died, with what looks like the same modus operandi."

"Did you ask Danny about it? The night you arrested him?"

"Oh aye. He denied it, just before he passed out in the cell. Then claimed he couldn't remember saying anything about it in the morning."

"Did Mary Devitt know about all of this?"

Andy nodded, before taking another gulp of his coffee. "Yes. I told her. She said she'd talk to him." His tone softened. "She's the greatest wee woman. I've known her all my life. She was like a second mother to me; she used to look after me when I was a kid."

"And you didn't tell Molloy?"

"Sounds stupid now, but I was trying to deal with it myself. I was hoping it wouldn't have to go any further. You see, if Molloy had found out, he would have had Danny arrested for harassment and charged on the spot. Danny would have had to appear in court and God knows what would have happened. I couldn't do that to Mrs. Devitt."

I couldn't deny that he was probably right, but then maybe Danny would still be alive if he had been charged. I didn't share this thought with McFadden though; he looked miserable enough.

"Then when his DNA was found on the blanket," he said, "I thought maybe it was another example of him prowling about, messing with things that didn't concern him. I wondered if he'd been poking about around the church again and had found the bones and decided to wrap them in the blanket or something. It was the kind of thing he might have done. Thinking he was doing the right thing. He could be a bit childlike sometimes."

I liked this image better than the one of Danny digging up a skeleton or stealing a body.

"Maybe that's what he did do."

McFadden sighed. "That's why I told Mrs. Devitt. I thought she might know something."

"The problem is, Molloy is going to be looking at who would have had a motive to kill Danny, and his nocturnal activities might have had something to do with that," I said.

He ran his fingers through his hair. "I do know that."

I watched as McFadden drove off, wearing the expression of a man about to face his executioner. I couldn't blame him. Molloy was going to be furious. But Jesus, what the hell had he been thinking?

As I opened the door of the Oak again, I was hit by a waft of very expensive perfume: Lisa Crane. I felt suddenly guilty, as if she had heard me talking about her with McFadden.

"I got your letter," she said.

"Oh, good."

"Have you time to see me at half one before I have to go back to Buncrana?"

I checked my watch. It was quarter past. "Um . . ."

"Alan's free and I want him to be there, too."

I put off my plans to go and see Mary Devitt.

"Sure," I said. "I'll meet you at the office in ten minutes."

It would be a short lunch.

Chapter 25

"So, is it possible to do this?"

Alan Crane's tone was prescriptive. Lisa had removed her coat before arranging herself neatly on the chair. She was wearing her navy Bank uniform with a name badge pinned to the collar of her jacket. Her blond hair was loose around her face. Alan sat beside her, knees spread, hands clasped between them, his fingers stained with nicotine.

"It seems the application should include an affidavit from a relative," I said.

Lisa's shoulders slumped. She looked immediately at Alan: his expression betrayed nothing.

"Why is that exactly?" he asked.

"When a person goes missing for a long time, there is no simple way of legally presuming them to be dead, Mr. Crane. Under the law, a missing person is presumed alive for seven years, after which time they are presumed to be dead. I've explained this to Lisa already."

"Yes." He nodded impatiently. "I know, go on."

"Well, when I spoke to Lisa before, I was aware that a relative could apply to the High Court to have a person declared presumed dead after seven years. But I thought at the time that there might be a difficulty in Lisa applying herself, being only a fiancée."

"Ex."

"Ex-fiancée. And it seems I was right. It should be corroborated by a family member."

Alan leaned back in his seat.

"Well, that's the end of that then."

Lisa looked anxiously at me as if there must be more to come, but there wasn't.

Alan smiled, showing his teeth. A smile totally lacking in mirth. "Looks like we're just going to have to put up with the whole Conor Devitt bullshit coming up every few years then, doesn't it?"

"I don't think a presumption of death would necessarily change that anyway, Mr. Crane," I said. "It's still not known what happened to Mr. Devitt. A presumption of death won't change that. This application deals only with the person's estate. There would be no issuing of a death certificate, for example."

There was no response from either Alan or Lisa. As usual in the face of taciturn clients, I found myself babbling.

"It's possible that Claire or Mrs. Devitt could do it, of course," I said. "They might be willing to, if you spoke to them about it. I know there is the issue of the house: they might see that as a valid reason to do it."

"Claire Devitt?" Alan laughed. "Sure, that one is away with the fairies."

Lisa played with her rings, twisting them to and fro on her fingers.

Alan grinned unpleasantly. "What kind of a woman, Miss O'Keeffe, would leap on a man at her own brother's wake? And that man only just married. Lucky I'm not a fella to take advantage, eh, Lisa?"

Lisa stared at the floor, eyes now brimming with tears.

"And Danny was supposed to be the crazy one?" he sneered. "I wouldn't be surprised if there was a hit of the crazy stick running right the way through that family. Starting with the father."

Lisa began to say something, but changed her mind.

"What do you mean by that, Mr. Crane?" I said coldly.

"Ach, old Jack Devitt taking a gun to himself, and then Danny doing his Peeping Tom bit around the town. Breaking into people's houses."

"You don't know that," Lisa said quietly.

Alan glared at her.

"What about Mrs. Devitt?" I asked, directing my question at Lisa. "She might be willing to sign an affidavit, if it would help get things in order for you. It might be worth talking to her about it at least."

Lisa shook her head. "I couldn't ask Mrs. Devitt."

"Lisa's afraid of old Ma Devitt, Miss O'Keeffe," Alan said, a spiteful grin on his face. "Just as well she didn't end up as her mother-in-law."

"It's fine. Really. Thank you for looking into this for us." Lisa looked up at me brightly, mask back in place. She stood up and started to put on her coat.

Alan didn't move.

"I'll ask her," he said firmly.

I followed them down the stairs to find Liam McLaughlin, the estate agent, chatting to Leah at the reception desk. He nodded to Alan as he passed.

"Fuck, I can't take that man," he said under his breath when the door slammed.

"Why is that?" I leaned on the counter beside him.

"Used to play golf with him. Had to stop – I couldn't take his temper. He nearly brained me with a nine iron one day. Had to be pulled off me."

"Seriously?"

"Seriously. He was losing badly in a charity tournament last summer in Buncrana – organized by Kelly, as a matter of fact – in aid of the hospice. I made the mistake of saying something smart while he was trying to take a shot."

"That's not like you."

"Scared the bejasus out of me, I can tell you. He wasn't kidding."

I noticed that Leah was looking at me as if she wanted to say something. She had an anxious expression on her face.

"What's up?"

"The man from the Law Society is here. He's in the waiting room. Shall I send him up to you?"

"I'll go in and talk to him myself in a minute. Was there something you wanted, Liam?"

"Oh aye. Ray Kelly's in hospital. I told Alison I'd let you know."

"God. Is he all right?"

"Don't know, to be honest. I know he collapsed a few months back on the golf course. I remember Alison was away at their pub in London and had to come back. But it was never said what was wrong with him, and I don't like to ask when it's not offered." He lowered his tone. "Although between you and me, I think he was in hospital in the States while he was over there."

"Oh."

"Alison said they were to come in and see you tomorrow?"

"That's right."

"She wanted to know if there was anything she could take Ray to sign and could you get it ready for her if there was."

"Will do."

The rest of the afternoon was spent immersed in Law Society financial regulation compliance. Hideous stuff. I was utterly trapped, with no hope of escape to see Mary Devitt. I ran to and fro from the filing cabinet on the orders of the auditor, finding receipts, tracing cheques and lodgements, my mind drifting constantly to what I would say to her when I finally got to speak to her. I left the office at half seven, head pounding, and decided I would drive up to her first thing in the morning.

I slept badly, got up early, and headed to Lagg Beach for a swim before breakfast. It was a beautiful morning, bright and crisp. As I clambered over the rocks down onto the beach, I thought about my last swim and my encounter with Claire Devitt. Alan Crane was a thoroughly dislikable man, but it didn't stop me wondering what he had meant by his comment about Claire's behavior at the wake. I remembered her sudden reappearance in the kitchen in that red dress.

The swim cleared my head and nearly gave me a heart attack at the same time: the intended effect. It also gave me an appetite for breakfast. A mound of toast and scrambled eggs later, I drove up the narrow lane towards the Devitts' old farmhouse. I had tried to ring before I left the cottage, but there was no answer.

In the daylight, with the cold blue sky behind it, the house looked quaint, like something from an old John

Hinde postcard. I almost expected to see a scruffy-looking red-haired child with a donkey and a basket of turf in front. I pulled into the yard and parked the Mini next to the porch.

The door was open. I knocked loudly. There was no response so I stepped inside and called down the hall. Finally, I heard a voice coming from the kitchen. I wasn't sure whether to follow it or not, but before I could decide, Mary Devitt herself strode up the hall looking surprised to see me. Her hair was swept back behind her ears and tied up with a red scarf. She was wearing blue overalls splattered in paint and had an equally splattered rag in her hand.

"So you're the artist?" I said.

"Sorry?"

"I noticed your paintings the night of the, er . . ." I looked again at the canvases of bright color on the wall. "They're very good."

"Oh yes, they're mine." She smiled. "Although you'd better not describe me as *the artist* in front of Claire. She's the one who went to art college, you know, as she'll be sure to remind you."

"I'm sorry for turning up unannounced like this. I did try to ring."

She wiped her hands with the rag. "Oh, I never answer the phone. In my experience it's rarely good news."

"How are you doing?" I asked.

"I'm fine." She corrected herself. "I will be fine."

"I thought we could continue the conversation we were having the other day, if that's okay with you?"

"Oh yes."

I waited for her to ask me in, but she didn't. She seemed to be working something out in her head.

"I presume you came by car?" she asked.

"Yes. It's outside. I parked in the yard."

"Maybe we could go for a walk on the shore. I need some shale for something I'm working on."

"Sure, of course."

"Just give me a minute. I'll see you outside."

I got back into the car and started the engine. A couple of minutes later, Mary joined me, dressed in a man's sheepskin coat, which looked like a relic from the 1970s. She had a large wicker basket on her arm, which dwarfed her even further.

"Lagg?" she said.

"Great."

As I drove out of the yard, a black-and-white sheepdog loped across in front of the car, head bowed. I braked suddenly.

"Jesus!"

"Sorry about that," Mary said. "It's Fred. He doesn't know what to do with himself. He's miserable without Danny. I just don't have enough time for him."

I drove on, heart still pounding, out the lane and down the hill towards the turn-off to the beach. Mary sat silently beside me with her basket on her knee gazing out of the window. Suddenly, despite all my planning, I wasn't sure how to broach things. But I didn't need to.

"The sergeant told me that Danny's accident is being investigated," she said.

"Yes."

"I'm glad. Andy tells me that you had something to do with that."

I wondered when he had passed on that particular piece of information. "Not exactly."

"Well, I thank you, Miss O'Keeffe – for whatever it was that you did. As you know, I was very disturbed by the circumstances of what happened to Danny. I'm relieved that it's being looked into."

I said awkwardly, "Garda McFadden mentioned something to me about Danny's behavior being a bit odd before he died."

She sighed and rubbed the condensation from the passenger window with her palm. "Danny was a very different boy from his brother. Conor internalized everything – you could never tell what he was thinking. He was a typical eldest child, I suppose, always had to handle everything himself. But Danny wore his heart on his sleeve. He was kind. You could see that he loved Lisa McCauley with all his heart, from the time they were kids. He never hid it."

I hesitated. "That still doesn't excuse him from hanging around her house at night though."

She continued to gaze out of the window. "Have you looked closely at that relationship, Miss O'Keeffe? The relationship between Lisa and her new husband?"

"Well yes, a little."

"It's not good, is it?"

I made a noncommittal noise.

"Alan Crane is a violent man," she said quietly.

"How do you know that?"

"Have I seen him hit her, you mean? No, nothing like that. But I know the signs. Believe me, I know them very well. I spent fifteen years trying to cover them up."

I looked across at Mary Devitt. She was staring straight ahead of her. Suddenly I understood why this woman had coped so well with her husband's death. It had been a relief.

* * *

The beach was deserted, and the tide was out. It was no less cold than it had been an hour earlier, but it was clear as a summer's day. Glashedy Island was visible in the distance, looking like a lump of coal that had been flung there by some giant, thousands of years before. I walked along the shore beside Mary Devitt as she peered at the rocks on the ground in front of her, stooping down every so often to pick up something that caught her eye – a shell, the remains of a crab, a bit of seaweed.

"Do you think Danny was trying to protect Lisa then? From her husband?"

"I couldn't say for sure because I don't know and I didn't ask. You have to allow your children to make their own mistakes, Miss O'Keeffe. I do know that even if Danny got things wrong sometimes, he would have been trying to do what was right." She paused. "I also know that he loved Lisa with all his heart, and that husband of hers is a most unpleasant man."

I bent down to pick up a particularly striking piece of pink quartz with silver veins running through it. I handed it to her.

She arched her thin eyebrows. "You have a good eye."

"You mentioned something to me about Danny the day of the funeral, something that you said you didn't want to share with me at that stage. Do you mind me asking what that was?"

She replied, this time without hesitation. "Danny told me he had killed his brother."

I stopped in my tracks. "*What?* When did he tell you that?"

"Not long before he died. I didn't believe him, of course. I thought he meant it in a metaphorical sense – that he had wished him dead. Danny thought like that, like a child. If he wished someone dead, that meant he was responsible for them dying."

"Why would he have wished him dead?"

"Lisa, of course. Conor took Lisa away from Danny, or at least that's the way he saw it."

"Did Conor see it that way, do you think?"

"No. I think Conor was just trying to take care of Lisa. Her father died young, you see."

"Yes, I heard. He was killed, wasn't he? The night the *Sadie* was blown up."

Mary nodded. "He was the pilot on duty the night of the hijacking. He was manning the pilot station when he was shot. It can have repercussions when that happens to a child: losing a parent in a violent way like that. It can leave them insecure and needy if it's not handled properly. I think Conor could see Lisa needed caring for."

"And he wouldn't have thought Danny could do that?"

"Conor is one of those people who feels he has to take responsibility for everyone else." Mary sighed. "It can be a bit smothering at times, and I know his siblings found him a little controlling, but he means well."

I noticed her use of the present tense when she referred to Conor. This was a woman who wasn't going to be signing any affidavits, I thought. Especially if the request came from Alan Crane.

She gazed into the distance. "Poor Conor. I think when he was young he tried to protect us from his father's presence, and then to make up for his absence after he was gone. An impossible task, especially for a child."

"Do you think he actually loved Lisa?"

She smiled. "You'd have to ask him that, Miss O'Keeffe."

Chapter 26

It was after ten o'clock by the time I made it into the office. Leah looked at me curiously, but I didn't offer an explanation.

"Where is he?" I whispered. I kept expecting a gray suit to jump out from behind a filing cabinet and ask me to trace a cheque.

"He's in the front office going through the books. He says he won't need you this morning. I can get him whatever he needs."

I looked at my watch. "Just as well. I have to be in court in half an hour."

She nodded in the direction of the waiting room. "Alison Kelly is waiting for you though."

"Damn it, I was supposed to get back to Liam before she came in."

"It's all right, she's four hours early. Her appointment wasn't until two."

I stuck my head in the door of the waiting room. Alison was sitting, legs elegantly crossed, staring at the wall opposite. When she looked up, her dark eyes appeared deeper set than usual, with heavy shadows underneath.

She stood up. "I'm sorry. I know I'm not supposed to be here till this afternoon, but I have to get to the hospital."

"It's okay. I have a little time. Come on up."

She followed me up the stairs. Even her tread seemed somewhat heavier than it should be.

"How is Ray?" I asked as I closed the office door behind us.

"Not great, I'm afraid."

"I'm sorry to hear that. Is there anything I can do?"

"I wish there was. There's nothing much anyone can do." She took a deep breath. "Ray has a brain tumor. He was in remission, but it's back. We've only just found out."

"Oh, I'm sorry."

"He was given the all-clear about two years ago. But we've lived with the possibility of it returning for a while."

"And it's serious?"

She nodded. "We had a scare a few months ago, but it's definitely back this time. With a vengeance. That's why we went to the States recently. New treatment, last-ditch attempt. But it didn't work, unfortunately."

"I see." I offered her a seat.

She sat down heavily as if she'd just run a mile rather than walking upstairs.

"Ray was exposed to radiation on a building site he worked on in the States when he was about nineteen, long before there was an awareness of the dangers. We have an ongoing civil case over there; another reason we went over. But I can't see it resolving in time to be of any use to us now. That's why we're so desperate to sell this damn church."

I sat down opposite her. "Oh?"

"We need cash. So we can get away for a while in the time that Ray has left."

"It's at that stage?"

"Yes. He hasn't long. To be honest, the church was the last thing I thought we'd have to sell. I hoped we'd be able to hold on to it. But none of our other properties are moving."

"Everything's a little slow at the moment," I acknowledged.

"Although we're selling the pubs now, too. All of them. At least we know they'll sell, even if we have to take a cut on the asking price."

"Is that necessary?"

She sighed. "Unfortunately, yes. I'm just about to go and arrange it. We'll be gone by the time they're sold, but Liam's agreed to handle everything for us. We want to be able to spend the last bit of time we have left together without the stress of having to run a business. Do the traveling we always planned to do."

"Of course. I understand."

She gave me an odd look. "Do you?"

"I think so."

"I wonder." Her eyes flashed suddenly. "I've always thought that life was too damn short, that you should grab it by the throat and take whatever happiness you can while you can, but that's taken on a whole new meaning for me now. I'm not sure you can truly understand that, unless you're faced with losing the person you love." Her tone was unexpectedly angry.

I looked down, chose not to respond this time, not to play whatever game she was playing. I suspected she just needed to vent.

Maybe she realized it herself. For whatever reason, she pulled back. "Anyway, look, one thing's for certain. All our assets have to be sold, and I need to know that you can process the sales quickly when they come through. If you can promise to do that, and at a good fee, we'll use you."

"I'll do my best."

"If not, I'll find someone who can." The edge was back.

I started to go through the contracts for the sale of the church, and Alison was immediately in focused, capable mode. She took notes on the outstanding documents I required, said she would organize tax-clearance certificates, and took the envelope of declarations I needed her husband and herself to sign and return.

"There are some documents in there that need to be witnessed," I said. "Now, anyone can witness them, but if you'd rather I did, I can bring up a set to the hospital and do it. That's no problem."

"I'll talk to Ray and see what he wants. He may not be there very long. There's not much they can do for him at the moment, so he'll be sent home in the next day or two, I expect."

"Okay. Whatever you need, I'll do."

Her eyes softened unexpectedly. "You know, it's so strange, he doesn't even look that sick. Sometimes you'd never even know."

"I wish there was something more I could do."

She put the envelope in her bag. "This is all we need. To push this through as quickly as possible."

"Just as well that English couple came back on board," I remarked.

She nodded. "I hope to hell they stay put this time. Is that everything?"

"Almost. I'm still waiting on planning documentation from the County Council. They said they'd call us when they had the file copied. And I'll also need a copy of Paul Doherty's survey."

"You'll have that this afternoon." She stood up. "I'm going up to meet him now. He wants to check a couple of things with me."

Before she reached the door, she paused and turned. "Please don't mention Ray's illness to anyone. We're keeping it to ourselves for the moment. He doesn't want people to know."

"Of course."

Leah was finishing a call when I came down the stairs.

"I'm going to head over to the County Council offices," she said, standing up and reaching for her coat and scarf. "That planning file on their sale is ready."

"Good. I think we need to get moving on it as quickly as possible."

By six o'clock the audit was finished, and I felt obliged to take the man from the Law Society for something to eat before he started the drive back to Dublin. I hoped that didn't count as bribery. Leah came with us. He left shortly after seven, anxious to make the capital by midnight.

"Thank the Lord that's over for another while." I leaned back in my chair with a sigh. "Fancy a glass of wine to celebrate?"

I was still waiting for her to decide what she wanted to drink when I felt a breeze on the back of my neck as the door behind me opened and someone entered the pub. Leah looked up. I asked again what she wanted to drink, but she didn't respond. Her gaze was fixed instead on whoever had entered the pub as they headed up to the bar. Her mouth was slightly open.

"Are you all right?" I asked.

"Fuck. When did *he* reappear?" she said at last.

I turned to see who she was talking about. A man and woman were standing at the bar. Leah continued to stare openly at them, and I realized she wasn't the only one. As I glanced around, it looked as if the entire pub had stopped chewing at exactly the same moment and were gaping at the couple. Even Tony was standing stock-still behind the bar, looking utterly shocked. Unshockable Tony.

"You won't believe who that is," Leah hissed.

The man was of average height, dressed in a long coat. His curly hair was receding a little and starting to gray at the temples. As he turned to the bar to order, I finally got a view of his face. There was no question about whom I was looking at: the photograph in the newspaper had stayed in my mind as if I had glued it to a noticeboard. He was slightly heavier and was sporting a tan his ex-fiancée would be jealous of, but other than that, he had changed very little. The man was Conor Devitt and the woman with him was his sister, Claire.

"Conor Devitt," Leah breathed, staring at him as if he was liable to disappear if she took her eyes off him. She shook her head in disbelief. "Imagine just walking in here after all these years as if nothing had happened."

Tony served up two takeaway coffees. How he managed to hold it together I'll never know, but Tony's not scared of an audience. There was no conversation though, and that wasn't like him. The drinks were ordered, served, and paid for as if the man were a complete stranger, after which Claire and her long-lost brother turned on their heels and walked back down the length of the pub.

Conor kept his head up and his gaze fixed on the door. He must have been aware of the fact that everyone was looking at him, but he didn't speak to anyone and he didn't catch anyone's eye. Claire, on the other hand, appeared to be relishing the attention. She beamed broadly and her eyes darted around the pub like an insect.

The second door closed, the hum of conversation started up again, quietly at first, then rising gradually to a semi-hysterical din. After a few minutes I went outside. The Devitts had disappeared. The street lighting had come on and there was an orange hue over the square; the air was smoky and still. I dialed the garda station. Molloy answered, and didn't even let me finish my sentence.

"Before you say anything, yes, we know Conor Devitt is back. Yours is about the tenth sighting we've had. I think we can take it he's not considered missing anymore."

"Have you spoken to him?"

"He's just been in with us."

"Oh right."

Molloy sighed. "Says he got back last night. Went straight to his mother's house. We're going to talk to him again, but it all seems above board. That's one file we can finally close."

"So where has he been then?"

"England, he says. Won't give us any details as to why he left in the first place, although I guess he doesn't have to. He's an adult. But he's bloody well wasted a lot of police time."

"So why now? Why come back after all this time? Is it to do with Danny?"

"That's what he says, that he had to come back after his brother's death, for his mother."

"So now he's concerned about her," I said with more than a hint of sarcasm in my voice.

"We've no reason not to believe him," Molloy said. "Although yes, you'd think he'd have got in contact with her at some stage in the past six years to stop the poor woman worrying."

"How did he hear?"

"Hear what?"

"About Danny's death. Do you think someone was in touch with him? Someone who knew where he was?"

"He said he heard it on Highland Radio. He must be able to get it on the Internet or something over there."

"It took him five days to get back all the same," I said. "You'd think he could have made it in time for the funeral."

"And he arrives back to the news that there is to be a murder investigation."

As I hung up, it hit me that Mary Devitt must have known that Conor was back when I went to see her that morning. That was why she had been so anxious to get me away from the house. He was probably in the bloody kitchen. I felt duped.

Chapter 27

THERE WAS AN oddly tense feel about the town the next morning. Or maybe the tension was coming from me. I'd had a restless night. Danny Devitt murdered, Conor Devitt alive, and Mary Devitt trying her best to . . . what was she trying to do? Who was she trying to protect? I had assumed it was Danny, but maybe I was wrong. I was tempted to try to talk to her again – but what good would it do? I had thought she was someone I could trust; now I wasn't so sure.

Wispy white flakes swirled across the square. The cold accessed any little bit of skin that was covered in fewer than three layers. I bought a newspaper and turned the corner towards the office. A white van pulled up beside me on the footpath and a window was rolled down. A bare elbow in a short-sleeved T-shirt appeared and Mick Bourke beckoned me over, his eyes darting to the left and right as I approached him.

"Yes, Mick? Do you want to talk to me?"

He nodded. His face was less florid than usual. Pale beneath the red, making a rather unattractive shade of pink. He was chewing his lip.

"Do you want to come into the office for a minute?"

"Nah, haven't time. It won't take long. Can you get in for a wee minute?"

"If you want me to."

He leaned over to open the passenger door for me and with difficulty I clambered up.

"I'll just drive out the road a bit, if that's all right. I think better when I'm driving."

"Okay," I said slowly.

He pulled off from the curb with a screech and headed out onto the Derry road. After a few minutes he began to hum rather tunelessly and tap the center of the steering wheel with his open palm. It was all a bit disconcerting. I was just about to tell him that I had someone waiting for me at the office and needed to get back, when he stopped humming and started speaking.

"I want you to forget about what we were talking about last week," he said.

"The missing money?"

"Aye."

"Are you sure? You were very anxious about it at the time."

"Aye, I'm sure. I made a mistake. Got me figures all mixed up."

"I thought you said it was Eithne who had done your figures?"

"Aye well, she got them mixed up then."

I paused. "Does this have anything to do with Conor Devitt's reappearance, by any chance?"

"No, it doesn't. I got me figures mixed up, that's all." He had a stubborn expression on his face.

"So there's no money missing."

He shook his head vehemently.

"And never was?"

He shook it again. The van veered a little to the left.

"Right, okay," I said. "Whatever you say."

"So that's it then?" he asked.

"That's it. I did say there wasn't anything I could do for you anyway, that you'd have to talk to the guards."

His eyes widened in alarm. "You didn't say anything to them, did you?"

"No. I didn't."

He breathed out audibly.

Leah looked up at me with a grin when I walked back into the office. "Did I see you getting into a white van, by any chance?"

"God, there's no privacy in this town."

"New man?"

"Yep."

"Who was it?" She handed me the mail.

"Mick Bourke. He's a funny one, isn't he?"

She looked up. "Not the brightest, my father always says."

"He's Eithne's brother though, isn't he? She's sharp as a tack."

"Half-brother. Eithne's father died and her mother remarried – Mick's father. He was a bit of a thug, by all accounts. Mind you, Mick must have something going for him. Have you seen his wife?"

"I think she was at Danny Devitt's funeral with him. I didn't get a decent look at her though. Why?"

Leah whistled. "She's about half his age. A Derry one. Never seen her without some big rock or other expensive bit of jewelry."

"Really? I thought he said his wife had cataracts. You don't get cataracts when you're young, do you?"

She laughed. "That was the previous one. He got rid of her a few years ago. Replaced her with this new model."

"I see. He never mentioned that. Just referred to 'the wife' as if it was some kind of generic position."

"That's hilarious." She chewed absently on her pen. "I wonder if Conor Devitt will go back to work for him, now that he's back?"

At lunchtime I wandered over in the direction of Phyllis' book shop. I was dying to see what she made of Conor Devitt's reappearance. I knew she would be delighted to chew over this latest town drama. I pushed open the door, and the little bell rang as it swung back. Phyllis was perched on a stool at the counter immersed in a book.

"At last, someone to talk to," she said, taking her glasses off her nose. "The town has been like a morgue all day."

"There's a funny old atmosphere all right."

"I reckon everyone is hiding away gossiping about Conor Devitt." She grinned. "Speaking of which, fancy some tea?"

I beamed an assent.

A few minutes later, Phyllis reappeared with a huge earthenware teapot and a plate of homemade butter biscuits.

"So, what do you know?" she said, as she rested the tray on the counter. "I hear he made a grand entrance in the Oak last night."

"Well, not quite a grand entrance, but he certainly attracted a lot of attention. Claire was with him."

"I bet she was. Did you know he was back? Before last night, I mean?" she asked.

"I was as surprised as everyone else. Or as everyone else looked, at any rate."

She smiled. "I'd say there was a bit of fly-catching all right. You can't blame people. He has been gone for six years."

I took a biscuit. "And his family seemed pretty convinced that was him in the crypt."

"I wonder," Phyllis said as she poured the tea. "I think people kind of hoped it was him in a way." Then she caught herself. "Hope is probably the wrong word. I think they didn't want to believe that Conor would up and leave his family and his fiancée just before his wedding. He was always the kind of fella to do the right thing, you know?" She shrugged. "Maybe it was easier to handle to think that something had happened to him. It seemed like such a callous thing to have done otherwise. And then to not even get in touch for all that time."

I took a sip of my tea. Earl Grey this time. None of your tar-like builders' tea for Phyllis.

"He must have had his reasons, I suppose."

"That's no excuse for what he did to his poor mother. And Claire. I know what I'd do to him if I got hold of him."

"I'm sure Claire's had a few things to say to him. I got the impression she didn't appreciate being left alone to look after their mother." I smiled. "Though I know Tony seemed to think it was the other way round."

Phyllis frowned. "I wouldn't have thought that Claire would take him on. I always thought she was a little afraid of Conor, to be honest. He was the reason she stopped working for Eithne, you know."

"Really?"

"Yes. Conor disliked Eithne, I knew that. But I never got the full story. I heard he just marched into the chemist shop one day and ordered Claire out of there. I often wondered . . ."

"Wondered what?"

She hesitated. "I don't really like to say, but well – I often wondered if maybe Eithne was a little overfond of Claire, if you get my drift. Still is, in my opinion."

"I see. Would Conor really have taken a dislike to Eithne because of that?"

She shrugged. "He seemed to. Claire was very young at the time, and Conor was always pretty conservative."

"And Claire?"

"Oh, I'm pretty sure Claire likes men. At least she used to, which doesn't mean she doesn't take advantage of Eithne's affection, I suspect."

"What do you think of him?" I asked.

"Conor?" Phyllis made a face.

"I thought everyone liked him?"

"Was that something you were told when everyone thought his body was in the crypt?"

"Well, yes, now that you mention it."

"That was the *don't speak ill of the dead* phase," she said with a cynical expression. "Look, Conor Devitt might have been straight in his business dealings. And a good carpenter undoubtedly, and he certainly took responsibility for the family when he was very young, got a job straight after school and all that, and of course that's all very impressive . . ."

"But?"

"There was something about him I just couldn't warm to."

"Go on."

"He was controlling, in my opinion. I assumed it was because he had to grow up too quickly with what happened to his father."

That was the second time I'd heard the word "controlling" used in reference to Conor Devitt.

"Why did you think that?"

"Oh, I probably shouldn't mention this, it was so long ago."

"Go on."

"Okay. One day I was down at the shore below the Devitts' house, going for a walk after Mass. You know I said that I used to go to Mass in Whitewater, when the priest here was driving me nuts?"

"Yes."

"Now this could be twenty years ago, mind. It's funny the things that stay with you. Claire and Danny were down at the shore – they were only kids. They were down around the old pilot station – they'd stopped using it at that stage – just messing about with the dog, when Conor arrived with a face like thunder. He ordered them off the beach and home. He was only a teenager himself at the time, eighteen or so. But there was something about the way he did it that bothered me. He was furious."

"I'm surprised Danny obeyed him."

Phyllis tilted her head. "I'd have obeyed him myself, the mood he was in."

"Do you think it had something to do with what happened to his father?" I asked.

"I wondered that, too, at the time."

"Trying to protect them? Something like that?"

"Maybe. But they only lived up the hill from the beach so they couldn't exactly have kept away from it." She murmured, almost to herself, "But that's what it looked like – as if they weren't allowed near the shore. Very strange."

"Do you think it was coming from the mother?"

"Mrs. D? God, no." Phyllis grinned. "She's a lovely woman and all that, but not what you'd call hands on. She let those kids run wild."

"So Conor was a real surrogate parent?"

"That's right. He grew up too fast in my view. Cocky and charming, but you wondered if it was all an act, to show how grown up he was. Able to take care of everything, you know?"

I looked at my watch. It was five to two.

"I have to go. Thanks for the tea and biscuits."

"Right so. I'll see you at your office at quarter past anyway," Phyllis said.

"Huh?"

"That Glendara Poverty Relief Committee thingy."

"Oh right. Grand."

I was about to close the door behind me when Phyllis called out.

"Drama meeting on Friday, too, by the way. Here this time, upstairs in the flat. We have to have a look at those plays. Claire might even come."

I nodded.

"If Conor lets her," she added with a grin.

My phone rang in my coat pocket on the way back to the office. The words *home calling* flashed across the screen. I hesitated before answering.

"Sarah . . . Ben?" My mother's voice was cautious.

"Hi, Mum. How's Dad?"

"Good, better – he's managing to get up the stairs with a bit of difficulty. Glad to be back in his own bed."

"That's grand."

She paused as if she was working out how to phrase the next sentence.

"What's up, Mum?"

She cleared her throat before she spoke. "We – that is, your father and I – we want you to talk to the pathologist."

My heart sank. "Whatever for, Mum?"

"We want you to find out why she said what she did."

"I can't, Mum."

"Whyever not? You said she was up there, in Donegal. Couldn't you just ask her?"

"She's left, Mum. And even if she hadn't, what on earth good would it do to talk to her? Why open all of that up again?"

"Because she said some things that we know couldn't be true. Maybe if you talked to her, she would understand. Maybe there could be a retrial or something – an appeal. That happens sometimes, doesn't it?" My mother was talking breathlessly now, as if she had to get everything she wanted to say out all at once, before her allotted time was up.

"Mum, she simply gave evidence of her own scientific findings. She is not going to change that, or be influenced by anyone else's view. She wouldn't be doing her job if she were. In any case, it's too late for an appeal, and it would never have been up to us anyway; it would have been up to the Director for Public Prosecutions. He was convicted, Mum. There was no reason to appeal."

"But . . ."

"Mum, I'm sorry, I have to go. I need to get back to the office."

Chapter 28

A FAMILIAR WAVE of nausea hit me as I hung up, accompanied by a sense of dread that this nightmare was never going to end. My parents were not going to drop this. Why the hell had I told them about the pathologist? The whole reason for keeping my distance was to avoid these kinds of conversations, to allow the tragedy to settle into something less raw, a dull ache that could be lived with. The memory of my sister preserved in some way, however artificial, not ripped to shreds and trampled into the gutter. This was what happened when I let down my guard.

The basic rule of cross-examination is: never ask a question unless you're sure you'll get the answer you want. My parents were never going to get the answers they wanted if they kept asking questions. Never. And if everything came out, there was a possibility I could lose them entirely. My head was spinning. I walked through the square trying to suppress the sense of rising panic.

I couldn't go back to the office yet. I had Phyllis' committee waiting to see me and I needed to be able to think straight for that. Five minutes was all I needed. Five minutes of fresh air and I would be okay.

I walked on a little bit out the Derry road, down the hill towards the old fish factory, trying to work out what to do.

Lie? Tell them I had spoken to the pathologist and she had refused to change her story? Or that she had refused to engage with me at all? My real fear was that they would try to contact her themselves. I couldn't manage this one by myself. I realized I needed to talk to Molloy – properly this time. As soon as the decision was made, my breathing started to calm down, and I could feel the tides of anxiety ebb.

I looked up, and discovered with a jolt that I wasn't sure exactly where I was or how far I had walked. I looked around me to get my bearings. Across the road was the back entrance to the hardware shop: a dusty lane with high wire fencing on either side through which the builders' supplies and wood were delivered.

I was about to turn on my heel and walk back up the hill to the office when I heard voices coming from the lane. Which was odd, as it wasn't usually used by pedestrians. There were two stone pillars at the entrance. I crossed the road and stood behind one of them. A car drove by and suddenly I felt conspicuous. Like Danny Devitt, I was going to get a reputation for lurking. Taking my phone out, I pretended to be reading a text. I peered around the pillar but couldn't see anyone. The lane curved inwards so my view was limited to about fifty feet. I strained my ears to listen. The wind carried two voices towards me, one male and one female, but I couldn't hear what either of them was saying.

I walked down the lane a little, expecting at any second to hear the roar of a cement lorry behind me, but hoping not to. Then I turned a corner and saw Eithne. Leaning over her, talking to her in a low, threatening voice, his face almost touching hers, was a man in a dark coat. Eithne's face was bright pink, and she was clearly protesting vehemently about something. As I watched, the man threw something on the ground. As Eithne stooped to pick it up, he took a further step towards her and she jerked back, almost falling, her back colliding with the wire fence.

"Hey, what's going on?" I shouted.

The man spun around, his face calm, impassive. It was Conor Devitt.

I walked towards them. "What are you doing to her?"

"Who are you?" he said coldly.

"Don't worry about that. I said, what are you doing to her?"

"I'm not 'doing' anything to her. We're just sorting a few things out. Isn't that right, Eithne?"

Eithne nodded, said breathlessly, "I'm fine." She shoved whatever it was she had picked up into the pocket of her cardigan.

"You don't look fine."

"Honestly." Her tone was pleading.

"I'm not leaving you here alone with him."

"Really. There's no problem," she insisted.

Conor put his hands in his pockets. "It's okay. We've finished. I've said what I needed to say."

He gave Eithne one last look and strode past me, back down the lane towards the main road.

I put my hand on Eithne's shoulder. "Are you all right?"

She was shaking.

"I'm fine," she repeated. "Please go."

"Do you want me to call the guards? I can call Molloy." I took out my phone.

Anger flashed in her eyes. "I've said I'm fine! How many times do I have to say it?"

I put my hands up. "Okay, okay. But he looked like he was threatening you."

"Well, he wasn't."

Eithne refused to allow me to walk her back up to the chemist's shop, so I arrived back in the office five minutes later to a packed waiting room.

Acting for committees always frustrates me. The members never entirely trust each other; in this case, seven people had turned up to see what was happening. With Leah's help, I dragged a couple of extra chairs into the front office, and three people stood leaning against the wall. Phyllis, of course, managed to nab one of the chairs. And, true to form, did all of the talking.

"We need to set up a limited company," she said.

"Okay. You're a charity, aren't you?"

"Aye, we're like a wee local Saint Vincent de Paul, I suppose. We help out those families in the community who are in trouble."

"Very commendable."

I looked around the room to give an impression that I was engaging with more than one person, but I was looking at a sea of blank faces. Mere observers.

"Founded about . . ." Phyllis looked around her for assistance. . . "Fifteen years ago?"

The others nodded.

"And why do you want to set up a company now, if it's been working fine so far?" I enquired.

They looked at each other, silently nominating Phyllis to reply.

"We've come into some money. A considerable amount of money," she said. "And none of us relishes the idea of being personally responsible for it."

"I see."

"From a very generous, anonymous benefactor." She tapped her nose with her forefinger.

"Well, the best model for you then is a company limited by guarantee," I said. "And we'll see if we can get you charitable status. It'll exempt you from most taxes."

Phyllis lagged behind, the rest of them having trooped out of the office.

"Was there something else?" I asked.

She grinned. "I thought you might like to know who our generous benefactor is."

"Don't tell me if you're not supposed to," I warned her.

"I know you're not going to tell anyone." She put her hand in front of her mouth in an exaggerated stage whisper. "It's Mick Bourke."

"Really?" I probably shouldn't have let the surprise show in my voice.

"Yes," Phyllis said. "I was pretty astonished myself. The carpentry business must be doing well."

"How do you know it was him?"

"He was stupid enough to leave the money in an envelope along with an old receipt with his name on it."

"Maybe he didn't want to be anonymous, after all."

"That's exactly what I thought."

I nearly collided with the man in the dark coat standing on the footpath outside the office. Conor Devitt looked down at me, all heavy eyebrows and brooding, fixed stare. One thing he had in common with his brother. I managed to make some noise resembling a greeting, if not a particularly friendly one.

"So you're the solicitor O'Keeffe?"

"Yes."

"I'm Conor Devitt."

"I know."

He didn't react. He must have known that he was the talk of the town.

"Were you waiting for me?" I asked.

"Yes."

"Is there a reason why you didn't come into the office and sit in the waiting room like a normal human being?"

"I was on my way in."

"Right."

"I want to talk to you about my mother. I know you came up to see her the other morning."

I didn't respond. Didn't admit or deny.

"I was there. I saw you through the window."

As I thought.

"What were you talking to her about?"

"I can't tell you that, I'm afraid."

"Was it about Danny?"

I started to repeat what I had said. "I'm sorry, I can't—"

He cut in. "I'm not going to be around for very long, Miss O'Keeffe. I have some things I need to attend to and then I'll be gone. But I do need to make sure that my mother is all right."

"Your mother seems to be fairly self-sufficient, Mr. Devitt."

I stopped myself from adding: "She'd need to be, since you haven't seen her in six years." I knew it was rich, given my own circumstances. Also, something made me think Conor wasn't overly blessed with a sense of humor. Phyllis had been right about him.

He crossed his arms. "You seem to have taken a certain view of me."

"You can hardly be surprised by that. I've just seen you threatening a woman who is about half your size."

"You're quick to judge."

"I wouldn't say that particularly."

"Do you always assume that things are as they appear?"

I didn't like the way the conversation was going.

"So why were you shouting at Eithne then?" I demanded. "You know she could report you to the guards? That's a public order offense, threatening and abusive behavior."

He gave the smallest glimmer of a smile, and I saw a trace of the young man I had seen in the photograph from the paper.

"She is absolutely free to report me. Did you ask her if she wanted to?"

"Yes. She didn't," I admitted.

"No, she wouldn't. Now: Are you going to tell me what you were talking to my mother about?"

His patronizing tone really riled me. "What are you doing, Mr. Devitt – sorting out all the people in the town you don't like? Is that what you came back to do? And I'm on your hit list because I talked to your mother?"

He turned and walked away.

Chapter 29

AFTER THAT EXCHANGE I needed a coffee – and not an instant one. Molloy must have had the same idea. I met him in the doorway of the Oak, takeaway cup in hand.

"Why don't you get Tony to put that in a real cup and join me for a bit," I suggested. "I need ten minutes away from the office."

"Okay. What are you having?"

"Same as you, assuming it's black coffee."

I took a seat at one of the tables by the fire. Molloy reappeared a couple of minutes later with two mugs.

"So what's up?" he said.

"Why should there be anything up? Maybe I just want to shoot the breeze with you."

His eyes narrowed. "Quite apart from the fact that I've never once heard you use the expression 'shoot the breeze,' I'm sure there's something specific you want to talk to me about."

"Maybe."

"I suppose I should be grateful you're not lurking in the bushes somewhere spying on me." A smile played at the corners of his mouth.

I could feel the heat moving up my neck and into my face. I chose to pretend it wasn't happening, though I'm sure Molloy could see it.

I took a sip of my coffee. "Any developments in the investigation into Danny Devitt's death?"

Molloy sighed. "Not really. Eddie Kearney is still our only witness, and I can't exactly imagine him shining in the witness box, even if he had seen who was in the other car."

"Anything turn up on Danny's car?"

"Nope. We got nothing. It didn't help that it was a wreck of a thing he was driving to begin with. That wasn't the first crash he'd had in it."

"You don't think Danny saw something someone didn't want him to, do you, on one of his nighttime excursions?"

"It's possible."

"McFadden said he told Alan Crane he knew who was doing the robberies."

"You talked to McFadden?" Annoyance flashed across his face. "What the hell was he doing, keeping all of that from me?"

"I think his motives were good. He cares about the family."

"He's a guard. He shouldn't have let it skew his judgement."

"No, probably not. You're not going to do anything about it, are you?"

He shook his head. "Not this time."

I took another gulp of my coffee. "I ran into the infamous brother, by the way."

Molloy leaned back. "And?"

"I don't like him much." I was close to telling Molloy about the row with Eithne but I stopped myself.

"He's fairly humorless, all right," Molloy agreed.

"I thought he was supposed to be a bit of a charmer?"

"Maybe he's changed. He has been away for a while. And he's just lost his brother."

"A brother he hasn't seen for six years," I pointed out. "Is there a connection between his sudden reappearance and Danny's death, do you think?"

"You mean other than the obvious, that he came back to support his mother?"

"Other than that." I hesitated. "You don't think he had anything to do with it, do you?"

Molloy gave me a sardonic look. "Because you don't like him?"

"Of course not." I blushed. "But they did have their difficulties with one another – feelings for the same girl, that kind of thing. I believe Conor was a bit of a tyrant."

I knew I was floundering. Molloy knew it, too.

"I knew about Lisa, all right. McFadden mentioned something about it, when he finally decided to tell me about the Cranes' complaint. But didn't Conor steal Lisa from Danny? Surely that would give Danny a motive to kill Conor, not the other way around."

"I suppose." I remembered what Danny had told his mother.

"And in case you've forgotten, Danny was killed early last Wednesday morning – and if we are to believe what he tells us, Conor only came back into the country on Sunday night. Arrived up here on Monday."

"Are we sure of that?" I said suspiciously. "Have you seen his ticket?"

"No, but we'll check the passenger lists."

"Sibling rivalry can cause a lot of damage, you know . . ." I stopped. I wondered suddenly if I was allowing my own history to cloud my judgement.

"It's hardly enough for a conviction."

"I know. But there's something about Conor Devitt . . . he makes me uneasy."

He smiled. "Not enough, Ben, not enough."

"I know." I sighed. "Any other candidates?"

"No. It could have been anyone who drove Danny Devitt off the road. Six o'clock in the morning is a good time to be somewhere you're not supposed to be without anyone noticing. It's the *why* that we have to figure out."

"Hmm."

He drained his coffee. "They're reburying that young fella in the morning, by the way."

"That's good. I'm sure his poor father will be relieved."

Molloy stood up to go.

I stopped him. "You in a rush?"

He checked his watch. "I am now. Was there something else?"

"Could I have a chat with you later on? I need to ask your advice."

He moved to sit back down.

I waved him away. "No, don't, it's fine. There's no hurry, it's to do with what we were talking about at the weekend. Maybe later?"

"Want me to come over?"

"That would be great."

"About seven?"

I nodded. My mobile rang. It was Leah.

"Sorry, I'm on my way back now. I needed a stiff coffee."

"It's not that. Alison Kelly rang. She wants you to go up to the hospital and witness those documents for Mr. Kelly."

"Sure, I'll go straight away."

* * *

I drove up to Letterkenny in a fog of white. The snow had started again in earnest; tiny dusty flakes blew across the dual carriageway in gusts. I found Kelly's room easily – there are few enough private rooms in Letterkenny General. I knocked, but there was no reply, so I pushed the door open a couple of inches.

I was unprepared for what I saw. I guess it was Alison's comment about him not really looking sick, and I suppose in a way he didn't. Not physically, at any rate. He was a little thinner, his face a little grayer maybe. But it was his expression that disturbed me. It was full of fear, raw and sharp. He was alone and staring at a television screen above the bed, but not really watching it. A set of headphones led to an iPod on his bedside locker. When he heard the door click, he transferred his gaze to me. I smiled and the fear was erased. He removed the headphones.

"The Jam," he said. "You'd never guess I used to be a mod, would you?"

"Well . . ."

He gave me a weary smile. "It's a lifetime ago." He raised himself on his elbows and sat up, resting his head back against the pillow. "Thanks for coming. I wanted to come down myself. God knows why I'm still here. I thought they'd let me out today."

"That's okay. I'm happy to do whatever I can to help."

"I'm sure Alison's had something to do with it. She's so bloody anxious. She thinks I'm going to keel over if I get out of bed."

"It's understandable she's worried."

"She's told you?"

"Yes."

"I wish she wouldn't, but it helps her, I think, to tell people. It's obviously not something I want known."

"She did ask me not to tell anyone."

His expression clouded. "I know she needs comfort. I worry about her."

"As she does about you, by the looks of things."

He smiled again, weakly. "No need. She seems to think this bloody thing is going to kill me at some point, but I'm in no rush."

"That's good to hear."

He leaned over to open the door of his bedside locker and took out a folder of documents, saying, "Right, let's get this done. Is this the lot?"

I nodded and took a pen from my briefcase. His hand shook as he signed each of the documents.

"Sorry. It's these fucking drugs – they're worse than the bloody tumor." He handed the papers to me and leaned back onto the pillow.

I looked through the documents.

"Alison wants us to go away, you know – the three of us. I don't know if I have the energy. I'd be just as happy to stay here, but she says she wants us to do all the things we never had the chance to do." He added sadly, "That's the one thing I regret. We've done nothing but work to build up the businesses, and I regret that. I should have given her more. She deserved more . . ." His voice trailed off, then he saw me frown.

"Everything all right?" he asked.

One document wasn't complete. "This one here. It's called a Particulars Delivered form – it's for the Tax Office. It needs your tax number."

"Could you hand me my coat? It's on the back of the door there. My wallet should be in one of the pockets. I think there's a tax docket in it. If not, I'll get Alison to call the accountant."

Kelly pulled a leather wallet from the coat I brought him and opened it. While he poked about in the notes section for what he was looking for, I caught sight of a picture, a small photograph in a plastic sleeve at the front of the wallet. It wasn't difficult to recognize Alison, wearing a wide sun hat, smiling broadly. In the same sleeve was a lock of black hair. Kelly caught my gaze and closed the wallet with a slightly embarrassed expression. He handed me a slip of paper.

"Here's the number."

"Thanks, that's great. I'll get moving on this as quickly as possible. Is there anything else I can do for you while I'm here?"

He gave me a crooked grin. "You mean like a will?"

"Not unless you want one," I said gently.

"Nah, think I'm all right for the moment, thanks very much."

I walked out into the brightly lit corridor. White tiles, aluminium trolleys, antiseptic smells, the pale frightened faces of patients shuffling along in pink fluffy dressing gowns and sensible slippers. No wonder Kelly was anxious to get out of here.

I opened the swing door marked Exit and ran straight into Alison Kelly with Trevor.

"Oh good, you've seen him."

"All done and dusted."

"How was he?" she asked anxiously.

"Good."

Trevor yawned behind his hand.

"Trevor." His mother's tone was reproachful. She looked at me apologetically. "He's hungover – too many parties lately. That's the problem with working in a pub."

"I can imagine."

"Hopefully it won't be for much longer."

"The pubs are on the market?"

She nodded. "Fingers crossed."

"Well, good luck with it."

"Thanks."

Trevor yawned again and Alison tutted. "I wouldn't mind the parties except that it's muggins here who ends up having to go and collect him. He has me driving all over the peninsula."

Her son raised his eyes to heaven. "I have an overprotective mother."

I laughed. "Aren't you lucky?"

Trevor grinned at me, showing perfectly even white teeth. "She just wants to keep an eye on me. Afraid some girl's gonna get her claws into me."

Alison gave his shoulder an affectionate shove. "Poor baby."

I got back to the office about six and dumped the papers Kelly had signed on my desk. I noticed Leah had left the planning file there, too, but I decided I'd look at it in the morning.

The morning seemed a long way off at the moment. Before then I had to talk to Molloy and tell him things I had never told anyone. It was time; I had backed out too often. I called into the Oak to pick up a bottle of wine to take home, then I changed my mind and bought two. As I was handing the money to Tony, the door to the Ladies opened and Claire Devitt came out.

She climbed onto a barstool and picked up her drink. She didn't seem to notice me, which was odd as I was the only other customer in the place. Tony threw me a glance but didn't say a word. I tapped Claire lightly on the shoulder. She turned around and flashed me a broad smile. Her eyes were half-closed.

"Ah, how are you? Sit down and have a wee drink with me, why don't you?" she said.

"I can't, I'm afraid. I have to be somewhere."

Her face fell in an exaggerated sad clown expression. "Aw."

She took another gulp of her drink – a clear liquid with a slice of lemon in it. A gin and tonic or a vodka, I assumed. She waved her arm in a broad sweeping gesture while Tony showed impressive reflexes in quickly moving a mixer bottle to one side.

"So what do you think of all of this drama then? I can't keep up, I swear." She was slurring her words.

I picked up my bottles of wine. "I'm sure you're pleased to have Conor back at least."

"Of course. Who wouldn't be? It's absolutely wonderful. Excuse me for a minute." She was up off her stool again and heading back towards the door to the toilets.

"Is she all right?" I asked Tony.

"Does she look all right to you?"

"No. Is she drunk?"

"She's drinking water. Hasn't any money for anything else. Not that I'd serve it to her even if she had."

"Anything I can do?"

He shook his head. "I called her mother's house about twenty minutes ago. Conor's coming down for her. She sure as hell can't drive in that state."

As I crossed the road to the car, I heard a noise behind me and glanced around to see a man standing in the shadows smoking a cigarette. It was Conor Devitt. Back in the role of big brother.

Chapter 30

I LIT THE fire. The cottage was freezing, turning my breath to white mist. Molloy had said he'd get here at seven, but I was beginning to hope that he'd be late. I turned on the heating, opened one of the bottles of red wine, placed it by the hearth, and sat down on the couch to wait.

Two minutes later, I stood up again and went into the kitchen to put out some food for Guinness, who hadn't made an appearance yet although I was sure he would turn up eventually. I sat down again, decided I felt hungry myself, made a cheese and tomato sandwich, which I found I couldn't eat, then went to sort out a load of laundry instead. My mind was racing. This whole idea of pouring my heart out to Molloy was a bad one. He wouldn't understand, he would judge me. I should ring him and cancel. I looked at my watch. If he didn't arrive in the next fifteen minutes, I promised myself, that's what I would do.

Surprisingly, shoving dirty clothes into the machine helped to calm me down, and for the first time in a long time, I allowed myself to think about Faye, properly. To picture her as she was that last time I'd seen her. Always thin, she was gaunt then, but it only made her look even more striking. But she had been distant, taut and erratic, her eyes not meeting mine, despite a flashy show of affection. I remained glad my parents hadn't seen her then. They could remember her as she was.

I jumped at the knock on the door. Molloy was standing on the doorstep wearing a heavy blue sweater over his uniform, and carrying a heavy-looking brown paper bag in his hand.

"I thought you mightn't have eaten yet either, so I took a risk and brought Chinese."

The sitting room had warmed up, and I could feel my appetite returning. I disappeared into the kitchen and produced a couple of plates and glasses. To my surprise, Molloy accepted a glass of wine.

"Just what I need," he said. "Thank you."

"Long day?"

"You could say that."

I poured myself a glass. "Something happen?"

"You'll hear tomorrow, I'm sure. It'll be all around the town. We've arrested Mick Bourke."

"For what?"

"For all those robberies."

"You're kidding!"

"Nope."

"How do you know it's him?"

"He made a few mistakes getting rid of the stuff. We managed to trace it back."

"God. Do you think Danny Devitt knew it was him? Was it Bourke he was talking about?"

"No idea. We think there was someone else involved as well. Bourke wouldn't have had the wit to run something like that on his own, but he's not saying who helped him."

"Have you any idea who it might be?"

"It has to be someone with local knowledge. Someone who knew who was getting married and when, who was going on holiday and so on. Bourke made a blunder with Paul Doherty's place. He didn't have time to do the job properly and cover his tracks like he did with the honeymoon break-ins."

"That was him, too?"

Molloy nodded. "We think he did that one on his own and made a mess of it as a result. Got greedy. He had to change his contacts to get rid of office equipment rather than household appliances."

I thought about what Phyllis had told me earlier. Had Bourke been trying to get rid of dirty money by giving it to charity? Did he suspect someone was onto him? I needed to speak to Phyllis again before I could pass that information on to Molloy.

After we had eaten, I took the remains of the food into the kitchen. Molloy leaned against the sink, glass in hand, and watched me as I loaded the dishwasher.

"So do you still want to have that chat with me, or have you changed your mind again?"

I straightened myself and said, "No, it's time I spoke to someone. I should have done it years ago."

"It's entirely your business, you know, Ben. You're under no obligation to tell me anything."

"I know, but we're friends, and I should at least have told you before you heard it from someone else. Which, let's face it, was always a possibility."

He gave me a smile. "I will admit it was a bit odd discovering that I didn't even know your real name."

"You make it sound as if I'm using a false name. It's my second name and my mother's maiden name. I haven't done anything illegal."

He put his hands up in a gesture of surrender. "Conceded."

"And, by the way, for all your magnanimity now, you were pretty cold to me for a while there when your 'friend' was around."

His smile disappeared.

"You seemed angry with me," I said.

Molloy avoided my eye and gazed at the wall.

"I'm sorry for that," he said slowly. "But there was more going on there that I don't really want to go into. It wasn't to do with you."

My stomach did a flip. "Oh."

"You said you needed my advice?"

"I do." I paused, but I couldn't seem to drop the subject of the pathologist even though it was clear Molloy wanted me to. "What did she tell you?"

"Why don't you just tell me what you want to? As much or as little as you like."

"Okay." I opened the second bottle of wine and poured myself a glass.

Molloy refused a top-up. I took a sip and placed my glass on the counter.

"You know I've been in Inishowen for six years."

"Yes."

"And you know I was in the States for a year or so before that."

"Yes, you've told me that."

"Well, what I hadn't told you, but which you now know thanks to your friend, is that before I went to the States, my sister Faye was killed." I heard a slight tremor in my voice.

Molloy was silent, still leaning back against the sink and continuing to study me as I spoke, listening intently. I was grateful to him for not delivering some sympathetic platitude at that point. I didn't think I could have continued if he had.

"And as you know, there was a trial. A fairly public one. Her killer was convicted of manslaughter. He's serving ten years. That's the information in the public domain so to speak."

Molloy nodded.

I took a gulp of my wine.

"For my family, the whole nightmare started nine years ago. I was working in a big commercial practice in Dublin, one of the big five. A plum job that I got straight out of college. My parents were very proud. It was at the beginning of the boom and there was lots of money about." I paused again. "There was another young lawyer working there. Luke Kirby."

As soon as I said his name, I realized I hadn't uttered it since the trial. I took another mouthful of wine before continuing.

"Luke was handsome and successful, and very dynamic. He was used to getting what he wanted and good at getting things done. That was part of the attraction at first. We started a relationship of sorts. I think I realized very early on that it meant more to me than it did to him, but I thought that might change. I introduced him to my parents. They liked him."

I forced out the words. "And then he met my sister."

Molloy didn't move. He made no attempt at any kind of comforting gesture, such as putting his hand on mine or his arm around me, for which again I was grateful.

"As soon as I introduced him to Faye, I saw the look in his eyes. Luke wanted her – I could see it. It was the same expression he used to have when he was about to close a big deal. He looked at her like a lion contemplating his prey; it was all he could do not to lick his lips."

A scratching at the door made me jump. It was Guinness; he went straight to his bowl. I locked the door and continued.

"Faye had just qualified as a nurse. She was pretty and kind, but she'd always had a wild streak in her – a reckless-ness that I envied in some ways. I was so straitlaced. She was always the first to try the most dangerous things. We took a trip together once to the south of Italy, and the one thing she wanted to do was this Flight of the Angel stunt – *Il volo dell'angelo*, an adrenaline junkie's dream. You fly on a high-wire between two villages, with only a helmet and a safety harness. Terrifying – I couldn't do it. But Faye did. Halfway across, she let go of the safety line. The organizers were furi-ous with her. In fact, we were nearly kicked out of the place, but she just laughed. She said it was amazing, that you felt like you were really flying."

I smiled at the memory of it.

"Anyway, she and Luke started spending time together. It began with the odd coffee here and there when they ran into each other. She told me whenever they met – she was quite up front about it. But there was one thing I hadn't told my family about Luke. He was a cocaine user. A heavy one. It worried me when Luke and Faye started to meet up, since Faye had such an extreme and addictive personality. But Faye said that they were just friends who had a laugh together, and Luke never allowed anyone to tell him what to do – he made sure to tell me that. He said I should be glad he got on well with my family.

"I pretended otherwise, but it drove me crazy. I was besotted by him, and jealous, stupidly so. Eventually I split up with him, hoping that would bring an end to whatever was happening between him and Faye. It didn't." I swallowed. "They became a couple. I went to Luke's apartment one night to see if I could talk to him, and I saw them together outside. That night, something snapped for me. I decided I needed to cut them both out of my life. And to my parents' great distress, I did. I stopped returning Faye's calls, stopped seeing her, and gradually she stopped contacting me. It upset my parents greatly, because then she started to avoid them, too. When she died, they hadn't seen her in six months."

I could hear the shake in my voice, so I spoke quickly to get through it.

"One night, my phone rang. It was late, about two o'clock in the morning. It was Faye. I ignored it. Let it ring out. She couldn't leave a message because I'd taken my voice message off so I wouldn't be tempted by hearing her voice – or his, for that matter. It rang again a number of times. Each time it was Faye and I ignored it. Eventually I put it on silent, even put the handset in another room so I wouldn't see it light up. And I went back to sleep.

"The next morning, Faye was dead. She was found by her flatmate returning after a weekend away. She'd been strangled. The evidence given by the pathologist was that there was cocaine found in Faye's system when she died. Luke Kirby's DNA and semen were found on her. He was charged with murder, convicted of manslaughter."

I stared down at the floor, the black tiles blurring before my eyes. My throat hurt. "He presented what had happened as a sex session, an asphyxiation game – strangulation to enhance pleasure. He claimed that the sex was consensual, if 'a little rough' as he put it. As usual he sounded utterly plausible. They were both up for it and it went wrong, he said. Unfortunately your friend the pathologist was unable to say definitively that this could not have happened. So he was convicted of manslaughter."

I looked up at Molloy for the first time since I'd started speaking. His expression gave nothing away.

"What do *you* think happened?" he asked quietly.

I took a deep breath. "As I said, Luke Kirby was a man who was used to getting what he wanted. I think Faye said no to him that night. And he took what he wanted anyway. I think she was changing her mind about him and he didn't like it. He wasn't used to having people say no to him and that made him turn violent."

Molloy nodded silently.

"I also think she had started using cocaine." I stopped. "Wait a minute – that's not true. I *knew* she had. I recognized the signs. I ran into her one night in a club in town and she was in bad shape. I told her to be careful and she said she was fine, that she was happy. But I could tell she wasn't. Then I saw she was with Luke, and I just walked away from her. I still wasn't over him. How pathetic was that?"

I wanted to weep.

"That was about a week before she died. It was the last time I saw her." I cried out: "My jealousy blinded me to the danger she was in! What happened to Faye is my fault!"

"How could it be your fault?" Molloy said gently.

I looked up at him. "*I* was the one who brought that bastard into my family's life. *I* was the one who introduced him to my sister, and *I* was the one who ignored her calls on the night she died – because I was jealous." I spat the words out. "What kind of sister does that?"

Molloy took a step towards me. I pushed him away.

"What was she ringing to say? That she was afraid, that she didn't trust him anymore, that she needed my help, that he was hurting her?" My voice broke. "There were four missed calls on my phone that night – *four*. What the hell was wrong with me? How could I not have helped her?"

Finally the tears came, tears I had blocked for eight years. My vision blurred and I slid down along the cabinet and sank to the floor, my hands covering my face. I felt someone beside me, strong arms around me. Holding me as my body shook with grief.

The fire was still alive, if dormant. Molloy threw some extra logs on it and it crackled back to life. He poured each of us another glass of wine and handed me a glass of water to go with it. My head was pounding, my eyes dry and itchy. I clutched a white handkerchief, now considerably less pristine than when Molloy had given it to me in the kitchen.

"My parents know none of this. They don't know anything about her drug use, or the fact that I deliberately ignored her calls that night."

"It didn't come out at the trial?"

I shook my head. "At the trial there was evidence that Faye had tried to ring me and that the phone had rung out. Both phones were produced in evidence. But I never admitted to ignoring the calls. Only said that my phone had been in a different room and I hadn't heard it. My parents know that Faye had cocaine in her system, but they're so bloody innocent about these things, they've convinced themselves that Luke spiked her drink or something. And I've never told them otherwise."

"Was Faye taking cocaine before she met Luke, do you think?"

"I don't think so. But Faye would try anything once. Luke was the same kind of adrenaline junkie she was. I think that's what made me so jealous. I knew I couldn't compete, I was so different from both of them."

I concentrated hard on looking at the ceiling, trying to stop the tears from starting again.

"My parents were devastated. I couldn't destroy their memory of Faye as well as everything else. But I got to the stage where I knew I couldn't keep up the pretense. They wanted to talk about it all of the time. It was as if, after she was gone, they craved news about her, anything at all that they hadn't heard before. They mined the memories of all of her friends, for any little snippets of new information. I was afraid I would tell them too much."

Molloy leaned forward. "So you went to America."

"Yes. I went to America. I took a secondment from the firm and I ran away. I convinced myself that I was doing my parents a favor, that my very presence was a reminder of what had happened."

I sighed. "And then my old firm contacted me and offered me a big payoff. They didn't want me coming back to Dublin. They wanted to wash the firm of any trace of Luke Kirby, and with me still working there, they couldn't do that. So I took it."

"And came here."

"Yes. I saw an ad in the *Law Society Gazette*, offering a practice for sale. I looked at the map, saw how far away it was from Dublin, and realized it was perfect. I started using my middle name and my mother's maiden name, so no one would connect me with the trial, which, of course, my old firm were perfectly happy to facilitate. And here I am. Small-town solicitor."

Molloy smiled. "I'm not going to complain about that particular turn of events."

My eyes welled again.

"I'm glad you've told me," he said.

"So am I."

"You said you wanted my advice. Or was that just a reason to talk?"

"No. I did want your advice. *Do.* My parents want me to talk to the pathologist." I stumbled. "Laura."

Molloy's expression didn't change.

"They're convinced they can persuade her that Faye wasn't a drug user and that there could be some sort of retrial, which could result in a murder conviction. I've told them that that's not a possibility, but I'm terrified that they'll contact her themselves and that it'll only open up a whole other can of worms for them. That she'll tell them Faye was a regular user or something worse. It'll only hurt them more. It didn't come out in the trial, and I see no reason for them to know." I hesitated. "Maybe I'm wrong about that."

"Only you know your parents, Ben. You know what they can handle. But if it looks as if they're going to contact Laura, I'll talk to her first if you like, and let her know your concerns."

I was grateful to him, though oddly uncomfortable about the obvious intimacy betrayed by what he said.

"Thanks."

"I do have one other suggestion," he said. "But you mightn't like it."

"Yes?"

"Maybe if you spent a little more time with them, it would ease things for them, and they might stop trying to look for answers that aren't there."

Chapter 31

A NOISE WOKE me at seven. The smell of burning turf invaded my nostrils. I opened my eyes. I was on the couch again. But this time I felt refreshed, if a little stiff. I stretched and sat up. The room was cozy, the fire crackling, its flickering orange flame the only light in the room with the curtains still drawn. Someone had taken the duvet from my bed and placed it over me. They'd also removed my shoes and placed them neatly by the couch. Molloy. I realized he must have only just left – that's what must have woken me. I threw off the duvet, ran to the window, and pulled the curtain aside just in time to see car taillights pulling away from the curb. I watched as the car drove off in the direction of Glendara, closed the curtains, and glanced around the room. The wine bottle and glasses were gone. The woolen throw from the couch was folded up neatly on the armchair by the fire.

I picked it up. We had talked long into the night, exhaustion finally overtaking me when Molloy, despite his skepticism, had gone into the kitchen to make me a camomile tea to help me sleep. I remembered his last words to me before he left the room.

"Guilt is a hard thing to live with, Ben. It can eat away at you like a cancer if you bury it."

It was all the confirmation I needed that he hadn't judged me in the way I had feared he would. I must have been asleep when he came back.

The papers I'd had Kelly sign the afternoon before were still on my desk where I'd left them, along with the planning file from the County Council offices. I was about to pick them up when Leah buzzed me.

"Phyllis is on the phone for you. Have you got a sec?"

I held the handset away from my ear. Phyllis' voice has a tendency to rise when she is excited. Dispensing with any preliminaries, she launched straight in.

"Bloody hell. I'm going to have to let the guards know about Bourke's big donation now, aren't I? Now that he's gone and got himself arrested."

"Yes. I think you should."

"And I suppose it means we'll have to kiss good-bye to that nice wee injection of funds?"

"Probably."

"I could pretend I didn't know who it was from. It was supposed to be anonymous, after all."

"Phyllis." My tone was firm.

I heard a heavy sigh down the phone. "Bugger. We could do an awful lot of good with it."

"I know. When did you get it, by the way?" I asked.

"Tuesday. The day before we came in to see you. The envelope was posted in the door of the shop. I thought it was too good to be true."

"It's the right thing to do, Phyllis."

"Ah sure, I know. It doesn't make it any easier though."

I paused for a second. "Can I ask you something? Nothing to do with Mick Bourke?"

"Shoot." I could tell her interest was piqued.

"I met Claire in the pub last night. She wasn't in great shape. And I remembered Tony said something after the wake, something about Eithne giving Claire pills."

"Did he now?"

"I was wondering if you knew anything about it."

Phyllis lowered her tone; perhaps there was someone in the shop. "By the look of her, I'd say Claire's been taking benzodiazepines, those damn antianxiety drugs, for a while."

It made sense: the mood swings, the waxy skin, the glassy eyes.

"I know the signs," Phyllis went on. "I had a friend who got hooked on them a long time ago. They're certainly not doing her any good, but I can't imagine Eithne giving them to her unless they were prescribed. She wouldn't risk her license."

"That's what I thought."

"Although if she is giving Claire drugs, one thing's for sure: big brother won't like it."

Snow was falling again. I stood at the window watching the flakes waft gently past, thinking about last night. Molloy was right about guilt. It eats you up from the inside, and if you let it take hold, it can destroy you. I wondered how much guilt had played a part in what had happened to the Devitts. Jack Devitt's guilt after the death of his friends was something that he had found impossible to live with, but Danny had been carrying guilt of some kind, too, I was sure of it. He was haunted by something he had done, or not done. Wrapping Stephen McFerry's bones in a blanket and placing a pillow underneath the skull. Disappearing for weeks after Conor left. Selling the farm and handing the money to his mother. All were actions that reeked of guilt. But what had he felt so guilty about?

I looked at the calendar. Thursday. Something was happening this morning. What was it? All the days were merging into each other. Then it hit me. Today was the day they were reburying Stephen McFerry's remains. I hurtled downstairs.

"Have I an hour free, Leah?"

She nodded. "All your morning appointments have cancelled, as a matter of fact. The snow."

I was about to head out of the door when something else occurred to me. I raced back up the stairs and took a file out of the filing cabinet. I opened it, found what I was looking for, made a note, and put it back.

I decided to park at Whitewater Church and take the pathway to the graveyard, over the old stile. The guards had left it the way it was; the wooden piece slid out easily, and I climbed over. I emerged from the trees to a strangely eerie sight. The graveyard was silent, buried again under a muffling blanket of white. Five people stood at the grave: the local priest, Stephen McFerry's father, two gravediggers, and Hal. I was glad to see that Hal was involved, that he wasn't being blamed for what had happened, despite Phyllis' fears. I remained back a little, aware that I stood out like a sore thumb in the empty graveyard. When the religious formalities were completed,

I approached Mr. McFerry. He was unshaven and obviously distressed. I shook his hand.

"I'm sorry. I was passing and thought I'd express my condolences."

"Aye, thanks. It's not a recent death though. My son died six years ago."

"I know. I heard what happened."

He kicked the soil under his feet, the soil that had been freshly dug. The snow rested like flakes of sea salt on top.

"I'm staying put this time until it's all done. I want to see my lad safely in the ground, with clay on top. Proper. Safe. Not like the last time."

He clicked his teeth and stood there with his arms crossed as he watched the gravediggers do their job.

"Left him lying there in his coffin in an open grave, they did. They were supposed to cover it that night."

I remembered leaving the graveyard on the day of Danny Devitt's burial, his coffin in the ground, but uncovered. To be done overnight, too, I guessed – it must be normal practice. I stood beside the boy's father, hands clasped in front of me like a second sentry, ensuring everything was done properly, this time.

I read the date of death on the gravestone – June 14, 2007. Six and a half years ago. My suspicions were correct. The date I had taken from the file before leaving the office was June 15, 2007. It was the date on the draft affidavit I had started to put together for Lisa Crane, the last day she had seen Conor Devitt, the day before their planned wedding. Conor Devitt had gone missing on his wedding day, June 16, 2007. If Stephen McFerry had died on June 14, taking into account two days for a wake, it was highly likely that he had been lying in his coffin in an open grave on that very day. I hadn't figured out what it meant yet, but there had to be a connection.

I drove back to the office and ran straight upstairs. Sitting at my desk, I turned on the computer and opened the website for back issues of the *Derry Journal*. I soon found the edition from the day after Stephen McFerry's accident. The death notice was there, together with the funeral details. I was right. Stephen McFerry had been buried at 11 a.m. on the morning of June 16, 2007; the same day that Conor Devitt had been due to get married, the day he had disappeared.

At five o'clock my mobile rang. It was Maeve.

"Fancy something quick to eat in the Oak before you go home? I'm on call and I won't get a chance later. Spring has finally hit. I'm going to be up to my elbows in calvings all night."

The thought of food was appealing and I didn't much feel like cooking. But unfortunately for Maeve, her phone rang as soon as her food arrived. I watched her stomp out of the pub with her lunch in a takeaway carton on her way to a calving in Malin Head.

I was finishing my own meal with only a newspaper for company, when the door of the pub opened again and Lisa Crane walked in. She strode up to the bar, high-heeled boots clacking on the wooden floor, her blond hair tied in a high ponytail. I heard her ask for a bottle of red wine to take away. As Tony went looking for a brown paper bag to put it in, she leaned on the bar and cast her eyes around the room. She spotted me, nodded, and when she had paid, came over.

Beneath the war paint she looked wretched. I suspected the bottle in her hand wasn't the first one she had consumed over the past couple of days.

"I must settle up with you for that thing I was in about."

"It's okay. I didn't do very much and . . ." I stopped.

"And you won't be now, you were about to say."

I smiled apologetically. "Something like that."

"Why don't you come up to the house now and I'll give you a cheque."

"There's no need. Seriously. The fee will be minimal."

She looked down at my plate. "You're finished your food, aren't you?"

"Yes."

"Come on then," she said, a pleading note entering her voice. "You can have a glass of this with me." She lifted the paper bag. "Alan's out at the driving range. It'll save me drinking on my own."

"Okay. I'll come up for half an hour. I don't need a cheque though. There's nothing owing."

"All the more reason to let me get you a drink."

She gave me directions to her house, and I paid the bill and followed her up.

Lisa and Alan Crane's house was hard to miss. I'd noticed it before, about two miles out of town, but I hadn't known who owned it. I wondered if this was the house she'd built with Conor or if it was a new one. Whichever it was, it wasn't to my taste, for all its show-house faux-Tudor grandeur. Light flooded the tarmacadam driveway as soon as I drove in, coming from a movement-sensitive imitation street lamp to the right of the front door. The house was huge – six bedrooms at least, I guessed – built off the back of either Celtic Tiger carpentry or plumbing.

It was red brick, and for some reason the color of the door had been carefully chosen to match the brick exactly, which made it look as if it were completely bricked in, that once you crossed the threshold you would be locked in there forever. Luckily, Lisa had left the red front door slightly ajar. On the doorstep, I called her name.

"Come on through. I'm in the kitchen fighting with a corkscrew."

I followed the voice through a vast entrance hallway dominated by a huge pair of chandeliers. The kitchen was a substantial space, with a dining table big enough for ten, and an island. Lisa was standing at the island, extracting the cork from a bottle.

"Looks like you're winning," I said.

"Huh?" she said.

"Your battle with the corkscrew."

"Oh right."

She poured two enormous glasses of wine and perched on one of the stools. I joined her.

"So I guess I can't get him declared dead now that he's back?" she said, clinking her glass against mine and giving me a half-smile before taking a large gulp from her glass.

"I guess not."

"Bastard," she said.

"Has he been to see you since he came back?"

"Would you believe I haven't even clapped eyes on him? I must be the only one in town who hasn't."

"Seriously?"

She took another gulp of her wine. It occurred to me that her glass would be empty before I had even started on mine if she kept this up. "Want some crisps or something?"

"No, thanks."

"Bastard," she said again.

"Maybe he's afraid to face you," I suggested, taking a sip from my own glass.

She gave me a look that would have turned the wine to vinegar if what we were drinking hadn't been pretty close already, so I tried a different tack.

"I got the impression when you came to see me that you didn't really think he was dead. Was I wrong?"

She sighed. "I couldn't be sure and that's the truth. I know things weren't great between us, but it just didn't seem like him to run off like that. Conor always took care of me. Even before we started going out, he treated me like a little sister. I was Danny's friend first, in secondary school. But then Conor kind of took over. It was as if he sought me out." She smiled sadly. "I was flattered."

Yes. I knew what that felt like.

"He made a big thing of the fact that we'd both had to grow up without fathers. Said I needed minding. Then a few years after I left school, we started going out, and for a long time, it was good. But after we got engaged, he changed."

When she frowned, the tiny lines around her mouth became more obvious, as if she'd been a smoker. She took another drink, set the glass back down on the island, and gazed into it.

"He became obsessed with making money. Money had never been a big thing for him before that, he just worked hard. I was stupid enough to think it was the prospect of getting married. He was thinking of going out on his own, and I supported him in that. He wasn't getting on with Bourke. Said he was dodgy, that he was getting up to some things he didn't agree with." She paused. "Looks like he was right about Bourke anyway."

"God yes, your break-in," I said. "I hope you were insured."

She nodded, casting her eyes around the room. "All new stuff. I'm just glad Danny's not being blamed anymore. Although I hear Bourke's been released on bail. I hope to God Alan doesn't get hold of him." She looked towards the door with a slightly panicked expression, as if the thought of her husband returning unsettled her.

She switched her gaze back to me. "Where was I?"

"Conor going out on his own?"

"Oh aye. He seemed to be working all hours, trying to get new work. At first I was pleased – as I said, I thought that he was doing it for us. And then I started to wonder if maybe he was doing it to try to spend time away from me." Her eyes filled with tears. "He stopped talking to me, too. He was never the most open fella in the world, but he closed up completely." She cleared her throat. "He wanted to pitch for work on that new development at Whitewater Church – the big heritage centre they were planning up there."

I looked up in surprise. "Oh yes? And did he?"

She said a little uncomfortably, "To be honest, I tried to put a stop to it."

"Why was that?"

"I saw him with the wife of the man who was doing it and I didn't like it."

"Alison Kelly?"

"Yes, her. Conor came into the bank one day and she was there. It was just after we got engaged. I could see them talking in the doorway. There was something about her – I could tell immediately that she fancied him. Women can tell within seconds if another woman is a friend or an enemy, and they're rarely wrong. And that bitch Alison Kelly was no friend of mine, I can tell you that much."

I remembered Lisa's reaction to Alison the night of Danny's wake. Now it made sense. But if what Lisa said was true, why had Alison claimed that she hadn't seen Conor since she was a child? Could Conor have been the man outside the Station Inn on Sunday night?

Lisa drained her glass. "I asked Conor about it, and he said I was imagining things, that she was a useful contact, and that she could persuade her husband to give him the job. But there was more to it than that, I'm sure of it. And if you'd seen the look on Conor's face when Alison Kelly's husband walked over to the two of them that day in the bank, you'd have thought the same."

I leaned forward. "What do you mean?"

"The color drained from Conor's face as if he had seen a ghost. It was weird. And then it kind of hardened. I'm telling you, the look that Conor gave Ray Kelly that day was not the look of someone wanting a job. It frightened me. He looked as if he wanted to kill him." Lisa rubbed her eyes. "I think that was the beginning of the end for us. I had been so happy before, but after that I just knew . . ." Her voice trailed off.

"You knew what?" I asked.

"I knew I wasn't his priority anymore."

Lisa stared at the wall, her eyes glazing over, tears running down her face. She had obviously been drinking before I met her in the Oak, but it was as if this latest drink had pushed her over the edge. It didn't stop her pouring herself another, but when she offered the bottle to me, I put my hand over my glass. My mind was racing. What was going on between Alison Kelly and Conor Devitt? And why had both Kellys lied about how well they knew Conor? Ray had claimed he had never met him.

"Did Conor go ahead and pitch for work at Whitewater Church, do you know? Even though you tried to put a stop to it?" I asked.

Lisa grabbed a tissue from a silver-plated box by the sink and mopped her face.

"I think so. He said he was going up there to have a look and see the plans before the wedding. I don't know if he ever got there though."

"Is that why you thought the bones might be his?"

"I didn't know," she repeated stubbornly.

"When exactly was he planning to go up there?"

"The night before, or even the morning of our wedding, maybe. I didn't see him at all, the day of the wedding. We weren't due to get married until three o'clock, and he didn't stay with me the night before. He was at his mother's."

"Did you say this at the time?" My tone was sharper than I intended.

She looked at me blankly. "What?"

"Did you tell the guards that Conor was planning on going up to the church?"

She shrugged. "I told someone. It mightn't have been the guards. But Danny checked up there when he couldn't find him before the wedding and there was no sign of him."

I took a second to digest this.

"Had Conor arranged to meet someone at the church, do you know?"

"I don't think so. He said he just wanted to have a look. I didn't think there was anything strange about it. He was always very attached to that place for some reason. And the planning notice was up on the gate." She gave me an odd look. "Anyway, why are we talking about this? He's back, isn't he? What does it matter now?"

I didn't know why exactly, but it did matter, I was sure of it.

"Imagine – I actually thought that it might be him up there when they found those bones. I thought it might be him, after all, that he might have fallen or something. I even began to feel guilty, for judging him wrongly." Lisa laughed bitterly as she waved her empty glass about. "But I was right all along, wasn't I? Nothing happened to him. He just ran away, didn't he? The day of our fucking wedding."

"He didn't run away with Alison Kelly though, did he?" I said. "She's still here, with her husband."

"Whatever, she's a bitch anyway."

Lisa leaned across the worktop to pour herself another glass of wine, then discovered that the bottle was empty. She clambered off the stool, swaying.

"I'll go and get another bottle. I'm sure there's a bottle of white out here somewhere."

"No, please, not for me. I have to go."

"Go on. It won't kill you."

"It might. I'm driving."

Her eyes widened as if something had just dawned on her. "We have six bedrooms. You can stay the night."

"No, thank you, honestly. I have to go."

I stood up, collected my bag and keys, and pointed myself in the direction of the door.

Before I reached the hallway, the doorbell sounded, a loud church-like peal that wouldn't have been out of place in a Beverly Hills mansion.

"Are you expecting someone?" I asked.

Lisa shook her head. A look of fear flickered across her face, and her eyes darted towards the door. She leaned precariously against the banisters.

"Do you want me to get it?"

She nodded.

I opened the door. Standing on the step was an unsmiling, unshaven Conor Devitt. He didn't look too thrilled to see me. I heard Lisa emit a small sound behind me, like a tiny whimper of pain.

"Is this where Lisa McCauley lives?" Conor asked.

"Yes."

Lisa didn't move.

His mouth was fixed in a tight line. "Is she here?"

I hesitated. I didn't want to turn around and draw attention to her. But suddenly, she was beside me.

"Hello, Conor." All sobered up, no trace of a slur. It's incredible what a shock can do.

His face was expressionless. "Lisa," he said.

"Long time no see." Sober and sarcastic.

He ignored the tone. "Can I talk to you?"

She opened the door wide and pointed. "Go into the kitchen, it's over there." As he walked past us, she whispered to me, "Will you stay?"

"Are you sure you want me to?"

"As my solicitor? You can do that, can't you?" she hissed anxiously.

"I suppose."

She walked into the kitchen, and I followed her.

Conor was standing in the middle of the room. He glanced in my direction as I walked in behind Lisa, but showed absolutely no curiosity as to why I was there.

"What do you want to say to me, Conor?" Lisa squared up to him, her composure completely restored. I wondered how long it would last.

"I thought I owed you an apology," he said.

Her face crumpled. "Oh well, that's all right then. That makes it all grand, doesn't it? That makes up for the past six and a half years."

Conor didn't react. His face remained set in the same expression he had been wearing on the doorstep.

"And I wanted to let you know that I'll sign over the house to you," he continued. "It's yours."

Lisa sank onto one of the stools. I stood behind her, feeling like an intruder, voyeuristic.

"Is that really all you have to say to me after all this time?"

"I presumed you would want that. You can sell it, or do whatever you like with it."

Tears were flowing down her cheeks. "Seriously? That's it?"

"I'm sorry," he said. "I don't know what else I can do." There was no trace of discomfort in his face.

"You always do the right thing, Conor, don't you?" she said. "Always what's expected of you. Except with me, of course."

"I'm trying to, Lisa. You're married now. I'm happy for you."

As if on cue, I heard a key turn in the front door. Lisa's face froze. She started to rub frantically at her eyes, which only served to make her eye makeup look even more panda-like.

Her husband strode into the kitchen. "Who owns the Mini parked in the driveway?"

"Alan." Conor nodded at him, hands still in his pockets.

Alan paused for a second and then walked towards him, right hand outstretched. Conor shook it.

"Welcome back, sir."

"Thanks."

"We must get a pint."

"Aye, sure."

"I'll give you a shout."

There was a pause. The two men looked at each other. Then Conor turned and walked out of the room. Seconds later, I heard the front door close with a gentle click, followed by a loud clatter as Lisa's stool fell against the island and she put out her hands to steady herself. Alan moved to place his arm around her. He looked pointedly at me.

"Thanks for getting her home safely. I think I can take it from here."

Chapter 32

THE FOLLOWING MORNING I went straight to the filing cabinet and took out the conveyancing file for Whitewater Church, flipping through it until I found the planning file Leah had attached. Something had been bothering me all night. The sheet on top was a copy of a "change of use" planning permission, permitting the change of use of the property from religious to cultural and recreational. That permission had been applied for before the church was even sold to Ray and Alison Kelly. The new buyers would have to change the use again, this time to residential, if that was what they were still planning. I expected they would want to make the contract subject to that permission issuing.

At the back of the file was a bulky envelope that I hadn't yet opened. I did so now and pulled out a sheaf of papers. It was a copy of the planning permission file for the construction work the Kellys had wanted to carry out to the church. I knew from what Kelly had told me that this permission had been refused. I had a quick flick through. Unusually, the Council had been very careful to give us every detail, including copies of any objections that had been lodged at the preliminary stage. There was only one. I pulled it out and opened it up. The name on the top was Conor Devitt.

I sank back in my chair. Why the hell would Conor Devitt have objected to planning permission for a development he wanted to get work on?

I checked the date of the final refusal. It was December 15, 2006. The development had been a non-runner for a good six months by the time of Conor and Lisa's wedding . . .

The phone rang. It was Molloy. My stomach did a weird little flip.

"How are you doing?" he asked.

"Good. Thanks for the other night." I lowered my voice. "Thanks for staying."

"That's all right," he said gruffly. I hoped we weren't going to revert to professional politeness. I didn't want that.

He cleared his throat. "I wanted to let you know that you were right."

"About what?"

"Conor Devitt came back into the country on Tuesday."

"Last Tuesday?"

"Yes. The day before Danny was killed."

"Jesus, he lied. Why would he do that?"

"No idea. But we're sure as hell going to find out."

I hung up the phone deep in thought and jumped when Leah buzzed.

"Mary Devitt's here with Claire. Can you see them for ten minutes?"

Looking at the two women sitting opposite me, I saw a likeness between mother and daughter for the first time. It was the furrowing of the brow, the lines under the eyes, the mouth; I hadn't noticed it before. But there was a delicacy about Mary Devitt's features that she had not passed on to her daughter. Conor had inherited the fine bone structure and brown eyes of his mother, while Claire was lighter in coloring, with more sturdy features and pale eyes. Danny had been a combination of the two. The dark coloring with the larger features.

The two women looked closer in age than they should. The past couple of weeks had aged Claire, and by the looks of things, Conor's reappearance had done nothing to relieve that. She sat with her hands clasped tightly together in her lap. Her mother seemed considerably more at ease. Claire spoke, quickly, giving the appearance of wanting to take charge.

"My mother wanted to speak to you."

I looked at Mary Devitt.

"She wanted to talk to you about Danny's estate."

I was surprised. Maybe I shouldn't have been.

"I wondered if there was something I should be doing?" Mary asked, her tone almost apologetic.

"Did he leave a will?" I asked.

"I don't think so. What do you think, Claire?"

Claire's eyes darted about the room.

"Claire?"

The daughter shook her head. "No. No, I'm sure he didn't."

"That's something we need to be sure of before we do anything else," I said. "You should probably check the other local solicitors' offices. I could do that for you, if you like?"

Mary nodded. "Yes, that would be very helpful."

"And then, if we're sure there's no will, we'll need to draw up a list of his assets and debts."

"I can do that," Mary replied. "It will only be his house and the money he gave me for the sale of the land, I expect. I never touched that money."

Claire looked up with interest. She started to pull on a lock of her hair.

I took an attendance sheet from the drawer of my desk and started to take some notes.

"The procedure is firstly an Inland Revenue affidavit, which is a schedule of assets, and then an application to the Probate Office," I explained. "If there is no will, his assets will be divided between his next of kin. Since he had no spouse or children, that would be you, Mrs. Devitt, as his mother."

Suddenly Claire stood up. Without a word she turned and stalked out of the room and down the stairs, leaving the door to the office wide open.

Mary sighed. "I'm sorry about that. She seems incapable of staying in one place for longer than five minutes at the moment. She's always been a bit fragile, but ever since the bones were found in the church, she's been suffering from some kind of panic attacks. I want her to see someone about it, but she refuses to do so. I put my life in the hands of the gods letting her drive me in."

"Is there anything I can do?"

"No, thank you. Conor is dealing with it, or so he says. He's told me to stay out of it, whatever is going on. Although she seems upset with him, too, at the moment. Anyway, I'm afraid the money is more important to Claire and Conor than it is to me, Miss O'Keeffe. Is there a way I can gift it to them?"

I stood up and closed the door before explaining the tax implications and procedure involved. She said she would talk to her children and get back to me.

"I'm sorry I lied to you the other day," she said. "I know you were trying your best to help me."

"Well, you didn't exactly lie to me."

She smiled. "I was a little economical with the truth. I didn't tell you that Conor was back."

"I assume you wanted to keep his return private for a few days. That's understandable."

"No," she said. "That wasn't it. We were anxious that people know as soon as possible. He went to the garda station himself the day after he arrived."

So Mary Devitt didn't know her son had been back in the country since the Tuesday before, I thought.

"I wanted to have a chance to talk to you alone, you see, and that wouldn't have been possible if you'd come into the house."

"No, I can see that." I looked her in the eyes. "Do you mind if I ask you a question? It was something you said at Danny's funeral and you said it again on the beach."

"Go on."

"You said it was far more likely that Danny was trying to be kind, to do the right thing, and that even though he got things wrong sometimes, he would have been trying to do what was right. It sounded to me as if you knew something you weren't saying. Maybe I'm reading too much into it?"

"I suppose it's not going to make much difference now – not to my poor Danny, anyway," she said in a low voice. "Now that we know that the poor young lad in the crypt wasn't murdered."

I waited.

She looked down at her hands. "I saw Danny coming from the church very early on Christmas morning."

"Last Christmas?"

"Yes. Since Jack died I always go for a walk first thing on Christmas morning. It's just something I do."

"Go on."

"Danny was coming out the church gate. It was barely light and he didn't see me, but I got the impression he had spent the night there. I didn't say anything to him about it at the time, but then when the bones were found . . ."

"You were afraid they were Conor's?"

"Yes."

"And you thought Danny might have been telling the truth, after all, when he said he had something to do with Conor's death?"

She gave me a weak smile. "You can see why I began to worry when Andy McFadden told me that Danny's DNA had been found in the crypt. I was so relieved when the body wasn't Conor. It seems now that all Danny did was to wrap that poor Derry boy's body in a blanket." She added slowly, "Although I have no idea why he did that, nor how he knew that boy's body was there in the first place. I don't like to think of him moving it there himself. I can't imagine what would make him do something like that."

"Did you know it was Christmas Eve when Lisa told him she was getting married?" I said.

"Was it?" she said thoughtfully. "That would have upset him."

"I think it did. I believe he walked out of the pub."

"And went up to the church? But why?"

"I don't know yet, but it's a bit of a coincidence. Do you mind me asking you something else?"

"I suppose I do owe you." She smiled.

"Why do you think Conor came back?"

A shadow crossed her face. "If I'm being honest with you, I'm trying not to think about that. I'm trying to accept that he came back for his old mother."

"But you don't believe that?"

"Something changed in Conor before he left," she told me. "I think over the years while he was gone, we tried to forget that. We hoped he might be different if he ever came back, that he'd have got whatever it was out of his system. Unfortunately, he's still the same."

"Lisa said something similar."

She looked up with interest. "Did she?"

It occurred to me that the two women had probably never had a proper conversation about Conor's disappearance. It seemed so odd while at the same time utterly unsurprising.

I hesitated. "I'm not sure I should tell you this, but Lisa thinks he was having an affair before he left."

Mary raised her eyebrows for a few seconds before gazing out the window. "Poor Lisa was always so insecure. It happens sometimes when a father dies, you know. Sometimes I think that's Claire's problem, and then sometimes I think she was just spoiled." She sighed. "But I'm afraid for once I think poor Lisa is right."

"So he was seeing someone else?"

"I can't be sure it was a love affair. But something was involving him, in a way nothing ever did before. Conor was always ensuring everyone else was okay, intrusively sometimes. But in the months before he left, he lost interest. There was something else there, too. A kind of suppressed anger, almost."

She paused before asking the question, as if she wasn't sure that she really wanted to know the answer. "Did Lisa say who she thought it was, that he was having the affair with?"

"Alison Kelly."

She looked at me blankly. "Who?"

"She was at Danny's wake. They were childhood friends apparently," I offered.

"Oh, Allie McDaid." Her face softened. "She was a cute wee thing. Had a rough time in the school, I think. The other kids used to call her *the Yank* because of her accent and she was a wee bit on the chubby side, which didn't help. But she and Conor were inseparable." Her brow furrowed. "She was at the wake, you say? I don't remember seeing her. I thought the family went back to the States years ago."

"They did, but she lives in Buncrana now. She's married to Raymond Kelly, the man who owns Whitewater Church. They moved back eight years ago."

Her eyes widened in surprise. "Well, I can tell you one thing: Conor hated the man who owned Whitewater with a passion. I assumed it was because he was renovating the church he associated with his childhood and he didn't like change. But maybe it was because my son was having an affair with this man's wife?"

"Maybe."

She heaved a sigh and stood up to go. Before she reached the door, I asked one final question. "When was the last time you saw Conor before he disappeared?"

She turned to face me, frowning. "Why do you want to know that?"

"Humor me."

She looked to the ceiling as if struggling to recall. "I saw him early on the morning of his wedding day, about eight o'clock, in the house. He said he was going out for a walk."

"Do you think he could have been going up to Whitewater Church?"

"Possibly." She shrugged. "He didn't say."

"Lisa said he wanted to pitch for work on the development up there."

Mary Devitt gave a brief laugh. "If there's one thing I can be certain of, it's that he would never have done that."

Chapter 33

THE REST OF the day passed in a haze of appointments, allowing me little time to think about what I had discovered. So at half past five when Leah shouted a good-bye up the stairs and I heard the door bang, I spent the next little while pacing up and down my office trying to put those discoveries in some kind of order.

My restless agitation was interrupted by a loud thumping on the door. I went downstairs to answer it. It was Liam. I don't think I have ever seen a more miserable-looking expression on anyone's face.

"God, what's up with you?"

"That damn English couple have pulled out again."

"Ah, Liam. You're kidding!"

"I wish I was." He followed me inside and dumped his phone on the reception desk so hard I checked to see if it had cracked.

"I thought they'd got over their squeamishness," I said.

"Well, they had – until someone decided to warn them off."

"Warn them off how?"

"They were up at the church having a look around and some guy came and threatened them. Can you believe it? Ordered them to leave and said that if they bought the church, they'd never have a day's peace."

"Jesus. Who would do that?"

"That's what I want to know."

"When did this happen?"

"Just now. They rang me to tell me about it. They just flew in last night to tie things up."

"Did they say what he looked like?"

"They couldn't see him properly. It's dusk. And he kept his distance, apparently. If I could bloody well get my hands on him . . ."

"Have you told the Kellys yet?"

Liam walked through the open door of the waiting room and slumped onto one of the seats. "I've been trying to get them all day, but neither of them is picking up. I'm dreading it."

I stood in the doorway with my arms crossed. "It's hardly your fault."

"No." He looked up at me. "This isn't. But I'm on thin ice with them as it is."

I was confused. "I thought you were their pet estate agent. I thought they'd asked you to sell all their properties?"

"Aye. For no fee." He put his head in his hands. "It's all such a mess."

I followed him into the waiting room and sat beside him. "What's going on, Liam?"

"I should have told you this before but . . . I wasn't supposed to be showing the church," he said in a muffled voice.

"What?"

He lifted his head and stared at the wall. "Before he went to the States, Ray Kelly asked me to sell a few properties for him – sites, a couple of houses he owns in Buncrana, an old cottage. He mentioned that he might have to sell the church, too, at some stage, but not yet. He said he'd talk to me about it when he came back from the States.

"After he left, I had a call from this English couple. Out of the blue. They'd been touring about up around Malin Head and they'd come upon the church and fallen in love with it. Wondered if there was any chance it might be for sale, and if so, could they have a look at it." He paused. "So I showed it to them."

"But the gate and the church were both padlocked. How did you get the keys?" I said.

Liam looked sheepish. "Kelly gave me a key ring full of keys and the keys for Whitewater were on it." He shrugged. "I thought it was fate. The church was exactly what the English couple had been looking for, they said. They wanted to restore it, turn it into a holiday house."

I remembered the broken padlock in the grass. "Was there a key to the crypt?" I asked.

"No. I'm sure of that. I told you, I didn't even know that crypt existed. I didn't go near it."

"Did you let Kelly know you were showing the church?"

He looked down. "No."

"Ah, Liam."

"I know, I know. I need my head examined to have done something so stupid. But none of his other properties were selling. And I thought, if I can have a solid offer for him on the church when he comes back – well, at least that's something. He'd have to be pleased. And it's not as if he would have been tied to anything until he signed a contract . . ."

"You don't need to give me a conveyancing lesson, Liam."

"I thought I was doing him a favor."

He looked so defeated, I immediately felt mean for having snapped at him.

"And what about the survey? I assumed that was arranged on Kelly's instructions."

Liam shook his head. "No. That was me, too. I was under a bit of pressure, see. The English couple were only here for a few days and they wanted the place surveyed before they confirmed their offer. I tried to ring Kelly at that stage but I couldn't get him. His phone was off so I couldn't even leave him a message."

"So you just went ahead anyway?"

"Yes. I know I'm an idiot, but it's just my bloody luck that the first time I show a property without instructions, there's a body in it."

I tried not to smile. "No wonder Kelly was furious when he came back."

"That's an understatement. He threatened to report me. Then agreed not to, if I sold all the rest of his properties on a no-fee basis. I'd no choice. I can't afford to lose my license."

"And, of course, you couldn't tell Molloy that you'd shown the church without instructions either?"

Liam looked miserable. "That's right. I've been having sleepless nights about that. But the padlock to the crypt was cut open, wasn't it? That's what Kelly told me anyway. So it's not as if it was him who put that body there."

"Yes, it was cut."

Liam looked relieved.

"So Kelly basically blackmailed you?" I said.

"Well, it was the wife who did the blackmailing. She was the one who struck the no-fee deal with me. She plays a tough game, that one." He stood up. "To be honest with you, it's her I'm not looking forward to telling now. She scares the bejasus out of me."

"I think she's under a fair bit of pressure with Kelly in the hospital."

"He got out last night." Liam walked over to the reception desk and picked up his phone. "Still no call back."

I followed him. "Is there anything I can do?"

"I need them to know about this as soon as possible. Is there any chance you could tell them? I'd take a run up to Buncrana myself, but I have a viewing in half an hour. It's my only viewing this week and having lost this bloody one again, I don't really want to cancel it."

"It's all right, Liam. I'll get hold of them. If I can't get them on the phone, I'll drive up myself after the drama meeting. I'll leave early, if it's going on too long."

He didn't even attempt to conceal his relief.

After Liam left I tried both Kellys' phones a number of times, but even the pub number was ringing out. I suspected there were staff there, but no one was bothering to answer it. I was tempted to drive up to Buncrana straight away, but knew I had nothing to gain by rushing things. I needed time to think. So Kelly hadn't known that Liam would be showing the church. How did that change things? We had assumed that the body had been placed in the crypt without Kelly's knowledge by whoever broke the padlock. But had Kelly just been happy for people to think that? Had he known it was there all along?

It was clear that Molloy needed to know what Liam had told me as soon as possible, but I knew it would be better coming from Liam himself; I didn't want to get him into more trouble than he was in already. But Liam had barreled out of the office so quickly after I had agreed to pass on the bad news to the Kellys that I hadn't had a chance to tell him that. I dialed his number and left a message for him to call me back. I looked at my watch. If he was showing a property, he could be twenty minutes or more. I tapped my fingers on the desk. I badly needed a distraction.

The two plays Phyllis had given me and which I'd promised to read before the drama meeting were sitting on the counter. I opened the first one. It was *Mary Magdalene* by Feargus O'Connor. I began to read the first scene. Distracted as I was, I could see it was beautifully written. I turned to the back; this was the play that had been written in Long Kesh Prison, the one Phyllis had said might be a step too far. But my curiosity was aroused. I turned on Leah's computer and Googled his name.

Newspaper account after newspaper account of O'Connor's recent trial for dissident republicanism appeared before me. No photographs though. I was curious to know what he looked like. I picked up the play again: there was no image there either. I did a search for images of Feargus O'Connor and a raft of photographs appeared in front of me, the vast majority of them having nothing whatsoever to do with the Feargus O'Connor I was interested in. But some did. There were press photographs of him being taken into his recent trial in handcuffs, and photographs, too, from a much earlier trial in the 1990s, when he was convicted of involvement in a bombing in London. He was thin, with a gray beard in the later photographs, and a shock of red hair in the earlier ones.

I scrolled down through the other pictures. A team picture after a hurling match published in the *Derry Journal* caught my eye. I clicked on the image to enlarge it. It was dated September 1985. The familiar red-haired youth was there again, standing in the back row, a member of an Under-21 team from Derry who had won some local league cup. I guessed he must have been about nineteen at the time. My eyes scanned the rest of the team. In the center of the picture was a large cup being held proudly aloft by a dark-haired young man with a wide grin and a mod haircut. I froze. The grin was familiar: it was a younger, stronger version of the one I had seen only two days beforehand in a hospital bed. It was Raymond Kelly.

My breath quickened. Feargus O'Connor, a leading Republican with a string of convictions for explosives, had known Raymond Kelly in 1985 when they were both in their late teens, only months before the *Sadie* was blown up by the IRA. Coincidence?

I scrolled down through the rest of the images for Feargus O'Connor, clicked randomly on a black-and-white photograph of what looked like a funeral cortège, and the full picture appeared in front of me. It was the funeral of a convicted IRA kidnapper. O'Connor was one of the pallbearers, his name mentioned in the caption underneath if I was in any doubt. I checked the crowd following the cortège. The faces were grainy, but there, unmistakably, wearing a mod suit with a skinny tie and walking with his head bowed, was Ray Kelly. I checked the date on the caption; the funeral had taken place exactly three months after the hurling picture was taken and a matter of weeks before the bombing of the *Sadie*.

My mind started to race. Alison had told me that by the time Kelly was nineteen, he was working on a building site in America. That meant that he must have emigrated only months after those photographs were taken. And he had remained there for nearly two decades. It was beginning to look very much as if Ray Kelly had been forced to leave Ireland in a hurry. Had he been involved in the bombing of the *Sadie*? If so, where did Conor Devitt fit in? He was just a child when his father's ship had been blown up. But he certainly seemed to hate Kelly.

Suddenly, I remembered what Claire had said at the wake, about Conor loving ships and going down to the shore to watch them. Could he have seen something that night?

I dialed the Devitts' landline. It rang out. I tried again, the same thing. I cursed Mary Devitt's refusal to answer the phone and Claire for not being there. And then I remembered: the drama meeting! Maybe she was there. I ran down the stairs and out of the office, slamming the door loudly behind me. I raced across the square towards Phyllis' shop. The windows were lit, but the shop door was locked, with the Closed sign hanging in the window. I banged on the door. Phyllis appeared within seconds, a startled look on her face.

"Ben. What on earth?"

"Is Claire here?"

"No, she's over at Eithne's. They're coming together."

I bolted back across the square, leaving Phyllis standing open-mouthed in her doorway. I knocked on Eithne's door, but there was no answer. I looked frantically up and down the street – and then I spotted Claire coming towards me, a confused expression on her face.

"Do you want Eithne, too?" she said. "I can't find her anywhere. I've been looking for her all day."

"No," I said. "It was you I was looking for."

"I need to speak to her. I'm afraid . . ." Her voice was slurring again.

"Never mind about that," I said urgently. "I want you to tell me something. The night your father's ship was blown up, you were only about eight — is that right? Can you remember it?"

She frowned. "Aye."

"You said at the wake that Conor loved the ships, that he went to the shore to watch them. Did he ever sneak out at night to do that?"

She shook her head. But her eyes avoided mine.

"To watch for your father coming home maybe?"

"He told me never to tell. I promised."

"That doesn't matter now, Claire." I wanted to shake her. It was like talking to a child. "You need to tell me. Think carefully: Did he go out that night?"

She heaved a big sigh. "All right. I saw him leaving the house, in his pajamas, and his coat. He said he was going down to the shore to watch for Dad's ship. He used to do that all the time; he'd sit up behind the pilot station where no one could see him. He made me promise not to tell as he knew he'd be in trouble. Gave me sweets not to tell."

"And did you?"

She shook her head again. "With everything that happened that night, I was scared. I thought he'd be in even bigger trouble."

"Do you think he could have seen something that night?"

"I don't know. I went back to bed, and we never talked about it again."

* * *

I jumped in my car and drove the fifteen miles to the Devitts' house in fifteen minutes flat. The only thing that saved my neck was the fact that I didn't meet a single car on the road, but I nearly wrecked the poor Mini's undercarriage on the lane to the house. I turned into the yard, braked sharply, and leaped out, the engine still running. I rapped on the door, and Mary Devitt answered after what felt like minutes, but was probably only a matter of seconds. She had a knife in her hand, covered in oil paint.

"Conor, is he here?" I asked breathlessly.

"No. He's gone," she said sadly.

"What do you mean, gone?"

"He's left. Said he'd done what he needed to do and now he had to go again. I have to let him live his life."

"Where has he gone?"

"I'm afraid I don't know."

I took a deep breath. "Mrs. Devitt, did you ever think that Conor knew something about what happened to his father's ship?"

Her expression clouded. "You mean the *Sadie?*"

"Yes. Could he have seen something? I know he was only a child at the time."

"Eleven," she offered.

"Well?"

Her eyes drifted over my shoulder. "So much happened that night," she said vaguely. "It's hard for me to remember."

My tone grew impatient. "Claire said he used to sneak out at night to watch for his father's ship."

She leaned against the doorframe for support. "I didn't know that."

"She said he went out that night, the night of the bombing. Do you think he would have told you if he had seen
something?"

With an effort, she pulled herself together. "This doesn't
reflect very well on me, Miss O'Keeffe, but it's possible he
wouldn't have. His father – well, all our attention went
on him, on coping with him. Conor was used to keeping
secrets."

"And Raymond Kelly? Conor never told you why he hated
him so much?"

"The man from the church? No, why?"

"I think he may have had something to do with the
bombing."

She paled.

"How long is it since Conor left?"

"A couple of hours." Then her eyes widened in horror.
"You don't think he . . . ?"

She dropped her knife on the floor with a loud clatter
and pushed past me. I watched as she dashed across the yard,
her skirt flapping wildly against her ankles. She ran to what
looked like an old turf shed. I followed and stood beside her
as she pulled open the door and switched on a light. She
dropped to her knees and crawled under an old workbench,
and with some difficulty managed to drag out a wooden box.
She lifted the lid and turned to face me with a look of horror,
her face white in the weak light.

"Jack's shotgun," she said. "It's gone."

I drove down the lane as if I were in a rally car, my head almost hitting the roof as the springs tried their best and failed.

I dialed the Kellys' numbers again as I drove, but there was still no answer from either of their mobiles. I tried the pub again. This time a young male voice answered.

"Trevor?"

"Aye." There was the sound of music in the background.

"Are either of your parents there? It's Ben O'Keeffe, the solicitor."

"Nah. Mam went out a while ago, to some sort of a meeting, I think. She said she wouldn't be back till late, and I don't know where my dad is."

"It's very important I get to speak to them."

"Okay. If I see my dad I'll ask him to give you a call."

I hung up and immediately dialed the garda station. McFadden answered.

"Andy, is Molloy there?"

"He should be back in ten minutes. Will I get him to call you?"

"Do."

"You all right?"

"Just get him to call me as soon as possible, would you?"

I stopped the car at the entrance to the main road. The wind was building again. I could feel a draught sneaking in the door where the rubber had worn away. My head was spinning. What the hell should I do now? Drive back to Glendara to find Claire? But what good would that do? She was unlikely to know where Conor was.

I decided to drive to Buncrana to try to track down the Kellys. I looked right and left before turning back onto the road. Across the fields to the cliffs I could see the moonlit sea. Then a glinting to my right suddenly caught my eye.

The lighthouse at Malin Head, I guessed. I looked again. No. The light was coming from much closer inland . . . My heart pounded. The church – it was coming from there!

With a screech of gears, I turned the car around and drove back in the direction of Whitewater Church.

Chapter 34

THERE WERE TWO cars parked at the entrance to the church. I dialed the garda station again, a feeling of dread in the pit of my stomach. Silence. Not even a dial tone. I looked at the screen of my phone, the white light ghostly in the dark of the car. Of course, no bloody reception. The road was in a dip – I had only been able to phone from outside the church when we had found the bones, from higher ground.

I looked at the gate. If my suspicions were correct, the last thing I wanted was to be in the same company as the Kellys, Conor Devitt, and a shotgun. But I had no choice: if I drove to get help, by the time I got back it could be too late. At least I had a hope of calling for help up at the church.

The wind battered me as I tried to close the car door; my coat flapped wildly around my legs. The moon was hidden now by black clouds that had moved in front of it, making the light eerie and unpredictable, lightening and darkening with no warning. A storm was coming.

I opened the gate, took a deep breath, and entered the darkened avenue. Bushes and brambles thrashed about like crazed Medusas. I caught sight of the beam of light again for a second, when I emerged into the clearing – a weak flash through the gaps in the walls of the church where the windows had once been. It was a torch, or maybe two. Silently,

I ran the rest of the way up the hill and reached the entrance to the church, my lungs burning, my feet wet from the icy grass. I stopped at the huge corrugated-iron door, which was ajar, maybe a foot and a half, a pale shaft of light escaping along the rough ground. I held my breath and peered in as the wind carried the murmur of voices towards me.

I saw two faces, each illuminated by the other's torch. One transformed utterly from the determined stoic I had encountered the day before, the other calm and controlled, like a mother speaking to a small child.

"Please, Conor, just go," Alison Kelly said.

"Not unless you come with me." It was Conor Devitt.

"I can't."

"I'm not going to leave you here with him. Not again." He touched her face. "It was a mistake to leave without you in the first place."

She removed his hand. "I couldn't have left without Trevor, you know that. He was only a child."

"We could have taken him with us."

Alison shook her head. "I would never have done that. Whatever you think of him, Ray's still Trevor's father."

"I should have stayed then. Whatever it took for us to be together. Anything would be better than the way things are, only seeing each other every few months."

"Don't be stupid."

He flinched. Her tone was sharp.

"I don't know why you're here at all," she went on. "I told you not to come back."

"There was no reason for me to stay away anymore. Not now that he knows I'm not dead."

"Surely that's even more of a reason?"

"I'm not afraid of him, Allie."

She ran her fingers through her hair. "Well, I am. If he had known I let you out of the crypt that day, he'd have killed you. You knew too much for him to let you go. God knows why you had to confront him in the first place."

Conor's expression darkened. "You know why."

She heaved a sigh. "He had no idea that you were the kid who had seen him all those years ago – until you decided to go and tell him." She looked skywards. "I still don't know what the hell you were thinking. And why choose to tell him here, of all places?"

"It had to be here. How he could buy this church after what he did . . ."

She cut across him, impatient. "That was me – I *told* you that. *I* talked him into buying it. He didn't want to come back at all; he knew what risks he might run. He did it for me."

"It was time, Allie. I needed to show him what he'd done, the community he'd destroyed."

"And tell him about us? Even though I didn't want you to?"

"He needed to know."

"No, he didn't."

"You were afraid of him. It was up to me to tell him."

"The morning of your own wedding?"

"I couldn't go through with a wedding to someone else, you know that. Not after I'd found you again." He put his hand on her shoulder. "I wanted to take care of you. Like I used to. I still do."

She pulled away. "I'm an adult, Conor. I'm not that fat little kid who needs a friend anymore. I wasn't then and I'm not now. We could have continued to see each other, but oh no, you had to force my hand. Just like you're trying to do now. I can't believe you scared our buyers away like that."

"I didn't think I'd need to force your hand. You were supposed to follow me, remember? When Trevor was old enough."

Conor kicked at a weed growing amidst the rubble. "I should have gone after him, back then when you let me out. I should have gone after him and told him about us and that you were coming with me. Not let you talk me into taking that young lad's body and putting it in my place." He stared at the ground, one hand in his pocket. "That was a crazy thing to do."

"It was the only thing to do. You needed to get away."

He looked up at her and, for the first time, a note of anger entered his voice. "No. I did that for your sake, but it was a mistake. It was a terrible thing to do to my family. I should have come back long ago, but I didn't – for you. It was only ever a matter of time before that body would be found."

He took a step towards her again and leaned in close. "It's time to face things. We can do it now."

Again, she pulled back. "No. You need to leave. Just go, Conor, please."

The wind changed direction, and I could no longer hear what they were saying. I peered cautiously around the edge of the door. Suddenly, I heard movement behind me – a footfall, the rustling of grass. I whirled around, my senses on overload. I thought I could make out a form about ten feet away, but when I looked again, it was gone. Had it been a trick of the shadows? The wind was churning the heavy storm clouds, daring them to break.

I'd turned back to face the door, my ears straining to hear what was being said, when I felt warm breath on the back of my neck. My heart jolted as someone grabbed my arm, wrenching it almost out of its socket, then hauled me inside and shoved me roughly between the two people in the church. They drew abruptly apart, and I heard a torch drop onto the ground. The light dimmed immediately. I stumbled forward and put my hands against the wall to stop my fall, scraping them painfully in the process. I managed to regain my footing in time to see Raymond Kelly, looking gray and thin and wretched, walk calmly over to his wife.

"Did you know your show had an audience?" he asked.

Alison's eyes widened in horror. "Ray. What are *you* doing here?"

"Your boyfriend called me – didn't he tell you? We had a nice little chat. Brought back memories of the last rendezvous he and I had up here, on the day of his wedding, no less." Kelly's voice was hard. "You'd think I'd learn, really. I only ever get a nasty fucking surprise when I'm summoned up here."

"Ray, please, I—"

"I'm disappointed you fell for him, sweetheart. It's me he's after, not you. He's only trying to get at me."

Conor moved towards the far wall. "Not true, Kelly. That's the way it started, but it hasn't been that way for a long time."

Without switching his gaze from Kelly for a second, Conor placed the torch, now the only source of light in the church, onto the window ledge, and picked up what I now saw had been resting against the wall the whole time. I stiffened. I heard Alison's sharp intake of breath, and instinctively I took a step away from Conor and towards the Kellys.

Conor slowly raised the shotgun in his arms and, feet planted firmly apart, aimed it directly at Kelly. "At first, all I wanted was to destroy you, to make you pay for what you had done, but it's been more than that for several years now. I love her. We love each other."

Alison's eyes darted from one man to the other. "Ray, it's *not* like that! Look at him – he's crazy."

I stole a glance at Kelly. He was impassive. Not at all the panicker I was used to, despite having a gun pointed at him. Which one was the mask, I wondered.

"No more lying, Allie," Conor said. "I refuse to walk away again. I need to finish what I started."

I reached for the phone in the pocket of my coat and felt for the on button, my eyes fixed on Conor. I thought I could remember where the redial button was. My mouth was dry, my throat constricted.

"Come and stand by me," he said, beckoning to Alison. She shook her head.

I gasped suddenly as Kelly took a swipe at the side of my head, so hard I bit my tongue. The phone shot violently out of my hand and hit a stone, ricocheted, and skittered across the concrete floor well out of reach. For a brief second all three pairs of eyes were on me.

Conor started to laugh – a low, bitter laugh. "You are one nosy solicitor. Everywhere I turn, you're there."

I put my hand to the side of my head. I tasted blood in my mouth.

"Why are you doing this?" I asked quietly, my ears still ringing.

"I want him to take responsibility. It is long overdue and I am calling him to account." He waved the gun in Kelly's direction. "You see this fine businessman here, this pillar of the community? This man is a murderer: he killed three people and as good as killed my father. Who knows how many others."

"*No*," Kelly said. "It was my first time, and my last."

"It was your last because you were stupid enough to allow your face to be seen by a wee boy," Conor spat. "Some brave volunteer you were!"

"I was the fucking lookout, for God's sake. I was only a kid myself."

"You were old enough to kill Lisa's father."

"If you're talking about the pilot, I panicked. It was an accident."

Fury flashed across Conor's face. "*Accident?* You shot him in the back of the head as he was running away from you. I saw you do it! I actually grew up thinking it was my fault somehow, because you were looking at me when he made a run for it."

"It *was* your fault. You distracted me. What the hell were you doing out that night anyway? Hiding behind the pilot station in your fucking pajamas. Everything went wrong after that. Stupid little fuck."

"You wouldn't know what guilt means, would you, what it means to have a conscience," Conor said disgustedly. "You'd rather blame your actions on an eleven-year-old boy."

"No one was supposed to die that night. Mistakes were made. Not just by me."

"That wasn't much use to the people you killed. Or their families. No one was ever punished for the lives lost or the damage that was done to this community. When I gave you a chance to man up – right here, six years ago – all you could do was knock me out and run. You're nothing but a pathetic coward, Kelly, and you always will be."

"So where have you been for the past six years then?" Kelly sneered. "I don't know how the fuck you got out of that crypt, but if disappearing and letting your family think you're dead isn't running away, I don't know what is."

Conor's jaw tightened. "If you really want to know, it was your wife who wanted people to think I was dead. She knew I couldn't stay here and marry someone else, not when I was in love with her."

"It wasn't like that," Alison said, but Conor ignored her.

"If she hadn't been so terrified of you, we could have run away together, been happy together."

Kelly laughed scornfully. "Alison afraid of me? I don't know what she's been telling you, son, but you don't know my wife very well . . ." He stopped suddenly. Confusion flickered across his features and his face fell. "Oh Christ, it was you. *You* let him out of the crypt that day, didn't you? It's been going on that long."

Alison looked silently at the ground.

"Looks like you're the one who doesn't know your wife very well, Kelly," Conor gloated as he repositioned the gun. "Now, are you going to let us leave, or do I have to do what I should have done six years ago?"

Kelly faced him. "You wouldn't have the nerve, son." His sunken eyes made him look skeletal in the dim torchlight. "It takes a certain type to kill a man, doesn't it, sweetheart?"

Alison flinched. "How did you know?"

Conor's eyes darted from Kelly to Alison. "Allie?"

"It didn't take a genius to work it out when I got the call from your boyfriend tonight. Heading off to collect Trevor at a party on the Malin Road on the same night as the accident, and then leaving him to get home in a taxi? Not like you, babe. Taking the Merc to the garage the next day before I could get a look at it."

Conor's face froze. "What is he talking about?"

Kelly ignored him. "What I don't understand is – why? I thought Danny Devitt was a harmless old eejit. Isn't that what you called him?"

Alison looked at her husband. "I did it for you." She touched his sleeve. He recoiled immediately from the contact and her eyes glistened with tears.

"Go on," he ordered, avoiding her gaze.

"Last week, after he found out the bones weren't Conor's, he came looking for you at the bar. He wanted answers. He'd seen you and Conor come up here the morning of the wedding and he saw you leave alone. He found Conor in the crypt."

"So why the fuck didn't *he* let him out?"

"We had a row," Conor said quietly.

Alison pivoted. "What did you say?"

"He was going to let me out, but I made the mistake of shouting at him. He was upset with me, said he knew about us."

"*What?*"

Conor shrugged. "He must have seen us together. He said that I didn't deserve Lisa. That he was going to make sure I missed the wedding. He left me there."

Alison's eyes sparked. "Why the hell didn't you tell me any of this before we started taking bodies out of coffins to put in your place?"

"I didn't want to involve my brother."

"What is wrong with you? He could have told anyone, any time in the last six years."

"Well, it seems he didn't, doesn't it?"

"Or did you hope he *would* tell, and then you'd have to come back?" she spat. "Was that your plan?"

"Would that have been such a bad thing?"

"Jesus fucking Christ!" Kelly's roar echoed around the walls of the church. "Am I really expected to listen to this shit?"

Alison ran her hand through her hair, her eyes brimming with tears. When she spoke again, her voice was choked. "The next day, Danny came back to let Conor out of the crypt but all he could see through the gate was a body wearing Conor's jacket. A body with a head wound."

"My poor brother." Conor sounded broken. "He thought it was me. That's why he didn't tell anyone. He thought he'd killed me."

There was a pause. No one spoke for a few seconds. It was starting to rain. I could hear the drops hitting the iron door, just a few at first, big heavy drops, splattering against the metal like the plucking of guitar strings. I imagined I heard an engine on the road. But maybe it was just the wind.

"My mother said he had some kind of a breakdown after I went missing. He must have kept it to himself for years. Thinking that was me in the crypt." Conor's voice was shaking.

Kelly applauded with a slow handclap. "Well, if that isn't fucking hilarious. Your plan worked."

"Danny couldn't understand it when the bones turned out not to be Conor," Alison said. "When he came to the bar last week, he was really drunk. He was all over the place – he could have said anything to anyone."

"So you killed him," I said. "Just like that."

Alison looked at me, confused, as if remembering for the first time that I was there. I hadn't realized I'd spoken aloud.

"It wasn't planned. At first I sent him away. I told him to come back the following day. But that night Trevor wanted me to collect him after a party. It was about five o'clock in the morning. I remembered Conor saying how Danny was a night owl, so I drove by his cottage and there was a light on. I called in to see if I could persuade him not to say anything." Her voice hardened. "He wouldn't listen. He was talking about going to the guards. I couldn't let him do that. I told him that if he came back to Buncrana with me that Ray would talk to him and explain everything."

"And instead you ran him off the road." I felt sick.

"It was easy. He drove ahead of me. His old banger was no match for the Merc." Her expression was defiant. "I had no choice. I had to protect Ray."

"That's bollocks," Kelly said. "What you were really afraid of was that he'd tell me about you and lover boy here."

Alison shook her head. "No."

"You were afraid you'd lose everything. Just like before."

"I swear. It was nothing to do with that."

"Oh come on. Penniless carpenter versus wealthy businessman? Not much competition there. *Dying* wealthy businessman." Kelly laughed bitterly. He sounded tired.

Alison looked stricken: it was as if his words had caused her physical pain. "No, that's not it. I couldn't let it all come out. I couldn't let you go to prison, not now."

"You're lying, Allie." Conor waved the gun at Kelly. "He did it. He killed my brother. Why are you trying to protect him?"

Alison looked down, her voice barely audible now against the sound of the rain drumming on the roof and the door, battering the ivy creeping in through the open windows.

"I'm not. I was protecting him when I killed Danny."

Conor's eyes widened in horrified comprehension. His features contorted as a whole gamut of emotions crossed his face: rage, anguish, grief, followed by searing, wretched desolation. Slowly, he switched the angle of the gun towards Alison.

Suddenly, I found myself shoved roughly aside as Kelly leaped forward and wrestled Conor for the gun. Alison screamed. Blood pounded in my ears. My thoughts flew in a thousand different directions as I watched the struggle, my body paralyzed by fear. It didn't last long; there was no contest physically. Weakened by illness, Kelly was no match for a man ten years younger. A shot rang out and Kelly slumped to the ground.

Alison cried out and ran forward. She fell on Kelly and curled herself over him in a fetal position as if trying to cover him with her body. Conor stared at them for a second, confused, as if unsure of what had just happened. His confusion was replaced quickly by understanding, by pain. Slowly he lifted the gun again, eyes only for her. Alison looked up at him, frozen.

I saw her face in the torchlight and heard a click as the trigger was pulled into position again. I saw the dark hair, the dark eyes, a face full of fear. My head started to spin and everything around me receded into nothing . . . all I could see was the gun. I lunged towards it.

I heard a shot. Was aware of the warmth of blood, a metallic smell. The last thing I remember was a searing pain in my leg – and then nothing.

Chapter 35

I CAME TO, my head pounding. There were bright lights all around and my eyes hurt. I was confused to see Molloy's concerned face peering down at me as I struggled to speak.

"Where am I?" I tried to sit up.

"Glendara Hospital. Don't move. You've been shot."

"What?"

"It's okay. You were only grazed, but you shouldn't move for a bit. You were knocked out when your head hit the wall."

I lowered myself back down. "What happened?" was all I could manage. Two- or three-word sentences seemed to be my limit.

"Raymond Kelly's dead. Conor Devitt shot him."

"And Alison?"

"Alive – thanks to you. She's in custody with Conor. The bullet grazed you en route to its actual target: you deflected it."

I nodded – then winced. It was beginning to come back to me.

Molloy sat on the seat beside the bed, his long legs stretched out in front of him. "We arrived as the second shot was fired. Too late to save Kelly, unfortunately, but in time to stop anything else from happening. You were unconscious. I thought . . ." His face clouded. "Anyway, I'm glad you're all right. Though why the hell did you go up there?"

"I'm nosy," I croaked.

Molloy produced a slight smile.

"How did you know?" I asked.

"Mary Devitt called us. We found your car at the church."

My throat was dry and I asked for water. Molloy handed me a plastic cup from the bedside locker. I drank thirstily, feeling a tiny surge of energy as I did so; my brain was starting to wake up.

"Why didn't Ray Kelly come armed?" I asked. "He must have known what he was facing when Conor called him."

"He probably didn't care enough to put up a fight, especially when he knew about Conor and Alison. He was aware he was going to die anyway – it seems he only had weeks. Alison is singing like the proverbial canary. She keeps saying it was Kelly she loved. It's a shame he had to be dying for her to realize it. Strange woman."

"Conor seemed to think she was too afraid of Kelly to leave him."

"It probably suited her for him to think that. She certainly knew all about Kelly's past, but I suppose it was the only way Conor would have understood her staying with Ray."

"So she had two men who were prepared to risk their lives for her." I shook my head. It hurt a lot. "What about Conor? How is he doing?"

"He hasn't said a word since we brought him in. It's as if he's in shock."

"He saw Kelly, the night of the *Sadie*, as a child," I said.

"So I understand. Kelly was in the IRA briefly in his late teens. After the bombing of the *Sadie,* he took off to the

States for twenty years. Thought he was safe enough to come back by then, I suppose, persuaded by his wife. But Conor recognized him and vowed revenge."

"And fell in love with his wife in the process," I added.

Molloy nodded. "They hadn't seen each other since they were children, apparently. When they met again, they started an affair. But it seems it meant more to Conor than to Alison. He wanted her to leave Kelly, which she wasn't prepared to do, but she couldn't end it with Conor because he knew about Kelly's past. She was trapped. It all came to a head the morning of Conor's wedding. Alison had told Conor that Kelly was going to the States for a few weeks to bring back some equipment for the bar, so Conor decided to confront him before he left. He got Kelly up to the church by pretending he was going to withdraw his objection to his planning application."

"And instead he confronted him about the bombing," I put in. "But why didn't he tell him about the affair, if he was trying to get Alison to run away with him?"

"He didn't have a chance. Kelly quickly overpowered him, knocked him out, and left him for dead in the crypt. Kelly had told Alison he was going to meet Conor at the church, so when Conor didn't turn up for his wedding, and she didn't hear from him, she went up there on her own and found him that night. It was Alison who came up with the plan of dressing Stephen McFerry's body in Conor's clothes, and putting it in the crypt, so that Kelly would think it was him when he got back from the States. By that time the body would have been sufficiently decomposed to be unrecognizable."

"They must have used that passageway between the graveyard and the church," I said. "That explains why those planks came away so easily."

Molloy nodded. "Yes. As it turned out, Kelly was content to leave the body there untouched for years. It looks like all he did was put a padlock on the gate to the crypt. Didn't even go in to view his handiwork. I suppose the risk of leaving the body there would have been less than moving it. Especially since no one knew about the crypt."

"Apart from poor Danny," I said.

"Yes."

"I presume Kelly would have moved the body before he sold the church if Liam hadn't—" I stopped mid-sentence.

"Jumped the gun?" Molloy smiled. "It's all right – I know. He came to the station, told me the whole story. You're right. As a matter of fact, it looks as if Kelly started to dig a shallow grave in the old graveyard but he didn't get a chance to finish the job. Maybe he was too weak, or the opportunity to go to the States for treatment came up."

"So, Conor did what Alison wanted and disappeared – went to England?"

Molloy nodded. "He's been working there on the building sites in London. Amazing no one happened to run into him really, over the years. He was sure he'd convince Alison to leave Kelly and start a new life with him. It turns out they've been meeting up every few months for the past six years. She was afraid to end it because of what he knew about Ray, and so it went on, until the body was found."

"And poor old Danny got caught in the crossfire," I said.

"Yes. He was using that cottage of his beside the church as a workshop at that stage. It seems he saw Conor and Ray both go up there the morning of the wedding, but only Ray come back. So he went up to investigate and found Conor locked in the crypt, with a cut to his head where Ray had hit him. They had a row, shouting at each other through the gate, and Danny ended up leaving Conor there so he'd miss his wedding."

"Danny must have thought it was his big chance to get Lisa back." It was very sad. "His mother said he was like a child in many ways. And of course he knew about Conor and Alison – he'd seen them together. Another reason for him to want Conor to miss his wedding." I paused. "But when he went back the next day to let Conor out and saw the body through the gate, why didn't he go in? He'd have immediately seen it wasn't Conor if he had."

Molloy shrugged. "Danny was the one who found his father's body. Maybe something snapped when he saw what he thought was his brother's body and he just couldn't handle it. He'd left Conor alone for twenty-four hours with a head wound, after all. He must have been horrified by what he'd done. He disappeared himself for a while after that. Had a bit of a breakdown, by all accounts."

"Poor Danny," I said. "Imagine carrying that guilt for all those years, thinking he was responsible for his brother's death, when all the time local people were wondering what had happened to Conor. He must have been completely haunted by it. I wonder if that was why he moved into the cottage – so he could maintain some sort of a vigil over what he thought was his brother's body?"

Molloy sighed. "Possibly."

"So, on Christmas Eve when Lisa told him she was getting married, he was so overcome with guilt again that he went up there and wrapped the bones in a blanket and put a pillow beneath the skull." I shuddered at the thought. "He couldn't bear the idea of Conor being there alone in the cold crypt, because of him. As far as he was concerned, he'd caused his own brother's death for a girl who was now marrying someone else. Not only did Conor not get to marry Lisa, but he didn't either."

"His big mistake was talking to Alison, telling her what he knew. He couldn't have known how dangerous she was. And how desperate. Especially with the pressure Conor was putting on her."

"And she really did it to protect Ray?"

"Who knows what her real motives were," Molloy said. "Whether she actually loved him, or loved the security he provided, who can tell? If Danny had talked to us or even to Ray, it would all have come out and she would have lost everything. Her parents lost everything here when she was a child. She wasn't going to let that happen again."

The door opened suddenly and a nurse stuck her head in. She saw Molloy, mouthed the words, "I'll come back," and closed the door again. The garda uniform has that effect.

Molloy stood up. "I'd better get going. Your bag's in your locker, by the way. We took it from your car."

"Thanks for coming."

His brow furrowed. "You had me worried."

I smiled weakly. "Sorry."

He paused. "Ben, you know . . ."

I held my breath.

"I'm sorry I haven't . . ."

"Yes?"

He shook his head. "It's nothing. I'm just glad you're all right."

Before he reached the door, he turned back. "I nearly forgot. Two messages. Maeve's feeding Guinness for you and Phyllis said to tell you she'd be in later. She's a little busy this afternoon. You see, she's acquired a new dog."

I could feel a smile creeping across my face. "Fred?"

"Yep. And she also has to get over her shock at Eithne O'Connell being arrested for her involvement in those burglaries."

"What did you just say?" I forgot, and tried to sit up again. Not such a good idea. Pain shot through my leg and I felt sick.

Molloy quickly came back over. "Careful." He pushed me gently back onto the pillow.

"Eithne? Robberies? Really?"

"Yup. Someone put Bourke under some serious pressure to give her up."

"Conor Devitt?"

"That's right. Looks like he put his father's shotgun to use before he even made it to the church. Threatened Bourke with it." Molloy grinned. "Bourke's made a complaint against him. Thinks there might be money in it. It's not going to be much use to him where he's going."

"But how did he know? Conor, I mean."

"About Eithne? I don't think he did. I think he was just trying to make Bourke keep Eithne away from Claire before he took off again. But faced with a shotgun, Bourke of course got the wrong end of the stick and in a stunning display of chivalry told Conor that it was his sister who was behind the robberies, but that all the money was going to charity. No doubt thinking that would absolve him, get Conor off his back."

"I saw Conor having a row with Eithne a couple of days ago. I thought it was about her giving Claire drugs."

"I think that's what it *was* about. Eithne denies it, despite what Conor thought. Says she was trying to help Claire get off them, that Claire has been buying them on the Internet for a while. But who knows? She denies any involvement in the robberies, too, of course."

"Do you think Bourke's telling the truth?" I asked.

"Well, Bourke's business suffered badly after Conor left, and he robbed a couple of places he was doing work for. Bourke's greedy, always has been. And he has an expensive taste in wives. Eithne found out what he was up to through doing his books, and she agreed to keep it to herself on the basis that they split the proceeds and she gave her share to charity, or had Bourke do it for her. Convinced herself everyone was insured so it didn't matter. But it seems she couldn't stop herself from managing the whole thing, feeding Bourke information about when people would be away. A pharmacist would be in a perfect position to do that; selling makeup for weddings, anti-malaria tablets for exotic holidays, that kind of thing. It makes sense. Bourke's not the sharpest tool in the box. He'd have been caught long ago if it weren't for Eithne."

"Jesus."

Molloy gave a wry smile. "According to Bourke, Jesus is why she did it. Running the local chemist in a small town gave her a view on the shallow nature of the way people lived, after her time in Uganda. Big weddings, cosmetics, perfume, expensive jewelry, holidays. She thought society was becoming too unequal. Thought that she'd do a little redistribution of wealth, even things out. Must have seen herself as a latter-day Robin Hood. We arrested her last night while you were on your way to the church to do your own superhero bit."

After Molloy left, the nurse came in and gave me some pain-killers. But I couldn't get to sleep. I switched the light back on, reached across to the bedside locker, pulled out my bag, and found the book on Inishowen I had bought on my way to Dublin. I turned to the back, the chapter on the twentieth century, and leafed through it slowly. A word caught my eye. *Sadie.* I stopped, turned back the pages.

In 1985 a British cargo ship the Sadie *was hijacked and blown up by the IRA. The IRA's intention at this time was to disrupt the maritime traffic in and out of the port of Derry.*

A band of eight IRA volunteers came on board the Sadie *via the pilot boat, which left from the tiny maritime community of Whitewater. They entered the pilot station and took the pilot hostage, with the intention of forcing him to take them to the cargo ship on board the pilot boat. Unfortunately the pilot attempted to escape and was shot. The IRA men nevertheless succeeded in boarding the ship from the pilot boat. They then informed the captain of their intentions and evacuated the crew of the tanker onto lifeboats, which were set adrift close to the shore. Charges were planted in the engine room and detonated. Two explosions occurred. The first set the ship on fire, the second caused the ship to sink, watched by the crew from the lifeboats. Tragically, two crew members remained on board the* Sadie *— it is assumed this was unbeknownst to the captain or the IRA cell. These two men, along with the pilot, lost their lives.*

Many others were affected by the tragedy. After the bombing of the Sadie, *many shipping companies stopped using the port of Derry, resulting in serious job losses. This had a devastating effect on the area, causing poverty and emigration. In particular, the small community of Whitewater – where the three deceased men lived and the pilot station was situated – was all but destroyed.*

No arrests were ever made in connection with the bombing of the Sadie. *The perpetrators all wore balaclavas and were never identified.*

I closed the book and felt it fall from my hands with a soft thud, as the painkillers finally began to take effect.

Acknowledgements

The bombing of the cargo ship the *Sadie* in this story was inspired by real events; two coal ships, the *Nellie M* and the *St. Bedan*, were sunk in the Foyle estuary in 1981 and 1982 respectively. The circumstances of the real bombings were very different to those in this book and no one was injured in the real attacks. But the bombers did board the ships via a pilot boat.

You will find neither Whitewater nor Glendara on the map of Inishowen, but many of the other places mentioned in the story do exist. Inishowen is well worth a visit. It's beautiful.

I'd like to thank the Arts Council of Ireland for their generous financial support during the writing of this novel.

Thank you to my agent, Kerry Glencorse of Susanna Lea Associates in London, and to Laura Mamelok of Susanna Lea Associates in New York. Thank you also to my new publishing family, Oceanview Publishing, who have welcomed me so warmly and pulled out all the stops to make this book as good as it can be and ready for a new American audience.

Finally, thank you to my family and to Geoff.

CPSIA information can be obtained
at www.ICGtesting.com
Printed in the USA
FSHW022035111019
62830FS